Don't Curse the Rain

Rain Mystery Trilogy Book 1

David Homick

"Many a man curses the rain that falls upon his head,
and knows not that it brings abundance."

~ *St. Basil of Caesarea*

CHAPTER 1

I couldn't possibly have imagined the shit storm I set into motion when I opened that letter. My past had somehow caught up with me. I wanted to feel something—after all, the man was family. *Family*. That F-word had been the source of all the pain I'd suffered for as long as I could remember. I folded the letter and slipped it back into the envelope.

Jenny Lee Myles watched me toss it onto the counter. "What's the matter, Dillon?"

"Pop died," I said in a flat voice.

I hadn't seen or spoken to Pop since I left for basic training ten years ago—seven years in Afghanistan and two more in and around the VA Medical Center in Dallas, less than fifty miles from home. My exile had been self-imposed—too many bad memories.

"How did it happen?"

I shook my head to clear it. "What?"

"How did he die?" She studied me from her seat at the small kitchen table.

"It doesn't say." Probably drank himself to death.

"Did he know you were back in the States?"

"I don't think so."

"Y'all want to talk about it?"

"Not really."

The kitchen shrank, as if the flowers on the wallpaper had grown and pushed their way into the room. Jenny Lee liked to talk about things, something I hadn't been able to do since my little brother, Luke, disappeared.

At first, I'd said plenty about the local police and their half-ass investigation. When people stopped listening to me, I left Bradley, Texas, and never looked back. I went to war, where I saw things that no one should see and did things that no one should do. A piece of shrapnel had sent me stateside during my second tour. Everyone wanted to know what I felt. Everyone except me.

"What else did the letter say?"

I squeezed the back of my neck. "Pop's attorney needs me to go home and settle his affairs."

"Like his funeral?"

The letter, postmarked two weeks ago and sent to a ten-year-old address, had finally found me. "It's probably too late for that."

"Do you think that's a good idea? Going home, I mean."

I stared at the floor. "I don't think I have a choice."

Not true. We always have a choice. Everything we do is a choice. I didn't exactly have the best track record when it came to making decisions, so I tried not to overthink this one.

Jenny Lee approached and rested her arms on my shoulders. "Do you want me to go with you?"

Her soft blue eyes felt more like home than Bradley.

"Thanks," I said, "but I reckon I'd better do this myself."

"Why do you think you have to do everything alone?"

The wallpaper pushed a little farther into the room. Jenny Lee had been hinting at moving in together, but each time I'd steered the conversation in another direction.

She sighed. "How long do you think you'll be there?"

I shrugged.

Her eyes searched mine. "What is it you want, Dillon?"

Another shrug. "I don't know."

"No. Not this time." She placed her hands on her hips. "I want an answer."

"What we've got here is pretty great, right?"

"Maybe so, but where is it going?"

I shifted my weight to the other foot. "What's your hurry?"

"I plan to move to Colorado at the end of the month," she said and returned to her seat at the table.

I tilted my head and studied her as she waited for a response. "What?"

Jenny Lee leaned forward and folded her hands. "I wanted to say something sooner, but—"

"What's in Colorado?"

"My dream."

I waited for her to continue.

"When my Uncle Roy passed, he left his six-hundred-and-forty-acre horse ranch near Colorado Springs to me and my cousin Seth. We spent our summers there when we were young. I've always thought of it as my little piece of heaven."

"You want to run a horse ranch?"

"I need to do this, Dillon."

I took a deep breath. "What about me?"

Jenn smiled and shook her head. "Don't be silly, y'all are comin' with me." Her expression fell. "I mean, if you want to."

Relief sank in for just a moment before the air left the room. Our eyes met, and I forced a smile. I didn't handle pressure well, or commitment, for that matter. I didn't want to move. But Jenny Lee had saved me, and I didn't know what I'd do without her.

"Well?"

"Of course that's what I want. It's just that…"

She folded her arms across her chest and waited for me to finish.

"I don't think you know what you're getting yourself into," I said.

"I'm a big girl. I reckon I can make my own choices."

"Sure. If you have all the facts, but you don't know everything about me. You can't imagine what I've been through. All I've ever wanted was a normal life."

"Normal lives are overrated."

"Easy for you to say. Your mama didn't run off. And your brother didn't disappear. And your daddy didn't spend all his time racing to the bottom of a whiskey bottle. I thought going off to war would have helped with the anger. It didn't. Now I can't even get through the day without medication."

"You're not the only one who's had it rough. You think I had it easy growing up with three brothers? I became an outsider, outnumbered even before Mama died. I tried desperately to join their boys' club, but nothing I did was ever good enough."

I walked to the sink and filled a glass with water, then leaned back against the counter. Jenny Lee's eyes burned with the intensity of blue lasers. I stared over the rim as I drank.

"Things change, Dillon. I can see that. Why can't you?"

The muscles in my neck and shoulders relaxed. I set the glass down. Perhaps I'd been a bit selfish.

Her expression softened. "It's time for us to write a new story."

"It's not that simple."

"Shouldn't it be?" She met me at the sink and held my gaze as we stood toe-to-toe. "Come with me, Dillon. My dream is big enough for both of us."

I couldn't imagine what I'd done to deserve this woman. I held her chin as I kissed her.

After a few moments, she pulled back and raised an eyebrow. "You do like horses, don't you?"

I smiled. "Do rocking horses count?"

"You mean to tell me y'all grew up in Texas and you've never ridden a real horse?"

"I wasn't that coordinated," I said ruefully, then grinned. "But I could fall off a bike with the best of 'em."

Jenn laughed. "I'm not sure what'll be more work, runnin' the ranch or teachin' y'all how to ride."

I felt a little better about what the future might hold for us. Maybe, just maybe, the light at the end of this long tunnel wasn't another oncoming train.

"Okay, Dillon, I understand. Go home and do what you gotta do. You need closure. That life is over." She sighed. "How long did you say it might take to settle things?"

"I didn't."

She waited.

"A week or two, I reckon. Believe me, I don't want to spend any more time there than I have to."

"Good answer." The lasers sparkled like blue diamonds.

Unfortunately, the road to Colorado would have to pass through Bradley, Texas.

CHAPTER 2

The Greyhound carried me down Route 67 toward what had once been the center of my universe—Bradley, Texas, population 5,228. I stared out the window at the sprawling desolation, punctuated occasionally by a stand of oil wells that bobbed up and down like giant mechanical cattle grazing on the scrubby vegetation. Until a few days ago, I had no intention of ever returning home.

The air conditioner on the bus struggled to keep up with the Texas heat. I set my hat on my lap, ran a finger along the brim, and thought about Jenny Lee. She liked it when I wore that old cowboy hat.

I'd found the hat in a thrift store in Dallas. After seven years in the Army and two months in the hospital, I had no clothes. That hat caught my eye as soon as I walked in, and I tried it on. A real Stetson, not the cheap knockoffs I'd worn as a kid.

I remembered how the girl behind the register smiled when I dropped a pile of jeans and t-shirts on the counter. She wore her dirty-blonde hair short and layered. A softness in her eyes undermined the strength and confidence in the way she carried herself. I figured she might be ex-military or maybe grew up with a bunch of brothers.

She eyed me with a curious expression after she rang everything up.

"How much do I owe you?" I asked.

"Y'all gonna pay for that hat?"

I raised my hands to my head, grinned, and nodded. "Forgot I had it on."

"It looks so good on you, it's almost a shame to charge you for it." She smiled, and a bit of mischief sparkled in her blue eyes. "I'll tell you what. You buy me coffee next door, and the hat's yours."

I glanced around the empty store. "Deal."

I paid for everything else and studied her as she set the bag on the counter. When I reached for it, she pulled it back.

"I didn't catch your name, cowboy."

"Dillon Bishop. And you?"

"Jennifer Myles. My friends call me Jenny Lee."

"Are we friends?"

"Let's have that coffee, and I'll let you know."

I turned the hat over in my lap and pulled a photo of Jenny Lee from inside the headband. She smiled up at me and I had to smile back. I returned the photo and hung the hat on my knee. My eyes closed when I leaned my head back against the seat.

After a few minutes, I turned toward the bus window and caught my reflection in the glass. My hazel eyes looked muddy as they stared back at me, and I wondered if anyone in Bradley would even recognize me. I'd grown a beard in the hospital, and my ash-brown hair hung six inches longer than when I left home.

The bus pulled into the station twenty minutes later. My left foot tingled as I stepped onto the pavement. I told myself that it had fallen asleep, but I knew better. My duffel bag hit the dusty platform, and I lit a cigarette. The bus belched a cloud of black smoke into the humid air as it pulled away, headed for Cleburne and points west. The exhaust swirled its way upward and disappeared into the low gray clouds that teased the thirsty ground.

A taxi rolled to a stop a few feet in front of me, and the driver looked my way. I held up my hand and shook my head. There's no way I'd ride in one of George Tucker's goddamn taxis. George had been mayor when they built the bus station in '98. He owned a fleet of taxis and decided that two miles outside of town would be the perfect place for the station. Good-ol'-boy politics. I slung my bag over my shoulder and set out on foot.

Dark clouds gathered ahead, and I turned my thumb out when I reached the highway. Halfway to town, a green Pontiac GTO skidded to a stop on the shoulder fifty feet in front of me. I ran up to the passenger door and looked inside.

The driver didn't look up as he lit a cigarette. "I'm only going as far as Bradley." A steady stream of gray smoke escaped through his nostrils. "But at least you won't get wet."

I hesitated. "Coop?"

Cooper Hill's head jerked in my direction, and he dropped the lighter onto the floor. He looked at me through squinted eyes. "Dillon Bishop? Day-um!" He took a drag on the cigarette. "What are you waitin' for? Get your sorry-lookin' ass in the car."

I threw my bag in the back seat and climbed in. His lighter rolled on the floor when he stepped on the gas. I picked it up and pushed it back into the dash.

"Jeezus, Bish, I figured you were dead." He took another long drag. "Where the hell you been?"

"Sweet ride," I said. "Gotta be, what, '68?"

He shook his head. "No, no. You ain't gettin' off that easy. My best friend in the whole world blows town after graduation, and I don't hear a goddamn word from him for ten years. You better start talkin', Kemosabe. I want details."

I watched the first few drops of rain pelt the windshield.

"I think I deserve at least that," Coop said. He took a final drag on his cigarette and flicked the butt out the window.

"Is Shady's still open?" I asked.

"That place will outlast both of us."

"Tell you what. Drop me off at Pop's house so I can get a shower and maybe a little shut-eye. Come back around seven, and we can go to Shady's for a few drinks and some barbecue. We'll get caught up then."

"You gonna shave while you're at it?"

I stroked the tumbleweed that hung from my chin. "What's the matter? You don't like it?"

He shook his head. "I don't know, Bish. You look a little like Jesus in a cowboy hat."

I laughed. "I've been called worse."

We pulled into the driveway of a small, single-story house. I stared at the front porch that Pop built when I was seven, remembering all the time Coop and I spent there playing with our GI Joe action figures instead of doing homework. Mama's favorite swing still presided over everything from its place of honor in the middle.

I thanked Coop for the ride and dodged the raindrops as I ran toward the house. Water poured from the corner of the porch where the rusted gutter had broken away from its straps.

A faded plaque on the front door welcomed me. My stomach bottomed out. I walked to the porch railing and looked out over the side yard, where a tire swing still hung from the lower branch of an old oak tree. The grass we'd worn down underneath it all those years ago refused to grow back. I closed my eyes and shook away the memories like a child shakes an Etch-a-Sketch, then walked back to the front door.

The wind shifted, and I felt the rain on my back. Paint chips fell like snowflakes as I ran my hand along the top of the door frame. After Pop locked me out a couple of times for missing curfew, I'd had a spare key made and hid it above the door. *Nothing.*

I tried the knob, surprised to feel it turn in my hand. Inside, I dropped my bag on the living room floor and looked around. Not much had changed. The same RCA TV that I used to watch as a kid sat across from Pop's favorite chair.

The day we brought that big La-Z-Boy home, Pop smiled for the first time in months. We didn't have much money, so we never had nice things. Pop had always sacrificed his comfort for Mama's. After she left, he said, "To hell with that bitch," and went out and bought the biggest, most comfortable chair he could find. Now, the stuffing hung out in too many places to count.

The smell of stale whiskey filled the room, forever infused into the thirty-year-old wallpaper. Despite the shabby furnishings, the room looked neat, like someone had just cleaned.

I picked up several pill bottles from the table next to his chair and read the labels. The cold hand of death had snatched Pop from this place. I'm glad I hadn't been around to see it, but I suddenly felt bad that I hadn't kept in touch.

A noise from the back of the house startled me. My combat training kicked in and I took up a defensive position against the wall. I backtracked quietly to the hall closet where Pop had kept a loaded shotgun. Parenting skills were never his strong suit.

I opened the door just enough to reach inside. A Winchester double-barrel shotgun leaned against the wall, exactly where I remembered it. I pulled it out, broke the barrel, and found two live rounds in the breech. With my finger heavy on the trigger, I peered into the kitchen. Empty.

A woman appeared from the pantry as I stepped into the room.

An invisible fist punched me in the gut. I lowered the gun. "What the hell are *you* doing here?"

"Hello, son."

CHAPTER 3

I broke the barrel and turned the gun upside down. The shells bounced on the floor. I set the gun on the table.

"Well?"

"I thought you might be glad to see me again."

I swallowed hard. "Sixteen years later?"

"I'm sorry, Dillon."

"You're gonna have to do better than that." My fists clenched at my sides.

"I know you probably hate me, and I don't blame you, but—"

"Why now? Cause Pop's gone and you figured you could move back in without having to explain yourself?"

Mama shrugged. Her eyes swam in their sockets.

Mama had run off with some rodeo cowboy before I turned eleven. Yeah, I know, it sounds funny, but I didn't see it that way. Pop hit the bottle hard after she left.

I folded my arms across my chest. "What happened? Your boyfriend dump you?"

"He died of a heart attack six months ago," she said as she dragged a finger under each eye.

"Poetic justice, wouldn't you say?"

Her eyes narrowed. "That's cruel."

"Really? You know what I think is cruel? A mother who abandons her children. A mother who doesn't care when her baby disappears. A mother who has the audacity to show her face again after sixteen years."

"I guess I deserve that." Her shoulders fell. "Isn't it better late than never?"

I shook my head. I honestly didn't have an answer for that, but I leaned toward *no*.

She pulled a chair from the table and sat. "Dillon, I'm your mother. Doesn't that mean anything?"

Her tired eyes held more than their fair share of pain. The lines and creases on her forehead and around her eyes had doubled in number from what I remembered.

"Apparently, it didn't to you."

"I made a mistake." Her eyes filled again.

"I think it's only a mistake because you're alone now, not because you have any remorse for how you left us."

"I love you, Dillon."

"Stop it!" My back stiffened. "You don't even know me." She cried.

"If you loved me, or Pop, or Luke, you wouldn't have left." I stood at the edge of the table and looked down at her. "People don't just leave the ones they love."

What could she say? She looked up at me with sad eyes, and her long brown hair fell across her face. She tucked it behind her ear. As much as I hated to admit it, she remained an attractive woman despite the obvious wear and tear.

I waited for her to say something. When she didn't, I turned and walked away. I pushed through the front door and it shuddered on its hinges. I'd just survived an ambush and needed to retreat and regroup to prepare for our next inevitable confrontation. Unfortunately, I'd left my meds in my bag on the living room floor.

The rain slowed while I walked to Coop's house, only to find he didn't live there anymore. *Artillery boomed in the distance. Small-arms fire crackled from somewhere in the next block, so I picked up my pace and kept a sharp eye on every door and window.*

Confusion stopped me in my tracks at the end of the block. I didn't remember any 7-Elevens in Kandahar before today. Coop's car pulled into the parking lot. More confusion.

"Dillon?"

I watched him approach and told myself to be careful. Something didn't feel right.

"Dillon!" He reached for me.

I grabbed his wrist and twisted it behind his back. In less than a second, I had him in a choke hold. "Where's the boy?"

"Are you crazy? Let me go!" He jabbed an elbow into my side.

A flash of white light brought me back to the present, wrestling with Coop in a 7-Eleven parking lot. I let go. "What are you doing?"

He tugged at his collar and looked at me wide-eyed. "Seriously? What am *I* doing?"

"Did I stutter?"

"C'mon, man. You're freakin' me out. Are you okay?"

I squeezed the bridge of my nose as the tension drained from my neck and shoulders.

"What just happened?" His eyes burned into mine, but I had no answer.

"I need a ride," I said and picked my hat up off the ground.

"Not until you tell me what's going on."

"I left my meds at the house."

Coop drove me back to the house. I didn't mention that I'd seen Mama. The house appeared empty, and I didn't stick around long enough to find out. I grabbed the pill bottle from my bag, and we drove to Shady's.

Coop pushed his plate away and sat back in his chair. "Not hungry tonight?"

Ten years I'd spent hankerin' for Shady's famous honey-barbecue ribs. I used to put away at least a couple of racks. Tonight, I couldn't finish one.

"You're twice the size you were when you left. You didn't get that way eatin' like this."

"I had time on my hands. I guess I worked out a lot."

"What else did you do over there?" he asked, like I'd been away on vacation or something.

Coop had changed little in ten years. He appeared thicker around the middle and his five o'clock shadow contrasted his ever-present boyish grin, but his eyes still held a measure of the adolescent mischief that mine had long since outgrown. He would've made a good detective with all his questions.

I shrugged and took another pull on a tall, cold Lone Star.

"When you freaked out earlier, you said something about a boy. What boy?"

I didn't remember mentioning the boy. "It was nothing." I stared at the bottle in my hands as the silence grew uncomfortable. "Just somebody I tried to save over there. He reminded me of myself at his age."

Coop nodded, apparently satisfied with my answer. He pointed to my tattoo. "Nice ink. You get that over there?"

I turned my arm to hide the image of a wolf that I'd had tattooed on my right forearm. "Before I left."

Coop frowned. "What's the matter, Bish? You seem like you—"

"Nothing," I said with a look that indicated the subject was closed. An awkward silence followed.

"Did you kill anyone?" he asked.

"Did *you*?"

"Just curious."

"In a combat zone... you do what you gotta do." I pushed my plate away.

"So, what are those pills you take?"

I tilted my head. "You ask a lot of questions."

"I'm your friend. Remember?" He leaned over the table. "You lost it out there today, Bish. It might be helpful if I knew what I was dealing with here."

"Trazodone. It's an antidepressant." I pushed a pile of dirty napkins around.

"That didn't look like any depression I've ever seen."

"It helps me sleep," I said without looking up.

Coop leaned back in his chair. He said nothing.

"And with the flashbacks." I avoided eye contact. "Doc says I got PTSD."

"Jeezus, Bish. What kind of things did you see over there?"

"I didn't just *see* things." Our eyes met. "I *did* things." Time to change the subject. "Did I tell you I met someone?"

A smile flashed across his face. "As in… a woman?"

I nodded. "In Dallas. Name's Jenny Lee."

"I'm happy for you, Bish. After all you've been through, you deserve it."

I shrugged and looked away just in time to see Josh Wilkerson walk in dressed in a police uniform. I nodded toward the door. "A little early for Halloween, isn't it?"

"What do you mean?"

"Isn't that Josh?"

"Yeah." Coop snorted. "He's a cop now."

"Are you shittin' me?" I waited for Coop to take it back, but he just shrugged. I shook my head. "God help us."

"He's a bigger prick now than in high school. I can't believe they let him carry a gun."

Sergeant Wilkerson walked over to our table and put his hands on his hips. "Hey Cooper, who's your girlfriend?"

I stood, and we locked eyes. Josh held his ground even though I had a good thirty pounds and a couple of inches on him. I took a deep breath like they taught me in anger management.

"You remember Dillon Bishop, don't you?"

Josh's eyes grew wide, and the color drained from his face, but he made a quick recovery. "I thought I smelled something bad in here."

"Me, too." Another deep breath. "You better check your shorts."

He glared at me for a few seconds, then turned and walked over to the bar. He spoke to the bartender, looked at our table, then walked out.

I sat and shook my head.

Coop stared, slack-jawed. A few seconds passed before he said, "Who are you and what have you done with Dillon?"

"What?"

"Seriously?" He shook his head. "That was awesome."

I shrugged it off.

"Next round's on me." Coop raised his hand and motioned to the waitress.

He grinned like a proud papa about to buy his son his first beer.

Alcohol and antidepressants don't always play well together, and I'd had more than my share of both. Pop's house appeared dark when we pulled up around midnight. Apparently, Mama hadn't intended to stay there, which was fine by me. I didn't want to talk tonight, or any night.

"You gonna be all right? We've got an extra room. I'm sure Jolene won't mind if you stay with us."

"Thanks, Coop." I closed the door and leaned into the open passenger window. "I think I can handle it."

"Suit yourself."

I watched his taillights disappear into the night before I went inside. I turned on the light in the living room and thought I saw Pop in his favorite chair. He nodded like he used to when I made it in just before curfew. I closed my eyes and shook my head. When I opened them again and saw an empty chair, I turned off the light, shuffled down the hall to my old room, and collapsed on the bed.

I woke to the smell of bacon. Sunlight filled the room, and a warm breeze nudged the curtains in front of the open window. I panicked, sure that I'd overslept and would be late for school again until I sat up and saw my reflection in the mirror that hung on the back of the door.

Another deep breath to be sure it hadn't been a dream. *Bacon*. I threw back the covers, slipped on my jeans, and ran into the kitchen. Mama stood in front of the stove, the table set for two.

"What do you think you're doing?"

She turned and offered a warm smile that brought back fond memories. "I'm making breakfast. Do you still like your eggs over-easy?"

I pushed the memories aside. "You can't do this."

"This isn't the first time I've made your breakfast, Dillon. I think I know what I'm—"

"No. I mean, you can't just waltz back into the house after all this time and pick up where you left off."

"Why not?"

I took a deep breath to keep from suggesting something inappropriate. "Because… you just can't. You gave up your privileges sixteen years ago. You left Pop and Luke and me to make our own breakfast. And everything else a mother is supposed to do."

She cracked an egg on the edge of a frying pan like she hadn't heard a word I'd said. "I got the thick bacon… center-cut, the way you like it."

I scanned the room, at a loss for words. The painted cabinets that once boasted a brilliant white finish had yellowed over the years. The entire room looked dingy except for the icebox, as Pop liked to call it, which had been replaced with a newer model.

Mama looked up from her pan and smiled.

We had the same eyes, more gray than brown, with dark specks around the edges. At the moment, that bothered me. "I think you should leave."

"You'd better wash your hands," she said, and turned her attention back to the stove. "Breakfast is almost ready."

"Jeezus, Mama." I sat and rested my forehead on the table between the silverware she'd set out. Another ambush. I thought I'd have more time to prepare.

"Dillon Matthew Bishop! Get your head off the table."

I straightened in my chair, a conditioned response from childhood when someone used all three of my names. The muscles in my face tightened. "I'm not ten years old anymore."

"That's no excuse to put your head on the table." She set one plate of food down in front of me and a second in front of her empty chair. She sat and unfolded her napkin. "Don't let it get cold."

I looked at her, then at my plate. The food smelled terrific, and my stomach growled so loudly I thought she might hear it from where she sat. I needed to eat anyway, right? I picked up the fork.

"Thank you," I said without looking up.

"I must have fallen asleep before you came home last night," she said.

"What?" The fork stopped in front of my mouth. "You stayed here last night?"

"Of course." Bonnie Bishop smiled. "I live here."

CHAPTER 4

After a heated discussion over breakfast, I walked out to the garage and found my '69 Mustang under a tarp. The smell of paste wax and gasoline greeted me like an old friend when I slid into the front seat. My heart rate slowed, and I ran my hand affectionately over the leather-wrapped steering wheel. I hadn't driven her in ten years.

Pop had surprised me with the car on my sixteenth birthday. Since Mama left, our birthdays had otherwise gone unacknowledged. Like me, that car was in rough shape, but I guess we'd both recognized the potential. I took auto shop the next two semesters at school and threw myself into the project. It hadn't been fully restored by the time I left for the Army, but the work was well under way.

I turned the visor down, and the keys fell onto my lap. The engine cranked a couple of times with the first turn, then roared to life with the second. I blew out my breath and smiled. Pop took care of my car as if he'd been waiting for me to come back home.

The smile slid off my face when I thought about Mama sleeping in our house again. I couldn't believe Pop had taken her back, and she'd been living there for the last six weeks.

I backed out of the garage and left rubber on the road as I headed for Coop's new place, which he'd told me about over a few beers the night before. The GTO sat in the driveway with Coop's bottom half sticking out from under the open hood. I pulled in behind it, and he straightened up. He looked at the Mustang and then at me.

"Back in the saddle," he said as he wiped his hands with an oily rag.

"Mama's back."

"What?"

"You heard me," I snapped.

"Relax." He held up his hands. "Are you sure it was her?"

"She made me breakfast this morning."

His wide eyes narrowed. "You're kidding."

"I wish. She moved back into the house."

"Just like that?"

I nodded.

"How do you feel about it?"

"I haven't decided. She said her boyfriend died and left her alone and broke. She figured maybe Pop would give her a second chance. Apparently, he did."

"How long has she been here?"

"As far as I can tell, she showed up about a month before he died."

Coop's eyes glazed over, and he scratched his chin. "I haven't seen her around."

At Shady's, Coop had told me he watched a lot of TV. I guess that's what you do after you've been married for a few years. Crime shows like *CSI* and *Criminal Minds* were his favorite. His eyes cleared, and he looked at me. "Do you think she—?"

"Don't even go there." Unfortunately, I couldn't shake the feeling that she hadn't told me everything.

Jolene stood on the front porch and put her hands on her hips. "Dillon Bishop. Is that you under all that hair?"

I tipped my hat in her direction as Coop went back to work.

She ran down the steps and threw a big hug around me. "I couldn't believe it when Cooper told me you were back in town." She rubbed her hands on my furry cheeks and scrunched her nose. "What's all this?"

I shrugged. "Just lazy, I guess."

"Y'all gonna stick around for a while?"

"I'm only here to clean up after Pop's…" The sentence went unfinished.

"Yeah. I'm real sorry to hear about that." She stepped back. "If there's anything I can do to help, you be sure to let me know."

"Thanks."

She turned and slapped the GTO's fender. "Hey, Cooper."

Coop looked out from under the hood.

"Did you tell Dillon about the reunion?"

"Now, why would I do that? He hated Bradley High. I'm sure he doesn't want to see any of those assholes again."

"Maybe you should let *him* decide."

"Maybe *you* should go back in the house."

Jolene gave him a dismissive wave, then turned to me. "It's this Saturday night in the gym. Ten years. Can you believe it?"

Coop was right. There's no one there I wanted to see.

"Nicole will be there," she said, like we were sixteen again.

Well, almost no one. My thoughts drifted.

"Did you hear me, Dillon?"

"Of course he heard you," Coop said after he blew out a breath. "Why would you even say something like that? He doesn't want to see that—"

I held up a hand to stop him. "It's okay."

"Really, Bish? Nicole?" Coop wiped his hands and shook his head.

"Don't start," I said, pointing a finger in his direction. "We grew up together. Don't forget, I've known her longer than I've known you."

"Yeah, but I didn't treat you like shit in high school."

"You had your moments." I forced a smile. "She felt like family when mine fell apart."

"Until she got too big for her britches and left you behind. I hoped you would have gotten over her after all these years."

I shrugged. "I reckon I just need closure."

"See, Jo? I knew this would happen." Coop looked from Jolene to me. "There's no such thing as closure with you. You've never been able to let go of anything."

I met his stare. "Thank you, Doctor Phil."

"All I'm saying is that maybe it's time to move on. Nicole's gonna be nothin' but trouble for you if you keep this up." He frowned at me like a disapproving parent. "Don't you have a girl back in Dallas?"

"Really, Dillon?" Jolene asked, eyes wide. "What's she like?"

"She's just a friend."

"With benefits?" Coop asked as he picked up a wrench.

I smiled.

He shook the wrench at me. "Once you cross that line, they're never just friends."

"Trust me. Jenny Lee's different."

"No. *You* trust *me*." He nodded his head toward Jolene. "They're all the same."

Jolene smiled and shrugged.

"Jo works with Nicole at the hospital." Coop wagged the wrench in his wife's direction. "Go on. Tell him what a nut-job she is."

"Stop it, Cooper. She's not that bad. She just went through a rough patch after she broke off the engagement with Josh."

"Wait a minute." I took a half-step backward. "Nicole and Josh Wilkerson?"

"Yeah, but she ended it a couple of years back. I guess you wouldn't have known." She wrinkled her nose like she'd just smelled something awful. "It wasn't pretty."

"Oh yeah, one more thing." Coop said. "She has a kid."

I swallowed hard. "Really?"

"I shit you not. Shouldn't be too hard to guess who the father is."

His tone hurt more than his words. I removed my hat and wiped the back of my hand across my forehead.

"Still wanna go?" Coop asked with a sneer.

I studied Coop's smug expression through squinted eyes, then turned to Jolene. "What time?"

She smiled. "It starts at six. Bring your dancin' shoes."

Coop shook his head and disappeared under the hood.

The next day, Jolene offered to drive me to Cleburne and help me pick out some new clothes. She said she didn't want to see me at the reunion in anything from my thrift store collection. I'd never been one to dress up much.

Jolene parked in front of a barbershop. I raised a suspicious eyebrow.

"Okay, here's the thing, Dillon. The hair's fine, but the beard's gotta go."

"I thought you were *Coop's* wife, not mine."

She turned, rested her elbow on the console, and grinned. "We can do this the easy way or the hard way. Your choice."

I told her I needed a minute and dialed Pop's lawyer. The call went to voicemail again. I reiterated my desire to clear up this matter as quickly as possible and left a callback number.

Jolene watched me like a hawk, no doubt afraid I might make a run for it.

Forty minutes later, I climbed back into the SUV feeling a couple of pounds lighter. I rubbed my naked chin as Jolene watched from the driver's seat and nodded her approval.

"If I wasn't married," she said, "I'd seriously consider jumpin' your bones right here in the car."

"Does that mean you like it?"

She put the car in reverse and backed into the street. "Maybe we should finish your makeover first."

An hour later, we started back to Bradley with a new shirt, pants, and boots in the back seat. Jolene pushed hard for a sport jacket, but I had to draw the line.

About halfway home, the flat, dry landscape brought back disturbing memories. I stared out the side window during a lull in our conversation. When I turned my attention to the road again, the sun reflected off something metallic on the shoulder, less than one click ahead of our position. At our current rate of speed, we'd be on top of it in twenty seconds. I had to act fast.

"IED!" I grabbed the wheel and pulled it in my direction. At the same time, I jammed my foot on the brake, trapping Jolene's foot between mine and the pedal. She screamed.

The SUV skidded to a stop. A cloud of dust continued down the road while we sat sideways in an empty field.

"Dillon!" Her knuckles turned white on the wheel. "What the hell was that?"

I pushed the door open and ran up ahead.

"Dillon!"

I stopped a few feet away from an old paint can on the side of the road. Someone approached from behind. I turned. "Stay back." *Jolene?* I squeezed my eyes shut. When I opened them, I held Coop's wife, Jolene, beside a busy highway. The sun burned down from a cloudless Texas sky as a tractor-trailer passed and forced a wall of hot air toward us.

Jolene looked up with tears in her eyes. "Dillon?"

I shook my head. "What are we doing here?"

She pressed her face into my chest and sobbed.

CHAPTER 5

I checked the time on my phone as I waited for Coop and Jolene on the high school steps. 1830 hours. The military demanded punctuality, so I learned to expect it from others.

I dialed Coop's number. Jolene answered and said something about a problem with their regular babysitter. Coop's mother agreed to watch the girls and would be there in twenty minutes. Jolene suggested I go inside without them. Not a good start to the evening.

I stepped onto the polished hardwood floor of the Bradley High School gymnasium. I'd never played basketball there, but Luke had. The bleachers where I'd sat and watched had been retracted for tonight's festivities, the basketball goals raised and suspended parallel to the ceiling. A small crowd had gathered around a makeshift bar in the far corner while a DJ set up his equipment in the opposite corner. A handful of people watched a photo slideshow on a sixty-inch flat screen.

"Welcome to the Class of 2009 10-Year Reunion," a tall blonde chirped from behind the reception table.

I glanced at her name tag. Amanda Hughes. I remembered her as a friend of Nicole's, but I'd bet money she couldn't guess my name if her life depended on it. I felt her eyes study me while I scanned the tags laid out in rows on the table like so many lonely crosses at Arlington. Mine wouldn't be among them, but I wasn't looking for mine.

Memories surfaced, most of them bad, as I made my way down the long table. I reached the end, disappointed that I hadn't seen Nicole's name. I took a deep breath.

"Are these the people who said they would be here tonight?" I asked.

"Yes, but there's always a few who just show up."

I nodded. "Like me."

"Oh." She smiled. "Why didn't you say so?" She picked up a blank tag.

I waited until she uncapped the marker. "Dillon Bishop."

Amanda stared at me without moving.

"Do you need me to spell it?"

She shook her head and wrote quickly.

I thanked her, peeled off the back, and slapped the tag on my shirt pocket upside-down. Amanda shifted in her chair as she watched me. I'd expected a few surprised looks tonight, my second reason for being there, but Amanda's expression held more than surprise.

"Enjoy your evening," she said, the sparkle gone from her voice.

I nodded after a quick scan of the room. "We'll see."

I walked over to the bar. The heels of my new boots announced my approach on the hardwood. A few heads turned, looked away, then turned again. I smiled as I watched the squinted eyes struggle to read my tag from ten feet away.

Amanda paced behind the registration table as I leaned against the bar and waited for my drink. I'd spooked her, but why? I checked the door for Coop and Jolene, then checked the time on my phone. I noticed Nicole when I turned around. Her long raven hair shimmered under the gymnasium lights. She spoke with two other women, and her green eyes flashed at something one of them said.

Nicole's expression fell when she caught my stare. A frown narrowed her eyes for a moment. I didn't think my face had changed all that much, but I'd added fifty pounds of muscle and six inches of hair. The package is one that none of them could possibly remember.

She looked as nervous as a long-tailed cat in a room full of rocking chairs. I couldn't be sure if she'd recognized me or thought I was a reunion-crashing serial killer. Same reaction as Amanda.

I stopped a safe distance away and said, "Nicole Garcia."

Her green eyes studied me, her expression unreadable.

I reached for my hat before I realized I'd left it home, so I raked my hand back through my hair. I had a decision to make. Bitch-slap her for what she did to me ten years ago, or take the high road and let bygones be bygones. Ten years is a long time. I hesitated.

Her smile held a measure of recognition.

The high road it is. "I didn't think it was possible, but you look even better than the last time I saw you."

She glanced at my tag for verification, but her eyes told me she'd already made that connection. "Dillon Bishop. I... I hardly recognized you."

I smiled. "I get that a lot."

"Where have you been hiding all this time?"

"Afghanistan, mostly." We fell silent for a moment, like we had nothing else to say to each other.

"You still here in Bradley?" I asked.

"Unfortunately." She shrugged. "I work at the hospital."

"Nurse?"

"That's right." I noticed a measure of pride in her smile. "How about you?"

"Me? No, I'm not a nurse." I paused a moment, then grinned like a possum.

Nicole relaxed and covered her mouth to conceal a laugh. We made small talk for a few minutes, mostly about who was there and how much they'd changed in ten years. My anger had made a hasty retreat. She still had some kind of power over me. I should have been angry about that.

Coop walked in, took one look at Nicole and me, and shook his head. He said something to Jolene, who promptly punched his arm.

I excused myself.

"I see you've already locked on to your target," Coop said as I approached. "Hey, don't let us interrupt your little..."

Jolene glared at Cooper, then looked me up and down. She smiled. "You look very handsome, Dillon."

I nodded and gave Coop a sideways glance. "Thank you, Jo." I took a step back and gave her the once-over. "Day-um! I still say Coop doesn't deserve you."

"I'll take that as a compliment."

Coop rolled his eyes and shook his head.

"Well? Was she surprised to see you?" Jolene's eyes widened. "I didn't tell her you were coming."

Coop put his arms around our shoulders. "I'll let you ladies talk. I'm gonna go get a beer."

I held up my empty. "I'm ready for another."

"White wine," Jolene said.

Coop threw his hands in the air as he headed toward the bar.

I looked at Jolene. "Let's just say it went better than I thought it would."

We walked to the reception table where Jo picked up their name tags. Amanda stole a glance at me every chance she could.

Coop returned with our drinks just as Josh walked in with a couple of the Bradley jocks. They walked past us without a word, like they were still too good for us. I let it slide.

A hand touched my arm. "Dillon."

I smiled when I recognized Mrs. Sanchez, my tenth-grade math teacher, at my side. Her close-set eyes matched her jet-black hair. They traveled up and down as she gave me a better look. "I thought that might be you. You're all grown up."

"I don't know if I'd go that far."

"How are you?"

I spread my arms. "I'm still here, ain't I?"

"It's a good thing you weren't in my English class," she said before we shared a laugh. "I'm sorry to hear about your daddy," she added after a moment of silence.

"Thank you, Ma'am."

She smiled. "You and Luke were two of my favorite students. Your mama taught you well."

"I reckon she did," I said as I nodded. "That is, until she up and left us."

Her expression fell. "Do you ever see her?"

"No, ma'am, I'm afraid I don't."

She wrung her hands and glanced around the room before her eyes met mine. "Nice to see you again, Dillon."

I gave a quick nod. "My pleasure, ma'am."

As she walked away, Jolene leaned in and whispered, "I can't believe you just lied to Mrs. Sanchez."

"Like the woman said, Mama taught me well."

Jolene let an elbow fly that caught me in the ribs. I took a step back and gave her a *what-the-hell'd-you-do-that-for* look. She turned and walked toward the food table. A carving station with a slab of roast beef and those itty-bitty rolls had attracted a crowd.

The DJ played an assortment of New Country and Red Dirt tunes from back in the day. After dinner, Coop and I met up with Jimmy Arroyo, the third of our *Three Amigos*. We'd done everything together in high school, then went our separate ways.

Jimmy had been the brains of our trio, a real computer nerd, so I wasn't surprised to hear he'd landed a job with a big tech firm in Arlington. We spent a half-hour catching up. He gave us each a business card with the words *Security Systems Product Manager* under his name and told us he could hook us up if we ever needed anything. I'm not sure what he meant by that, but good to know.

I kept an eye on Nicole throughout the evening. We talked again briefly before she ran off to dance with Amanda and a few others. About three hours into the tedious affair, I watched Josh and Nicole engaged in a heated discussion away from the main crowd. When Josh grabbed her arm, I set my beer down and walked toward them.

Nicole pulled her arm free. But by the time I reached them, he had her in his grasp again.

"Is there a problem here?"

"Keep walkin', Bishop. This doesn't concern you."

"If you don't let her go right now, it's gonna concern me plenty."

He maintained his grip as he turned toward me, eyes narrow and nostrils flared. The taste in the back of my throat wasn't fear, it was adrenaline—the fight-or-flight hormone. Josh wouldn't last thirty seconds with me in hand-to-hand combat.

Slowly, he released his grip on Nicole's arm and I stepped between them, my face only inches from his. "Why don't you go enjoy the rest of your evening?" I said as calmly as I could.

"You better watch your back, Bishop." His jaw tightened. "This isn't over."

I maintained my position until he walked away, then turned to Nicole. "What was that about?"

"It doesn't matter now." She composed herself. "Thank you."

"No one's gonna assault a woman and get away with it if I'm in the room."

"Good to know." She adjusted the strap on her dress and flipped a wall of long, black hair over her shoulder. After a deep breath, she took my hand. "C'mon," she said and pulled me onto the dance floor.

Fortunately for everyone there, the DJ played a slow song. Nicole held on tightly, and I'd be lying if I said I didn't enjoy every second. Halfway through the song, a crash echoed from somewhere behind me. I turned to see Josh slam his fist down on a table, producing another similar sound.

"He's really pissed," I said to Nicole.

She smiled and squeezed a little tighter. The image of Josh melted away.

"Let's get some air," she said when the song finished.

I'd bet money Nicole made sure Josh watched us leave.

The July night air felt heavy and warm, but I didn't mind. Stars twinkled above, and Nicole seemed to have a pretty good handle on their names and locations. Jenny Lee had tried to teach me once, but I hadn't been interested at the time.

"I don't want to go back inside," Nicole said, still gazing at the heavens. "Would you walk me home?"

"Uh..." Probably a bad idea. I looked back at the door. I'd have to listen to a rash of shit from Coop tomorrow. "Sure. Why not?" At least she wouldn't get into any more trouble with Josh.

Nicole owned a small house near the center of town, about a quarter mile walk from the school. I figured I could double back to pick up my car after I dropped her off. I kept an eye out for Josh and the boys along the way.

We had a few awkward moments at her front door.

"Do you want to come inside?"

I hesitated while my head, and possibly my heart, put down the hormonal mutiny. "I have someone back in Dallas."

A few seconds passed. "She's a lucky girl."

"The way I see it, I'm the lucky one."

For much of the night, I'd felt like a pawn in Nicole's game of sticking it to Josh. But the moonlight revealed a genuine disappointment in her eyes. I'd felt a rush spending time again with Nicole, but the last place I wanted to be was in the crosshairs of a jilted lover with a badge.

Nicole reluctantly accepted my answer, stood on her toes, and kissed my cheek. "Good night, Dillon Bishop," she said with a sigh.

I took my time on the way back to the school. I had no intention of going inside.

My car sat on its rims in the parking lot, all four tires slashed. I kicked one, then raked my hands back through my hair. A call to the police would do me no good. My gut told me this crime had been committed by one of their own.

CHAPTER 6

I avoided Coop the next day, but by Monday morning, I needed to do something about my car. Coop owned an auto repair and detailing shop on Market Street. I parked Pop's Silverado out front and went inside. The staccato blast of an air wrench reminded me of machine-gun fire as I walked through the service area and up an open stairway.

Stale exhaust followed me into a small, glass-walled office that overlooked the activity below. I closed the door behind me.

Coop looked up from behind an old wooden desk.

"I need a tow."

"Let me guess," he said, shaking his head. "You took Nicole for a drive and ran out of gas."

"I wish." I braced myself for one of Coop's *I-told-you-so* lectures. "It's in the school parking lot with the tires slashed."

"This is because of *her*, isn't it?" He stood and punched a fist into his palm. "I knew it! Didn't I tell you she'd be trouble?" He waited for an acknowledgment. When he didn't get one, he said, "Didn't I?"

I nodded.

"You need to report this."

"To who? The police?" I snorted. "Maybe they'll send Josh to investigate."

Coop sat and shook his head again. "Day-um!" After a few moments of silence, he said, "Okay, I'll take care of the car. But you need to stay away from that—"

"I don't know if I can do that."

Coop's shoulders dropped as he stared. A few seconds passed. "Leave your keys on the desk and get the hell out of here."

I obliged. On my way down the stairs, Coop called my name. I turned.

"You got something to drive in the meantime?"

I nodded. "Pop's truck."

He dismissed me with a wave of his hand.

My next stop: the office of Mortimer J. Anderson, Esquire. Mort had been Pop's lawyer for as long as I could remember. He'd finally returned my calls and asked me to meet him at his office on Monday morning.

A bell jingled when I opened the old wood-and-glass door. I entered a small but neat waiting room in a brick office building adjacent to the courthouse. An empty secretary's desk faced a half-dozen wooden chairs set up around the perimeter of the room. I called out, but no one answered. I sat and waited, grateful for the running air-conditioner.

Ten minutes later, Mr. Anderson, a portly gentleman carrying a large briefcase, strolled through the front door. The buttons of his short-sleeved shirt strained along his midsection behind a short, striped tie that hung loosely around his neck. He set down his case, pulled out a handkerchief, and blotted his forehead and inside his open collar.

He gazed at me over a pair of round, steel-rimmed glasses that matched the shape of his face. "Is that you, Dillon?"

"It sure is, Mr. Anderson." I hadn't spent much time with Pop's friends, but I recognized the voice from my childhood. I'd lay in bed on Saturday night and inhale cigar smoke while I listened to Pop and two close friends solve the world's problems over more than a bit of whiskey. Mort's gentle, almost jovial voice stood in stark contrast to the raucous "Wild Bill" McCutchen.

"Why, I barely recognize you, son." He smiled as he wiped his glasses, then hooked the stems, one at a time, around his ears. "How long has it been?"

"Over ten years, sir." I nodded.

"You can dispense with the formalities. Mort will do just fine." He slid his thumbs under his frayed black suspenders and snapped them against his chest. He picked up his case, then motioned for me to follow him through a door behind his secretary's desk.

The tidiness of the waiting room did not extend beyond the threshold we'd just crossed. Stacks of papers, folders, and legal-looking volumes covered every horizontal space in the room except for three chairs. Mort sat in a large leather chair behind what must have been a desk under all that clutter. I hesitated, afraid that if I sat, I'd no longer be able to see him.

"Have a seat," he said and methodically rearranged several piles. "It may not appear to be the most efficient filing system, but it works for me." He leaned forward and folded his meaty hands on the desk. "We had trouble tracking you down after your daddy passed. Your mama, too. I didn't know she was even alive until the police brought her in for questioning."

"Why? I thought Pop died in the hospital."

"Standard procedure." He waved a hand like he was swatting flies. "I've always had a soft spot for Bonnie. I went down there to make sure she got a fair shake. They didn't have enough to hold her, so I took her home."

"Did she say why she came back?"

"I didn't ask," he said, his eyes focused somewhere behind me. They never divorced, so that certainly affects the disposition of Eli's assets."

The bell above the front door jingled and brought him back. "In here," he called.

A thin man, probably in his mid-forties, entered the room. I stood.

"Dillon, this is Sam Granger. Sam, Dillon Bishop."

Granger nodded, and we shook hands. He wore snakeskin boots under new Wranglers and a suede sport jacket. His long, square nose, brown eyes, and large ears made him look like a beagle.

He sat in the empty chair and handed me his card. *Insurance Investigator.*

"Sam asked me to set up this little meeting," Mort said while I studied the card.

Granger nodded. "I'll get right to it. I'm investigating a claim by a Bonnie Bishop on a $100,000 life insurance policy purchased one month before the named insured, Eli Bishop, died in Memorial Hospital."

My foot tingled, and I shifted my weight in the chair. "I had no idea the policy even existed."

"I didn't think so," Granger replied. "Obviously, your Mama did."

"Mort? Did you know anything about this?" I asked.

Mort held up his hands and shook his head.

"I think we can all agree that the timing is suspicious." Granger cleared his throat. "Texas Star Mutual Life does not pay claims for suicide or for murder by a named beneficiary."

I looked at him through squinted eyes. "Did you just call my mama a murderer?"

"Frankly, I haven't ruled out that possibility."

I turned to Mort for help, but he just shrugged. "Is that what you think, too?"

"Perhaps if you'd let me finish," Granger said in a calm voice.

I studied him for a moment. Beagles have a distinctive expression that makes them look like they want something. I knew what Granger wanted—to get his company off the hook for Pop's policy. A sizable commission most likely awaited him if he succeeded. Judging by the boots and the oversized, diamond-studded bolo tie around his neck, I reckoned he had an excellent track record.

A few seconds of silence passed. "I did some digging into Bonnie's recent past," the beagle said. "Prior to her return to Bradley, she spent three months in a homeless shelter in Amarillo. During that time, I believe she started used crystal meth, which she received from a local dealer with whom she'd had an undetermined relationship."

Pictures of Mama on the streets with some low-life drug dealer played in my mind like a bad movie. I shook my head to clear it. "What does that have to do with anything?"

"Addicts need money." He avoided eye contact. "Your father didn't die of natural causes. According to the Medical Examiner's report, the seizure and massive coronary he suffered while in the hospital were induced by methamphetamine."

The air left the room, and I reached for another breath. "It doesn't prove Mama killed him."

His voice softened. "The police have provided me with video from the hospital security cameras that show her leaving Eli's room minutes before he crashed."

I leaned back in my chair.

Mort stood, walked around his desk, and placed a hand on my shoulder. "Your mama's fallen on hard times, but I can't believe she'd do something like this."

Too late. The seed had been planted. Mama had told me that her boyfriend died of a heart attack, as well. I decided not to mention it.

I wondered if Pop had watched her, knowing he was about to die. Hospitals are supposed to be safe. There's an unwritten agreement, an assumption inherent in the patient's bill of rights, that you needn't be concerned that someone—doctor, nurse, or visitor—might enter your room and kill you. I hoped he'd been asleep and didn't die choking on his own fear.

"What do we do now?" I asked.

Granger shook his head. "I'm sorry, Dillon. I've got a few loose ends to tie up, then I file my report."

"Couldn't he have just had a heart attack?"

"I think he had help, and the evidence points to Bonnie." Granger stood.

I took a deep breath as I found it increasingly difficult to argue with his suspicions. We shook hands, and he left.

"Dillon," Mort said from behind his desk. "Keep this under your hat until he files his report."

I gave a quick nod, then turned to leave. Fortunately, I'd left my hat at home.

CHAPTER 7

I met Coop for lunch at the Parkway Diner. We talked over chili dogs and Dr. Peppers about my meeting with Mort and the insurance investigator. Like me, his first reaction was disbelief, followed by growing suspicion. Part of me hoped he would see something I missed that might exonerate Mama. That didn't happen. In fact, he suggested I do some investigative work at the house after she fell asleep.

I called Nicole after Coop left. She worked the seven to three shift but agreed to meet me in the park behind the hospital when she got off. Nicole had been on duty the day Pop died, and I hoped she might remember something to help me understand what happened.

I arrived just before three and waited on a bench under a large cedar elm. Several more shade trees dotted the well-manicured acre tucked behind Memorial Hospital. Each had their own benches and picnic tables positioned for maximum shelter from the relentless Texas sun. A walking trail wound its way through the grounds for the more daring souls. Hospital staff who frequented this nameless park simply referred to it as *the park*.

Nicole approached a few minutes later, wearing a smile. "I was surprised to get your call."

"Not as surprised as I was to make it."

She sat next to me; her expression held equal parts of fear and curiosity.

"I need to talk to you about the day Pop died."

Nicole shifted in her seat. "What would you like to know?"

"Was Mama there?"

"She came by shortly after he died. I let her sit with him for a while." She lowered her head. "You know, to say goodbye."

"You're sure she visited *after* he died?"

"Things got crazy that day, but yes, I'm sure of it." Another curious look. "Why?"

"It's nothing." I shook my head. But it wasn't nothing. Granger had said the security video showed Mama leaving before he died. Why would Nicole lie? "What do you mean *crazy?*"

"A police officer had been shot in a hunting accident. The police chief and most of the force were there."

"What about Josh?"

She nodded.

"Did you talk to Pop at all?"

"Just for a minute when I gave him his meds. He seemed in pretty good spirits."

"When was that?"

She looked down at her feet. "It couldn't have been more than ten minutes before he died." She looked up and wiped her index finger just below one eye. "I was the last one to speak to him."

"Thank you." I placed my hand on hers and studied her for a moment as she wiped another tear. "I didn't mean to upset you."

"I hope I was able to help."

I nodded, unsure whether she'd helped or added to the confusion.

I waited for an hour after Mama had gone to bed before I conducted my covert op. My need to know if I'd been sleeping under the same roof as the enemy trumped my reservations about violating Mama's personal space.

Mama's purse sat on the kitchen counter. I listened for a good five minutes to the steady rhythm of the clock on the wall and the refrigerator hum. Convinced that Mama had fallen asleep, I dragged the zipper across the length of the bag and rummaged through the main compartment. Sunglasses, hairbrush, keys, various grocery and drug store receipts. Nothing out of the ordinary or incriminating. I exhaled, unaware I'd been holding my breath.

I moved on to the three zippered compartments. The longest one contained an envelope. Inside, I found the insurance policy that Granger had mentioned. But her knowledge of the policy was not necessarily an indictment.

A second, smaller compartment held a small glass vial of tiny white crystals. *Damn it, Mama!* I'd just found the smoking gun. I hesitated while I considered my options. If I put it back and she found out I suspected her, she might destroy the evidence. On the other hand, if I took it, there would be no way to prove how I got it. Or worse, I might incriminate myself.

A creak. Mama's door? A floorboard in the living room? I returned everything to its original place and zipped the purse. I scanned the kitchen for an excuse to be there. I opened the refrigerator door and stuck my head inside.

"I thought I heard someone in here. You're up late."

I turned to find Mama in her robe, standing in the living room doorway. "Sorry. I didn't mean to wake you, but I couldn't sleep."

"There's fresh pecan pie in there, and vanilla ice cream in the freezer." She glanced at the clock and smiled. "Let's have a midnight snack."

CHAPTER 8

The next morning, I answered a knock at the door to find Jenny Lee on my front porch in boots, cutoff shorts, and a Rascal Flatts t-shirt.

"If y'all are trying to ditch me, Dillon Bishop," she said, "you're going to have to try a little harder."

I stepped outside and smiled. "If I was trying to ditch you, we wouldn't be having this conversation."

Jenny Lee held her arms out at her side. "Y'all gonna kiss me or not?"

I planted one on her, unaware of how much I'd missed her lips. "What are you doing here?" I asked.

"That's what you're gonna open with? I expected something like, *Hey, darlin', I missed you so much, it hurt.*"

"I was gettin' to that." I opened the front door. "After you, d*arlin'.*"

She breezed past me into the living room.

"How long you fixin' on stayin' in town?" I asked.

"Not long. I'm here to drag y'all back to Dallas. We need to pack. We're goin' to Colorado next week." She raised an eyebrow. "Remember?"

My expression fell.

Mama walked in from the kitchen, and I forced a smile. "Shame on you, Dillon. You didn't tell me we had company."

"Mama, this is Jenny Lee. Jenn, this is Bonnie."

Jenny Lee shot me a sideways glance before nodding in Mama's direction. "Pleasure to meet you, Bonnie."

"Likewise, I'm sure," Mama said.

I cleared my throat. "We'll be on the front porch."

"I'll bring you some tea."

"That'd be nice," Jenny Lee said as I nudged her toward the door. The rusty springs moaned when we sat on the neglected porch swing.

"*Mama?*" Jenny Lee said, eyes wide. "I thought she walked out on y'all when you were a kid."

"Apparently, she walked back in a couple of months ago."

"Want to talk about it?"

"Not here."

"Okay, Dillon, but it ain't healthy to keep it bottled up inside."

Time to change the subject. "I've got an idea. There's a couple of good friends who'd love to meet you. Let's see if they want to have dinner tonight."

"Sounds like a plan." A smile returned to her face, and she kissed my cheek. "By the way, who finally convinced you to shave?"

"That would be Coop's wife, Jolene." I smiled. "You'll meet her tonight."

"I like her already."

Mama stepped through the front door with a pitcher of iced tea and two glasses. I took the tray from her and set it on a small table near the swing. I gave Mama a *that'll-be-all-for-now* look and she stepped back inside.

I pulled out my cell phone and made dinner arrangements with Jolene, then reservations at the

Longhorn Steak House. Jolene assured me that Coop would be on his best behavior.

Jenny Lee wanted to visit all the spots in Bradley that had meant something to me growing up. We drove to the old quarry, a popular make-out spot for young, fumbling, wannabe lovers. We got out of the car and sat on one of the big red rocks.

"I get the feeling that you're not ready to leave Bradley yet," she said as she stared out over the large hole in the earth.

I threw a stone into the water fifty feet below and watched the ripples spread across the surface. "I can't."

"Is it me?"

"Absolutely not. I love you, Jenn." The words spilled from my mouth like I'd been holding them there too long. I froze and waited for a response.

After a few seconds, a warm smile spread across her face. "Good answer," she whispered, followed by the best quarry kiss ever. When we finished, I collected my thoughts and told her everything that had happened since I'd arrived in Bradley. I explained my suspicions about Mama's return.

"If you think it would help, we could stay a few extra days."

I owed it to Pop to find out what really happened. It still tore me up that I hadn't been able to do that for Luke. "We'll see."

I wished I could have been more excited about driving off into the sunset with Jenn. My conflicted heart ached over the decision I would soon have to make. Nevertheless, we had a great afternoon, except for one awkward moment when we ran into Nicole and her daughter. I had an uneasy feeling, which I'm sure did not go unnoticed by Jenny Lee.

We stopped at Shady's for a beer on the way home. I led her to a table in the back and watched her casually check the place out along the way. I couldn't wait for Coop and Jolene to meet her.

"Y'all used to hang out here a lot, I reckon," she said as we sat.

"I sure did. Came here mostly for the food." I took a drink and licked my lips. "Until I got my fake ID."

"The place has a good vibe." She smiled and looked around before she met my gaze. "I wish I knew you back then."

I shook my head. "No, you don't."

"C'mon, Dillon, y'all must have been cute."

"Okay. How's this for cute? The first time I came here after I got the ID, I threw up under this very table." I drank my beer and watched her expression fall.

She wrinkled her nose. "That's not exactly how I'd pictured it."

Jenny Lee had been a big breath of fresh air in my otherwise stale existence. I'd nearly lost my left foot when an RPG ripped open our Humvee outside Kandahar. My recovery had been slow and lonely. I'm not sure what I would have done after I left the hospital if it hadn't been for her. I've always had this feeling that Luke had died and reached down from Heaven to put her in that thrift store in Dallas. He told her to wait for me like he knew she could save me.

"Are you ready to go?" I asked after I drained my bottle.

She peeked under the table. "I am now," she said in mock disgust.

We laughed.

After a quick stop home to change, we met Coop and Jolene at the restaurant.

Jenny Lee fit right in with our group. She made quite an impression, and she didn't hesitate to ask all kinds of questions about my past. Coop and Jolene launched into a medley of stories that could have been titled, *The Most Embarrassing Moments of Dillon Bishop's Life, Volume 1.* Jenny Lee spent a good deal of time laughing at my expense, but her eyes told me there wasn't anything they could have said that would change her mind about me.

I sat back and folded my arms across my chest. "Maybe next, we can hear stories about Jenny Lee."

"I'd sure like that," Coop said.

Jolene punched his arm, feigning jealousy. She stood. "C'mon, Jenny Lee." The two women headed toward the restrooms.

Coop looked at me, his expression serious. "I hope you don't need me to tell you that Jenny Lee's a keeper. 'Cause if you do, you need to get your head examined."

"I'm probably due for a head exam, anyway."

"I'm just sayin', if I were you, I wouldn't let that girl out of my sight."

I forced a smile, knowing that was exactly what I was about to do. "I need to tell you something."

Coop reached for his drink, then studied me for a moment. "This can't be good. Go ahead, Mr. Buzzkill."

I glanced around the room and leaned closer. "I found the insurance policy in Mama's purse last night."

Coop took a long drink. "That doesn't mean that—"

"I also found crystal meth."

"Jeezus, Bish." He swallowed hard. "What are you gonna do?"

"I don't know."

"Do you guys want to stay with us tonight? We've got an extra room."

"Thanks, but I need to talk to Mama first. She wouldn't try to hurt us."

The women returned, and Jolene placed her hands on the back of her chair. "You two look so serious. What did we miss?"

"Nothin'," Coop said. "Just guy stuff."

Jolene shot a suspicious glance at her husband, then turned to Jenny Lee and shrugged.

"Maybe we should call it a night," I said before the two sat down.

"One more drink?" Jolene looked from Jenny to me.

"Thanks," I said, "but I think we're gonna pass. It's been a long day."

Coop drained his bottle and set it on the table. "Yeah, I'll bet they're real tired."

Jolene's head snapped in Coop's direction. "Cooper!"

"I'm just sayin' that they haven't, you know, *seen* each other in a while."

"I know what you're sayin'." She turned to Jenny Lee. "I'm sorry, honey. Sometimes he's a real jackass."

"I don't mind it," Jenny Lee said, and flashed a mischievous smile in my direction. "I had a great time tonight."

"It's too bad you can't stick around for a while," Coop said. "I'd sure like to do this again sometime."

"Maybe y'all could come out to visit. Colorado isn't that far away."

Only seven-hundred-fifty miles, give or take. Colorado. The word held both promise and pain.

Coop slapped the table. "C'mon. One more round. I'm buyin'."

"They said no, Cooper." Jo smiled apologetically at Jenny Lee, then sighed as she touched my arm. "I'll miss you when you leave Bradley, but I'm happy that you can finally move on with your life. It's time. I believe that when one door closes, another one opens."

"I guess you're right."

Coop shook his head. "Sometimes when one door closes, you need to nail a board over it."

I knew he was referring to Nicole.

Jo shot him another look.

"We'll see you again," I said. "It's not like we're leaving in the morning."

They nodded, and we said good night.

Jenny Lee talked on the ride home while I worried about Mama and the real reason she'd come back.

We walked into the house to find Mama watching television in the living room. Something still rubbed me the wrong way about her sitting in Pop's chair.

"What are you watching?" I didn't care, but I felt like I had to say something.

"It's a new show this season called *How to Get Away with Murder*."

I told myself it was just a coincidence.

"How was dinner?" she asked without looking up.

"We had a wonderful night," Jenny Lee replied.

I slipped my arm around her waist. "We're off to bed now. See you in the morning."

She nodded without words.

We walked down the hall toward our room. Jenny Lee went inside, and I stood in the doorway watching Mama sit in the television's glow like it was just another night, in just another normal family, in just another normal house, in just another normal town. I took a deep breath, stepped inside my room, and closed the door.

CHAPTER 9

I stared up into the darkness from my bed, Jenny Lee's arm draped across my chest. Her soft skin and slow, rhythmic breathing couldn't calm the storm that raged inside my head. I wanted desperately to leave this life behind, drive off with Jenny Lee, and never hear the words Bradley or Texas again. But I knew I couldn't do that.

I walked into the kitchen a little after midnight. Mama sat at the table with her hands wrapped around a cup of tea. After a few seconds, she looked up and her sad eyes brightened.

"Can't sleep either?" She patted the table. "I can make you some Sleepy Time tea."

"No, thanks." I pulled out a chair and sat.

"You sure? It really works."

I shook my head.

"Is Jenny asleep?"

"Stop it, Mama. We need to talk. I know about the insurance policy."

She sipped her tea.

"There's an insurance investigator in town who believes Pop was murdered."

She set her cup down slowly. "What do you believe?"

"The medical examiner says Pop died of a meth overdose."

"You went through my purse?"

"I had to."

"You can't imagine what it's been like, Dillon. I spent three months in a homeless shelter where I met some bad people. I was in a dark place, and I thought they wanted to help me."

Mama, an addict? Living in a homeless shelter? It didn't seem possible.

"Eventually, I realized that I might have a place to stay, to start over, if Eli could find it in his heart to forgive me. Technically, we were still married."

"That was a big *if*, don't you think?"

"Not when you're desperate."

"So, Pop took you in, and that turned out to be a fatal mistake."

She took another sip of tea and set down her cup. "Do you really think your mama is a killer?"

I stared without words.

"You've got to believe me, Dillon. I could never kill anyone, especially Eli."

"When's the last time you were high?"

"Sixty-six days ago." She glanced at the clock and smiled tightly. "Sixty-seven."

"Why do you have meth in your purse?"

"Did you try to open it?"

"No."

"You wouldn't have been able to. I glued the top on."

"Why do you keep it?"

"It's a reminder. A one-way ticket to hell." She sighed. "Sometimes when I get depressed, I take it out and remember how much worse things could be, and how lucky I am to be right here, right now."

I felt sorry for her, but I had a question, one that I thought I'd never have a chance to ask. I set my palms on the table and leaned forward. "Why did you leave?"

She looked away while she thought about her answer.

"I'm not ten years old anymore, Mama. You can tell me the truth."

After a deep breath, she said, "I loved your daddy. I still do. That wasn't it."

"He loved *you*."

"I know, but he didn't show it all that much." She placed her hand on mine. "Your daddy was a kind man and a decent provider, but I needed something more. I needed him to tell me how much he loved me and maybe show me once in a while."

I let her hand stay, the first time I'd felt Mama's touch in sixteen years. The faint maternal smile that crossed her lips forced old memories to surface—memories that had tarnished over the years. "Did *you* tell *him*? Did *you* show *him*?"

"At first I did, but it got harder and harder as the years went on."

"And I suppose your new boyfriend did all that?"

"Wade was a little more open with his feelings, but he was a strong man like your daddy. I don't know why men think tenderness is a sign of weakness."

"Wade, huh? I never even knew the man's name."

Ironically, it'd been Mama who introduced me to the rodeo when I was eight. Twice a year, we would drive up to Fort Worth for a few days. Pop, who preferred gun shows and poker games, stayed home. I looked forward to those trips with Mama—not just for the rodeo, but for the one-on-one time.

After our first few trips, Mama got real friendly with some of the cowboys. One of them gave me his hat when Mama told him I dreamed of becoming a real cowboy someday. I suspected it would never fit quite right. I burned that hat a few years later, just in case it had belonged to the man who stole my mama.

"I'm sorry, Dillon. I'm sorry for everything. Hell, maybe your brother would still be alive if I stayed. Maybe that's what good wives do. They just put up and shut up. If I'd done that, perhaps you wouldn't hate me so much."

"I… I don't hate you…" My heart moved up into my throat and blocked any more words. Somehow, I found the strength to place my other hand on hers.

Mama smiled as a tear left her eye.

"They never found Luke's body," I said. "What makes you think he's dead?"

"A shaman told me."

"A what?"

"A Cherokee medicine woman named Leotie."

I said nothing.

"Your daddy made enemies trying to uncover the reason behind Luke's disappearance. He believed Luke was dead, and that someone killed him. He told me he found evidence that would blow the lid off this little town."

"What kind of evidence?"

"I'm not sure. I don't think he trusted me enough to tell me."

"Do you think he told anyone else?"

She shrugged. "I don't know. He kept a journal where he wrote it all down, but I've never seen it and I don't know where it might be."

"Do you think that's why Pop died?"

She nodded. "I think someone needed to silence him." Fear, like a shadow, crossed her eyes. "I think they want to do the same to me."

"Why do you say that?" I squeezed her hand. "Did something happen?"

"No. It's just a feeling. Like someone is out there watching the house, waiting for the right time to make a move."

I stood, walked over to the kitchen window, and stared out into the darkness. No movement, no sounds. My thoughts turned to Jenny Lee, asleep in my old bed. My chest tightened and my foot tingled. Some people's joints ache before it rains. My damaged foot tingled when something bad was about to happen. Perhaps trouble lurked out there just out of sight. Or perhaps Mama's been lying about everything like addicts do.

"When I came back to town," Mama said in an unsteady voice, "I felt embarrassed. I didn't want anyone to know I was here. If Eli didn't let me stay, I'd have disappeared again, and no one would have been the wiser."

I turned. "You were here for a month before he died."

"I barely left the house for fear of running into someone I once knew. I wore a hat and hid behind dark glasses, afraid of what they'd say if they recognized me." She cried.

More paranoia. Part of me wanted desperately to believe her, but I hadn't seen her in so long, I just couldn't be sure. Eventually, she said good night and went to bed. I knew sleep wouldn't come easily for me after that, so I sat at the kitchen table and played our conversation over and over in my mind. When my head became too heavy to hold up any longer, I rested it on my folded arms.

I felt hands on my shoulders, and I opened my eyes. Fortunately, I recognized where I was before I had a chance to jump up and subdue my unknown assailant.

"What are y'all doing out here?" Jenny Lee asked.

I raised my head and glanced at the clock. 0630. I shook my head to clear the cobwebs. "Sleeping, I guess."

"I can imagine how difficult this must be for you." She kneaded the muscles in my neck and shoulders.

I closed my eyes and took a deep breath. I felt relaxed and aroused at the same time.

"Why don't you come back to bed?" She removed her hands from my shoulders.

I hesitated, then turned.

Jenny Lee stepped away and held her arms out at her sides. "Y'all mean to tell me you'd pass up another shot at *this?*"

She wore one of my t-shirts, and when she raised her arms, I could see that she had nothing on underneath. I stared for a moment before I caught my breath. She smiled, clearly pleased that her gesture had its intended effect.

I followed Jenny Lee back to my room.

CHAPTER 10

I finished shaving and splashed cold water on my face. Two tired eyes stared at me from the mirror, taking me back to the time when I realized Mama was never coming home. I'd loved her and hated her at the same time, and I struggled once again with the same feelings. I didn't know how much of Mama's story I should believe, or if we were truly in any danger.

"Breakfast is ready," Jenn called from the hallway.

"Be right there."

The kitchen table had been set for two.

"Where's Mama?"

"I haven't seen her. She must have gone out."

Jenny Lee washed the dishes when we finished. I walked up behind her and slipped my arms around her waist. "Pack a bag, darlin'. We're blowin' town for a few days. Just you 'n' me." I kissed the back of her neck.

"Really? Where?"

"It's a surprise."

"Dillon, we need to get back to Dallas and pack. We've got a long trip ahead of us."

"Right now, I need some downtime." I kissed her neck again. "And I need to spend it with you."

She turned her head to the side and smiled. "Good answer."

I threw everything in the back of the Silverado, and we sped out of town. Pop owned a cabin on Lake Whitney, about an hour south of Cleburne. He used to disappear there for a week at a time with Mort and Bill to hunt, fish, and kill a couple bottles of Texas Single Malt. Women weren't allowed, so Jenny Lee would probably be the first to ever cross its threshold. I disclosed our destination on the drive down Route 174. I'd hoped for a more positive reaction.

When I parked the truck at the end of the gravel access road, the lake showed through the trees. The cabin stood on our left, an outbuilding on our right.

Jenny Lee looked at me, eyes wide. "Dillon, this is nicer than I'd pictured it. It's more like a... a lake house than a cabin."

I unlocked the front door and let myself in while Jenny Lee strolled across the wrap-around deck that overlooked the lake. I stopped in the middle of the large living room and dropped my bag. My muscles tensed as they did during recon patrols in Kandahar. Things felt a little out of place, so I listened for a moment before I checked every room. Satisfied we were alone, I let out a breath and straightened the cushions on the sofa and closed the kitchen cabinets that hung open before joining Jenny Lee on the deck.

She turned. "This is a great spot."

"I guess that's why Pop held on to it all these years."

"I expected a little shack with a fireplace, a few cots, and a gun rack. I was afraid to ask if it had running water."

I slipped my arms around her waist and gave her a quick kiss. "C'mon, I'll show you around."

We began the tour in the main living space, which had no interior walls and occupied the entire first floor. An oversized fan hung from the ceiling and twisted slowly above our heads. Three bedrooms and a bath made up the second floor, all remodeled since my last visit. The place had a rustic Old West feel, and I guessed Pop did most of the work himself. I recalled that a mason friend had built the massive stone fireplace that anchored the living room half of the first floor.

I dropped our bags in the largest bedroom, put away the food we'd brought, and walked down to the shore. I removed my shoes and sat on the dock next to Jenny Lee.

A motorboat cut through the water about thirty yards out, and we exchanged a neighborly wave with the passengers. We lay back on the dock with our feet in the water and watched the puffy white clouds drift across a royal blue sky.

Jenny turned her head and studied me in silence. After a few minutes, she said, "Somethin's on your mind."

"Been thinkin' about Mama." I hesitated, not sure that I wanted to burden her with my family problems. "The insurance investigator said he thought Pop died from a drug overdose. I found crystal meth in Mama's purse."

She sat up quickly. "You went through her purse?"

"C'mon, Jenn. I had to."

"What about mine?" she asked with a look of indignation.

I pulled myself up on my elbows. "What? No. I haven't touched your purse."

"Dillon, we have to be able to trust each other."

"I know. That's the problem. I don't trust Mama." I sat up and folded my arms across my chest. "What would you have done?"

"I would have come right out and asked her."

"Oh, I see. Somethin' like, 'Mornin', Mama. Gonna be another hot one today. Did you kill Pop?'"

"If you're gonna act like an ass, you can go do it with your friend Nicole."

I blinked back my surprise. "What's that supposed to mean?"

"It means I saw the way she looked at you yesterday… and then how she looked at me."

"I've known Nicole since we were seven. We're just good friends."

"Is that why y'all acted so nervous and jerky around her?"

"I don't know what you're talkin' about." I stared down into the water.

"Listen to me, Dillon." She put her hand on my arm and I met her gaze. "If y'all don't know exactly where your heart's at, you'll never be happy."

"Where's yours?"

She rested her head on my shoulder. "Since the first day I laid eyes on you, Dillon Bishop, my heart's been with you."

My chest tightened, and I had to catch my breath.

"I'd never ask you to do anything you didn't want to do, anything that wasn't in your heart." She hesitated. "But y'all have to stop running."

I recoiled. "Running?"

She lifted her head. "Running away."

"I'm not the one who runs. Mama, Luke, Nicole, they're the runners. I'm the one left behind to pick up the pieces."

"You ran away after high school and joined the army."

She had a point. I probably would have killed someone if I'd stayed. "I was doing my patriotic duty."

"Bullshit."

She was right about that, too. I stared into the water.

"I know you're still dealing with a lot, and I'm not sure if coming home has helped or hurt, but I don't want to add any more pressure."

Unsure where she was headed with this, I said nothing.

"So… y'all just let me know when you're ready to go to Colorado."

I nodded, embarrassed by my lack of commitment to this point. "I sure will."

She stood. "Now that that's settled, let's do somethin' fun."

I smiled tentatively. "We could go back to the cabin and—"

"Not that kinda fun."

I must have looked like the cheese fell off my cracker.

"We can do that later." She tilted her head. "Your daddy liked his guns. Did he leave any up here?"

If we weren't gonna have sex, firing off a few rounds to impress a pretty young thing like Jenny Lee was a close second.

I led her past Pop's truck to the outbuilding. A big padlock hung from a hasp on the door. "You want trust?" I squatted and motioned for her to come closer. I slid the bottom clapboard up, reached into the opening, and pulled out a key. I held it up between us.

She smiled and shook her head. "That's not exactly what I meant."

I shrugged. "I reckon it's a start."

I held the door open, then followed her inside. Light filled the small room from a skylight cut into the roof. Pop's cluttered workbench ran the length of one wall, while two gun racks hung on the opposite wall above an old wooden chair and a locked cabinet.

Pop kept the key for the cabinet hung from a finishing nail underneath the bench. I opened the cabinet, grabbed a box of 30-caliber ammo, and pulled the Mossberg down off the rack. I handed the rifle and the ammo to Jenny Lee, then reached into a barrel near the door where Pop kept some old cans and bottles to use for targets.

We walked about twenty yards down a dirt trail through the woods to a long, narrow clearing where an old target stand made of angle iron and two-by-fours stood at the base of a large oak. I set two whiskey bottles and two tin cans along the top of the stand, then walked in the opposite direction. Jenny Lee followed. I stopped next to a small metal sign attached to a piece of rebar that read *100 yds*.

Jenny Lee touched the sign, then looked at me and smiled. "You've done this before."

"Maybe once or twice. I helped Pop clear this land." I grinned and peered through the Mossberg's scope. A few seconds later, I squeezed the trigger and the first bottle shattered.

Jenny Lee rolled her eyes. "Anybody can hit a target that big at a hundred yards."

"You think so? Follow me." I shouldered the rifle and walked to the 200-yard marker, where I shattered the second bottle with one shot.

"Not bad," Jenny Lee said, then showed me a mischievous grin. "Is that all you got?"

"I don't like to brag, but even with this little huntin' rifle, I can shoot the balls off a squirrel at two hundred yards."

Jenny Lee raised an eyebrow. "That sounds like it hurts."

"Only for the squirrel."

"Can y'all hit anything from three hundred?"

"Let's go find out."

We walked past the 250-yard marker, the end of our makeshift firing range. Jenny Lee walked a few steps behind me, and I slowed to wait for her.

"Don't stop here," she said when I turned around. She kept walking.

The girl pushed my buttons, and she knew it. I couldn't back down now. When we reached the gravel road that we drove in on, I said, "This is as far as we can go."

"What do you reckon the distance is now?"

"I'd say three hundred, give or take."

"Let's see what y'all can do from here, hotshot."

Two cans remained. I spent a little more time locking in on the target, then squeezed.

"Sorry, cowboy."

I glared at her and chambered another round.

"C'mon, Dillon. It's my turn."

"From here?" I snorted. "I don't think so."

Jenny Lee's eyes flashed, and her back stiffened. "Why? 'Cause I'm a girl?" She held out her hand.

I studied her for a moment before I handed her the rifle. "Okay, but I gotta warn you, I finished second in my sharp-shooting class at Fort Benning. I trained on a Barrett M90, 50 cal. Makes this thing look like a BB gun." I grinned. "So, don't expect to hit anything from this distance."

"Your concern is duly noted."

I folded my arms across my chest and watched her sight the target.

"Wind speed. Best guess?"

I chuckled. "I don't know, maybe five miles. Out of the west."

She adjusted a knob on the scope. "Temperature's probably what? Eighty-seven, eighty-eight?"

Okay, Annie Oakley, I'll play along. "Sounds about right."

Another quick adjustment. She inhaled, held it, and squeezed the trigger. The round ricochet off something, but I could barely see the stand from this distance, let alone the targets. She re-positioned her weapon and fired another round. I heard the same sound and squinted toward the target stand.

"Gimme that." I took the rifle from her hand. I pulled the scope to my eye and scanned the target area for the two remaining bogeys. Nothing.

I turned to Jenny Lee, standing with her hands on her hips. We stared in silence at each other for a good ten seconds. "That was hot," I finally said. "I am so turned on right now."

"Good." She smiled. "Remember that the next time you're thinkin' about letting me go to Colorado alone."

I tried to ignore her last comment. I shook my head to clear it. "Day-um. Where did you learn to shoot like that?"

"Fort Jackson, South Carolina. I finished *first* in *my* class."

CHAPTER 11

I fried catfish in cornmeal and peanut oil for dinner. Turns out Jenny Lee handled a fishing pole almost as well as she handled a rifle. While she watched the sunset over the lake after dinner, I conducted a thorough search of the premises. Perhaps Mama couldn't find Pop's journal at the house because he kept it here where it would be less likely to fall into the wrong hands. An uneasy feeling surfaced. What if I'm too late?

I thought about where I might hide something. I'd either lock it up somewhere in plain sight or stash it in a secret compartment that wouldn't require additional security. The latter would be much harder to find. I reasoned that if he locked it up, the container would be heavy enough that you couldn't carry it away easily, like a safe or large desk. Nothing on the first floor fit that description.

I recognized a few of the furnishings in the largest bedroom and assumed it was Pop's. I sat on the bed and surveyed the room. My eyes moved past a bookcase to three framed photos on the corner of a wooden desk. The photo in front showed me and Luke and Pop in his boat. I remember Mama snapped it when we returned from our first fishing trip. I'd smiled for the camera as I held up three bullheads on a line.

The next photo caused my chest to tighten as I stared at our once-happy little family. Mama and Pop crouched on either side of me and Luke. I remembered the day—I was seven and Luke was five. Everyone smiled, unaware of the tragic events that waited in our path.

I picked up an older photo of Pop and another man to give it a closer look. They stood in a field with their arms slung over each other's shoulders and cigars in their mouths. They held a piece of paper between them. The other man looked familiar, but I couldn't place him. I set it back behind the others.

I found two cardboard boxes on the floor of the closet— one marked *Dillon* and the other *Luke*. I slid them out and opened the flaps of the box with my name. A wave of nostalgia—or maybe nausea, I wasn't sure which—washed over me. I fought the urge to seal it up and put both boxes where the past belongs—in a hole covered with dirt.

Something made me forge ahead. I removed the model of Apollo 13 that I'd built after Luke broke the three-foot mega-model that had been the centerpiece of my old room. Two of the World War II fighter planes that hung in formation from my bedroom ceiling were also in the box. My barely used baseball glove came out next.

After I unloaded a few books and other childhood trinkets, I stared into the empty box. What happened to my *GI Joe* and *Sheriff Wyatt Earp* action figures? I would have remembered something as traumatic as losing them. I might have given Wyatt Earp to Luke at some point, but I couldn't recall for sure. I ran my hand across the bottom of the empty box, like I could have somehow missed them inside.

I quickly returned everything to the box and pushed it back into the closet. After a few moments of staring at Luke's name on the side of the other box, I opened the flaps. I smiled when I recognized the cowboy hat that Pop had bought me on my tenth birthday. I loved that old hat and broke it in real good for Luke, who inherited it when my head no longer fit inside.

Bittersweet memories bubbled up as I pulled out Luke's well-worn baseball glove, a couple of Little League trophies, his harmonica, and a handful of prized baseball cards that had mysteriously disappeared from my collection.

The real blast from the past sat at the bottom of the box—Luke's favorite Halloween costume. Luke was seven when he dressed up as Sheriff of Johnson County. We called him *Lawman Luke*, because he went on and on about how he would catch all the bad guys and clean up the county. We couldn't get him out of that costume. He wore it well into November before Pop took it away from him. Neither of us ever saw it again.

I unpinned the silver star from the chest and slipped it in my pocket. Perhaps Lawman Luke could help guide me through this mess.

I glanced at the bookcase again and noticed the initials I'd carved into the side. Pop had built it for me after Mama left. I hadn't noticed it missing from my bedroom back home, but the room had been stripped clean. Even the posters on the walls had been removed.

I remembered the bookshelf because it contained a secret compartment to store my most valuable possessions, which at the time consisted of baseball cards, Playboy magazines, and a little cash. Coop had been in the habit of pilfering all of the above whenever I left him alone in my room.

I dropped to my knees and removed the books from the bottom shelf. I grabbed the front edge of the shelf and pulled it toward me, surprised to find my stuff still hidden underneath. I recognized everything except for the tattered green notebook that rested on a few magazines.

The back of my neck prickled as every hair stood at attention. I removed the notebook and peeled back the cover. *Pop's handwriting.* I leaned back on my heels and flipped through the pages.

"What y'all doin'?" Jenn asked from the doorway.

I closed the notebook and looked up. "Uh…"

"It's a simple question."

I considered my answer carefully. What do I have to gain by keeping it from her? Don't I trust her? If Mama was right about what it contained, I might be putting Jenn in harm's way, but at this point, I didn't have much choice.

"You'd better sit down," I said.

I sat next to her on the bed and told her everything I knew to this point about the tattered notebook in my lap.

After a few moments of silence, she said, "Well, don't just sit there. Let's see what's inside."

I shifted uncomfortably, nervous about reading the words out loud to anyone without having first heard them myself.

According to the first few entries, Pop had picked up where I'd left off. The police had undermined my efforts to find out the truth about what had happened to Luke. I'd become frustrated and angry and ran off to join the Army.

Pop called in his friend, Bill McCutchen, a ball-bustin' Texas Ranger who had connections all over the state. The Rangers deferred to the local police on this case, but Bill agreed to help Pop on his own time. They turned over rocks, so to speak, at the quarry, the site of three deaths over the last fifteen years. One appeared to be a suicide, while the other two involved drunken high school students who slipped on the large rocks and drowned in the water below. The diver Pop hired to search beneath the water came up empty.

Eventually, the two believed that Luke had fallen victim to a hit-and-run accident. It had rained hard that night and washed away most of the evidence. However, the small amount of blood they recovered from the gravel shoulder at the bottom of Quarry Road had never been tested, because the police lost the samples in transit. An eyewitness claimed to have seen a patrol car parked at the same location the night Luke disappeared, but the police had no record of any calls or cars dispatched.

While such an accident normally resulted in a body left on the side of the road, none was ever found. They maintained that someone with too much to lose may have disposed of the body rather than face charges—someone like a politician or government official, a local celebrity, or perhaps someone with previous DWI convictions.

Then, three years ago, Pop purchased a car at an auction in Fort Worth that he believed to be the car that killed Luke.

"Holy shit, Dillon. Did you know about the car?"

"No." I hadn't seen it on the property. I made a mental note to ask Coop if he'd ever heard Pop mention it.

"What y'all gonna do?"

I shrugged. "It might be the chance to find out what happened to Luke."

"It sounds dangerous."

"That's why you can't stay. I can't drag you into this."

She frowned. "So, I need to go to Colorado, and y'all need to stay here?"

"Just until I can sort this out. Then I'll leave. I promise."

"I can help you."

"Please, Jenn. This will be difficult enough. I don't need any distractions."

She exhaled sharply. "Is that what I am? A *distraction*?"

"That's not what I meant. It's just that—"

"Save it, Dillon. I'll get outta your way."

I closed my eyes and squeezed the bridge of my nose as she left the room. The front door slammed, and I hit my forehead with the palm of my hand. *Stupid!* If brains were dynamite, I couldn't even blow my nose. I set the journal down on the desk and studied the pictures again, reasonably sure now that the man with Pop was Bill McCutchen.

I told myself that Jenn and I just needed a little space. But by 2200, I reckoned we'd had enough. I walked out onto the deck and called Jenn's name. No answer. I called again and again with the same result. My heart hammered in my chest as I wiped the sweat from my brow.

A chopper's rotor thumped overhead, and I ran for cover. The night was as black as the devil's boots, and I cursed myself for not bringing my night vision goggles. I crawled along the ground until I reached a small building. I had no map, no intel. For all I knew, it could be a Taliban outpost. The building appeared to be empty; the door padlocked. I searched for a key and found one behind a piece of broken siding.

I felt my way around inside. Rifles hung on the wall, and I grabbed one. Semi-automatic, ten-shot clip. I slung it over my shoulder and set off into the woods, moving like a cat, careful not to make a sound.

I hadn't gone far when a noise stopped me in my tracks. A twig snap? I heard it again. Something moved out there at three o'clock. I spun on my heel and fired. The muzzle flash lit up the night. I squeezed off three more rounds before I doubled back.

When I returned to the makeshift armory, I noticed a house with a light in the window. Maybe the boy was inside. A perimeter sweep revealed no activity inside or out. I crept inside, secured the building, and locked the door. I turned the couch parallel to the entry and lay down behind it. At daybreak, I would try to reconnect with the rest of my unit.

I woke on the floor, disoriented. My shoulder ached from sleeping on hardwood. I pulled myself up to a sitting position. Pop's rifle lay beside me with five rounds in the clip and another in the chamber. That left four rounds unaccounted for.

Where's Jenn? I stood and stared for a moment at the rearranged furniture.

"Jenn!" I took the stairs two at a time and shouted her name again. I found our bedroom empty, the bed made, and our bags unopened on the floor.

I nearly fell down the stairs, unlocked the front door, and stood on the deck.

"Jenn!"

No answer.

CHAPTER 12

My stomach twisted its way up into my throat, and I raked my fingers back through my hair. I found the gun shed unlocked and prayed that she'd gone out for some early morning target practice. But when I examined the racks, the only rifle missing was the one on the floor in the living room.

I stepped outside. "Jenn!" After a few seconds, I shouted louder. "Jenny Lee!" I pulled up the bottom of my shirt and wiped the sweat from my forehead.

The truck's passenger door opened, and my heart stopped. Jenny Lee, her hair tousled, climbed down onto the gravel and rubbed her eyes.

I ran to her and wrapped her in my arms.

She pushed on my chest with both hands. "What the hell's wrong with you?"

I guess I deserved that. "I'm sorry, Jenn."

She folded her arms across her chest. "Yeah, well, I wish y'all felt like that when you locked me out last night."

My shoulders dropped. "Last night's a blur. I don't remember anything."

Jenny Lee studied me for a moment. "Another flashback?"

I nodded. "Roger that."

"I figured as much when I heard you shootin' up the woods. I was afraid to go back in the house, so I waited until you fell asleep, but you locked me out."

"I'm really sorry, Jenn." My pulse slowed, and I blew out a long breath. "I'm just glad you're alive."

"Yeah, me too. You're off your meds, aren't you?"

I shrugged. "I figured out here, away from everything, I could take a break. Maybe feel like a normal person for a few days."

She walked over to me, slipped her arms around my waist, and buried her head in my chest. We stood in silence for a good five minutes before she said, "Let's go get cleaned up. I'll make breakfast."

Inside the house, I picked up my phone and checked my messages while Jenn started breakfast.

One new message from Coop. "Sorry to bother you, Bish, but you need to get home ASAP. I'm at your house. It's… uh… eight-thirty. I'm supposed to be at work in half an hour, but I'll stay until you get here. Hurry."

My foot tingled as I dialed Coop's number. "Jenn, you better make that to-go."

We packed everything and left in a hurry.

"Did you take your meds this morning?" Jenn asked as we drove north on Route 174.

I glared at her for a moment, then nodded. She had every right to ask after what happened the night before.

"Did you ever kill anyone?" I asked.

She looked away. When she looked back, her eyes begged me to change the subject.

"They must have used you as a sniper over there."

"At first." She shifted in her seat. "I don't like to talk about it."

"I'm sorry, Jenn, but I need to know."

"Did *you*?" she asked.

"I did."

"If you must know, I had the opportunity once. I couldn't do it." She took a deep breath. "It wasn't a tin can, Dillon. It was a human being. I saw his eyes in my scope. I couldn't detach."

"What happened?"

"Someone else took the shot, and I got transferred to a non-combat position."

"How do you feel about it now?"

"Grateful that I'm back in the states shooting at tin cans."

A long silence settled in as the thrum of raindrops on the windshield and metal roof had a hypnotizing effect. Coop's message was as vague as it was urgent. Something happened to Mama. Something he didn't want to talk about on the phone. The rain came down harder.

As a boy, I welcomed the rain and played in the puddles it left behind. Today, I cursed it and the trouble it brought. One storm after another had blown into my life, harbingers of the destruction that left me to pick up the pieces.

They don't get much rain in these parts, but when it rains, it comes down in buckets. By then, the ground is so dry and hard that most of the water runs off. If the flash floods don't get you, the twisters will.

I'm not saying that the wind blows or the rain falls with any malice. They're just following orders—like I did for seven years. But in the end, the damage is done just the same.

I dialed Coop's number again. This time he answered.

I pulled the truck into the driveway at 1030 and parked behind the Mustang, which sat on four new tires. Coop had told me he came by to drop off the car and found Mama high and the house torn up. I threw open the truck door and ran up the front steps. Coop met me on the porch.

"Slow down." He held up his hands. "She's pretty banged up, but she's calmed down and she's resting now."

I took a breath. "What happened?"

"It's hard to tell. It looks like she got high and tore the place up."

"I don't believe it. She swore she'd never touch the stuff again."

"Would you listen to yourself?" He folded his arms across his chest and stood between me and the door. "That's what addicts always say."

"Get outta my way, Coop." My hands clenched into fists. "I need to see her."

He glanced over my shoulder at Jenny Lee, then stepped aside.

Mama sat alone on the sofa. A few things looked out of place, but not as bad as I'd imagined. I stared at her for a moment but said nothing. I found her purse in the kitchen and unzipped the pocket where I'd seen the vial. The top wouldn't budge.

"Where'd you get the drugs?" I asked as I sat beside her. She stared at me with vacant eyes, like she had trouble putting a name with my face. "Mama! I need you to talk to me. Tell me what happened."

A tear rolled down her cheek.

"She was talking when I got here," Coop said, "but she hit a wall about half an hour ago. She's been like this ever since."

"What did she say?"

Coop scratched his head. "Mostly nonsense. At first, she went on about some dude who forced his way in here and pushed her around. I believed her until she told me about the pack of wild dogs that broke in and stole the Christmas turkey from the kitchen table."

"Did she recognize the man who did this to her?" Jenny Lee asked.

Coop shifted his weight, looked at Jenn, then back to me. "Oh, she recognized him, all right. She claims it was George Bush."

"Senior or Junior?"

"Does it matter?"

I glanced at Mama, closed my eyes, and shook my head.

"I should go," Coop said. "I found drug paraphernalia on the coffee table when I got here. It's in a bag under the kitchen sink."

I patted his shoulder. "Thanks, man. I owe you one."

He said goodbye to Jenn and left.

I tried to talk to Mama while Jenn left the room. She stared straight ahead, her breath shallow. "I'm gonna get you some help." I pulled out my phone and made a quick call.

"Who was that?" Jenn said from a few feet behind me when I hung up the phone.

"I called Nicole."

"You did *what*?"

"She's a nurse. I want to have her check Mama out. That cut above her eye might need stitches."

"Shouldn't a doctor do that?"

I turned to face her. "We have to keep this quiet."

"I don't like it," she said, hands on her hips.

"I suppose it would've been okay if I'd called someone other than Nicole?"

She exhaled sharply. "Y'all do what you gotta do, Dillon," she said, then pointed to a chair in the corner. "I'll go sit over there and keep my mouth shut."

"Jenn…"

She watched from her chair while I sat with Mama. When I looked for her a few minutes later, I stared at the empty chair. Two weeks ago, Bradley had been nothing but a distant memory. I'd thrown my past, and everyone in it, down a deep hole and spent years shoveling dirt over it. Some things were harder to cover up than others.

I sat in Pop's living room next to my drug-addict mother, wondering if my girl planned to drive off to Colorado without me. I felt like a spectator as I watched my life unravel.

I wanted to go back to a time when living was easy. Back to lazy days on the tire swing with Nicole, or swapping baseball cards with Coop, or beating Luke at Pac Man down at the arcade.

Mama closed her eyes. I propped up a couple of pillows to help her get comfortable.

Jenny Lee returned to the living room, her suitcase in her hand.

"I can see that I've overstayed my welcome," she said. "I probably shouldn't have come. This is *your* home, *your* friends. I feel like an outsider."

"I never said that."

"You didn't have to."

"I'm in over my head, Jenn. I didn't ask for any of this." I stood. "I'm pissin' up a rope here. I need some help."

She forced a smile. "You'll be in capable hands soon enough."

"Stop it, all right?"

Jenny Lee set her bag down and walked toward me. I studied her face, hoping to see something that wasn't there.

"C'mon, Jenn. I'm sorry for whatever it is I did."

She leaned in, kissed my cheek, then patted my chest. "When you figure out what's going on in there, y'all let me know."

"Jenn…"

"You've got my number." She picked up her bag and walked out the door.

I followed her outside.

"Don't be surprised if you miss the crap out of me," she called from the driveway.

She stopped for a moment next to the door of her Ford Bronco as Nicole pulled in and parked between us.

CHAPTER 13

"Where's she off to?" Nicole asked as we both watched Jenn's taillights flash at the end of the street.

"Colorado, I guess." I didn't wait for a response before I walked up the porch steps.

Nicole followed. "How's your mama?"

I held the door. "I hoped *you* could tell *me*."

"Dillon, I'm not a doctor."

"You're a lot closer to one than I am. Just do the best you can."

Nicole knelt by the sofa and checked Mama's pulse. Mama stared with hollow eyes while Nicole examined her. She shot me a nervous glance, then leaned her head in close to Mama's. "Overdose. She's barely breathing. My guess is an opiate. Heroin, maybe."

"Heroin? Are you sure it wasn't meth?"

"Bonnie!" Nicole rubbed her knuckles on Mama's chest. "Bonnie. Can you hear me?"

"Are you sure?" I asked.

"Yes. Different symptoms." She pulled a syringe and a glass vial from her bag.

"What's that?"

"Narcan." She pushed the needle into the vial and pulled back the plunger. "If it's heroin, this will reverse the process and hopefully save her life."

Mama didn't even blink when the needle went into her arm.

"Now what?" I asked.

"We wait."

"How long?"

"It should start to work in a few minutes."

I told Nicole everything that happened that morning while we waited for Mama to show signs of improvement. Nicole explained that the Narcan would be active for about thirty to ninety minutes in the body and may wear off before the effects of the heroin. If that happened, Mama could overdose again and need another shot.

Mama's eyes opened, and she sat up.

"Dillon...?"

"I'm here, Mama." I sat on the edge of the coffee table. "How do you feel?"

Her eyes moved slowly to Nicole, then back to me. "Awful."

"She needs to go to the hospital," Nicole said.

"No. That's why you're here."

She hesitated. "You've put me in an awkward position. I have an obligation to see that she gets proper treatment."

"I'm sorry, but I can't let you do that. Please. Just trust me. No one else can know about this."

"Dillon, if she dies—"

"She's not gonna die." I stood and paced the length of the living room. *She can't die. Not like this.* "What can we do for her?"

"She needs to be monitored closely. If she even looks like she's about to relapse, I'm calling 911, and you better pray we didn't wait too long."

Mama's condition improved over the next two hours. She didn't speak much, but the color returned to her skin, and she looked more alive.

"Why, Mama?"

She shook her head slowly. "I didn't do it."

"I don't understand. You almost died from a drug overdose. You did *something*."

"He made me do it."

"Who? George?"

Mama blinked a few times, then squinted her eyes.

"Are you trying to tell me that someone forced their way in here and shot you up with heroin? Why? Why would someone do something like that?"

She shrugged.

"They wouldn't."

"I'm tired," she said. "Can we talk about this later?"

I let loose a deep breath. "Sure, Mama." I helped her get comfortable. "We can talk later."

I needed to talk to Coop about what I'd found in Pop's journal, so I asked Nicole to stay and watch Mama while I went out. She made a quick call and took the rest of the afternoon off. After another call, Nicole explained that she'd arranged for her daughter, Annabelle, to stay with her grandmother for a few days. Nicole would be all mine for as long as I needed her. Her words, not mine.

"What are you doing here?" Coop asked when I walked into his office.

"I need to talk to you about Pop."

"Where's your mama?"

"She's back at the house with Nicole."

"Nicole? Where's Jenny Lee?"

"She got mad and left."

Coop shook his head. "You're a real piece of work."

"Save it, Coop. This is more important."

He pointed to a chair in front of his desk. "First, tell me how your mama's doing."

"She's better now… thanks to Nicole."

Coop stared as he chewed his lower lip.

"I found a journal that Pop kept hidden out at the cabin."

"What kind of journal?"

"He and his Ranger friend, Bill McCutchen, had looked into Luke's disappearance together for years." As soon as I said it, I thought of the man in the photo with Pop.

I held up the notebook. "Pop wrote everything in here."

"No shit?" He leaned forward. "What's it say?"

"He thinks Luke was involved in a hit-and-run accident out on Quarry Road, then his body dumped someplace to cover it up."

"Did he know who hit him?"

"He didn't write it down. But…" I shook Pop's journal in my hand, "according to this, he's got the next best thing."

"What's that?"

"The car that hit him."

"What do you mean, the plate number?"

"No. I mean he bought the actual car at an auction in Fort Worth. He never mentioned it to you?"

Coop looked away and scratched his head. "Why would he…" His head snapped in my direction, and he slapped the desk. "Jeezus, Bish. Your daddy's been renting a garage out back for the past three years. Never told me why. I thought maybe it was for your Mustang."

"You've never seen the car?"

"I sure didn't. He walked in here one day, paid cash, and I gave him the key."

"Can we go take a look?"

He stood and walked around the side of his desk. "C'mon. I've got extra keys downstairs."

I followed him outside to a large pole barn behind his shop. Coop expanded his business five years ago when he added auto detailing and restoration to his regular repair work. He used the front of the barn for the new services, while he rented out the six individual garage spaces in back. He stopped near the back corner of the building, inserted a key into the control box next to door #3, and pushed a large green button. The door rumbled and shook as it climbed slowly up the tracks. When it reached chest height, Coop ducked inside, and I followed.

CHAPTER 14

Coop grabbed one corner of the tarp, and I grabbed the other. We pulled it back halfway to reveal a green 1970 Plymouth Road Runner. Fresh paint, and lots of tread on the raised white-lettered tires. I cupped my hands above my eyes and looked through the window. The Interior appeared to be clean.

"Can you find out who owned it?"

He nodded. "I can run the VIN through the Carfax database. That should tell us something about its past."

"It's been repainted. Any way to determine the original color?"

"If it still has the fender tag, I can look it up." He lifted the hood. "Found the tag. But I might be able to tell you right away. I've never seen a paint job that covered up everything. There are always telltale signs of the old color."

Coop pulled a small flashlight from his shirt pocket and opened the driver's door. He moved the light down the pillar to the door hinges. "Come here," he said as he pulled a rag from his back pocket. He reached in past the top hinge to wipe something.

I leaned in over his left shoulder for a better look.

He held the light steady. "This car used to be red."

I turned to Coop. "You thinkin' what I'm thinkin'?"

"The big, red douchemobile."

"You think it could really be Josh's old car?"

"Why did Eli think this was the car that hit Luke?"

"He didn't say, but he seemed pretty sure. Maybe Bill McCutchen can tell us."

"I'll bring some tools out here tomorrow and take the front end apart. Maybe I can find dried blood or..." Coop hesitated. "Sorry, man, I mean—"

"It's okay. If this car holds any clues, I want to know about them."

"Let's go. I've gotta get back to the shop."

Coop agreed to call me if he found anything. I drove home to check on Mama and found Nicole on the front porch. "How's Mama?" I asked.

"She's asleep. It's probably the best thing for her."

"Did she say any more about what happened?"

"Same story. A man forced his way in. She tried to fight him off, but he held her down and gave her an injection."

"Did he say anything? What he was doing? Why he was doing it?"

She shook her head. "I did a sweep of the house after she fell asleep but didn't find any drugs."

I sat next to Nicole on the swing. "Thanks for all this. I really appreciate it."

"I'm just glad I could help." She smiled briefly before lowering her gaze. "Where've you been?"

"Down at Coop's garage looking at a car. Pop believed Luke was killed in a hit-and-run. Apparently, he found the car that hit him and stored it in the garage behind Coop's place."

"A hit-and-run?" She swallowed hard. "How... when did he tell you that?"

"He didn't. He wrote it all down in a journal."

"Where's the journal now?"

I pulled it from my back pocket.

She fired off a couple of rapid blinks. "Can I see it?"

"I'm sorry, Nicole. There's personal stuff in here, and I wouldn't feel comfortable letting someone else read it."

"Sure. I understand." She looked away. "I'm sorry. I shouldn't have—"

"It's okay."

We sat in silence while the old swing swayed gently beneath us. The rusty hinges moaned with the movement. I resisted the urge to talk, to fill the void, remembering a time when Nicole and I didn't need to talk. We were just kids, but we had something special that could last a lifetime. Nicole rested her head on my shoulder, and I closed my eyes.

When I opened them again, I watched the taillights of a patrol car as it crawled down the street. If Josh was behind the wheel, I'm sure I'd hear about it, but at the moment, I didn't care. I couldn't tell you how many times I'd pictured a scene like this while deployed in Afghanistan or in the VA hospital in Dallas. A lazy summer afternoon on the swing or tangled up in the hammock with Nicole.

Eventually, I went inside and checked on Mama. She sat at the kitchen table with a glass of iced tea, looking better except for the cut above her eye that Nicole stitched. She'll probably have a nasty shiner by tomorrow morning.

"You don't believe me, do you?" she said.

"I'd rather believe your story than to think that you started using again on your own."

"I told you someone was after me. You probably thought I was paranoid, but you see—"

"Mama." I met her gaze. "I had a bad feeling about it, too."

She nodded, then sipped her tea.

I stood. "It's dinnertime. I'll fetch us something to eat."

I picked up pulled pork sandwiches and fries from Shady's, and the three of us ate dinner around our kitchen table. When we finished, Nicole told Mama that she would be happy to stay the night and check in on her from time to time. Mama accepted before I could object.

"You can stay in Luke's room," Mama said. "Dillon will make sure you have everything you need."

I shot a sideways glance at Nicole. "Sure, Mama, I'll take care of it."

Nicole had Mama settled by 2130, then sat and watched the Astros game with me. Except for the occasional glance at Nicole, my eyes were glued to the television, even though I had no interest in the game. Old feelings that I thought I'd buried long ago bubbled up. Frankly, I worried about sleeping under the same roof with Nicole.

After a few innings, she stood and yawned. Her fingers moved lightly across my arm as she walked by my chair on her way to bed. My body shuddered as if I had no control over its movements.

I watched another inning, but I couldn't tell you the score or who did what. I pressed a button on the remote and the screen went black. I stared for a few minutes, then walked down the hall and stood in front of the door to Luke's room.

I'm not sure how much time passed before I moved. My heart pounded in my chest as I raised my hand to knock. The door opened before my knuckles made contact.

"Dillon." Nicole's eyes blinked in confusion. "What are you doing out here?"

No words were necessary at that point. We'd known each other too long. She tugged my shirt, and I followed her into the room, closing the door behind me with my foot. I thought about all the times in high school that I'd dreamed of this moment. Nicole unbuttoned my shirt and slipped her hands inside.

My skin tingled under her touch, and my conflicted heart surrendered to those big, green kiss-me eyes. I leaned in and my lips brushed hers. I shuddered again in anticipation of yielding to the inevitable. Her hungry lips pressed against mine. I moved my hands to her lower back and pulled her in.

She bit my bottom lip until it hurt, then leaned back enough for me to see her playful smile. She had me now, and she knew it. Her eyes never left mine as she grabbed onto my belt and walked backwards.

Nicole stopped next to the bed, swung her hair over her shoulder, and unbuttoned her shirt as I watched. I slid the shirt off her shoulders just before her phone rang. She glanced at the nightstand, then back to me. She closed her eyes and let out a sigh. "I'd better check. It could be about Annabelle."

I gave her a quick nod, my disappointment tempered by relief.

"It's Cooper. He wants to talk to you."

"What?"

She held the phone out. "Cooper. For you."

I grabbed the phone, but before I put it to my ear, I blew out a long breath in the opposite direction. "Yeah, Coop. What's up?"

"I'm at the garage with the Road Runner. You'd better get down here. You're gonna wanna see this."

"I'll be there in ten minutes."

Nicole's expression fell. "What's the matter?"

I handed her the phone. "I don't know yet."

Nicole slid her shirt back over her shoulders. She raised her eyebrows. "Any chance I can get a rain check?"

I squeezed the back of my neck. The truth was yes, but I hesitated to make any promises. "I wouldn't rule it out."

CHAPTER 15

I pulled in behind Coop's shop. Light spilled out onto the pavement from door #3. I parked the truck and walked in.

"What are you doing out here?"

Coop grinned. "Just breaking your case wide open."

The Road Runner's front end had been disassembled, the pieces laid out neatly on the floor.

"I thought you were gonna do this tomorrow."

"So did I." He pulled a rag from his back pocket and wiped his hands. "But I remembered something about this particular model. I owned a '69 for a couple years, and had all kinds of trouble with the headlights. There's a design flaw that allows water and road grime to get up behind the bulb. Before long, it rusts, and you have to replace the whole assembly."

I shook my head. "Same ol' Coop. You get something in your head and you're like a dog with a bone."

Coop smiled. "Yeah, well, take a look at *this* bone." He held up a curved, metal object, about six inches long.

"What is it?"

"The correct question is: What's *on* it? And the answer is blood. At least I think it's blood."

"How do we find out?"

Coop gave me a sympathetic look. "You really need to watch more TV." He waited for a response, then said, "A crime lab can test this and tell us who it belongs to. Even if we don't have Luke's DNA to compare it to, we've got yours. They could do a sibling match."

"I don't imagine we can just go down to the corner crime lab and drop off a blood sample for testing."

"Duh! We'll need to get the police to do it."

"Not the Bradley police."

"How about your daddy's Ranger friend?"

"I guess I could give Bill a call. It's probably not a bad idea to keep him in the loop."

"You do that. I'll leave everything here just the way it is. Maybe he'll want to come down and look for himself."

"Good. It's been a long day, and I'm beat."

"Not so fast, Romeo. I think you're missing something here."

He didn't know the half of it, and I didn't want to tell him.

Coop folded his arms across his chest. "Luke disappeared the night of the Senior Dinner Dance, didn't he?"

"Roger that."

"Do you remember why you didn't go?" Coop raised his eyebrows and waited for an answer he already knew.

"Of course I remember. I asked Nicole, but she turned me down." I snorted. "She had a tough choice—star running back who could take the team to State, or a bench warmer who wasn't taking anyone anywhere."

"Sounds about right, but my point is that she went with Josh. She would have been in the douchemobile that night."

My stomach moved up into my throat and made it difficult to swallow.

"What's the matter, Bish? She didn't tell you?"

"What's that supposed to mean?"

"It means that I think you two have gotten a little too cozy."

"We're just good friends."

"Go on. Keep telling yourself that." He flipped off the light and walked halfway to the door before he turned around. "I called you five times. How come you didn't answer?"

"I left my phone in the truck," I said as I joined him outside.

"Well, you can imagine my surprise and disappointment when I called Nicole, and she put you on the phone." He punched the red button on the control box. "I hope I interrupted something."

"I wanted to kill you when that phone rang," I said as I watched the overhead door crawl down the rails, "but I should probably thank you for stopping me from doing something I might regret."

"Hey, what are friends for?"

I shook my head. "I don't know why I can't let that one go."

Coop slapped my shoulder. "Now who's a dog with a bone?"

Instead of answering, I climbed into the Silverado and drove off. My phone vibrated in the cup holder. A text message from Nicole: *coming home soon?* Before I put it down, I noticed five missed calls from Coop. I drove around for another hour, hoping Nicole would fall asleep.

The next morning, I thanked Nicole for her help and assured her I could handle things myself. She offered little resistance, and I guessed that she either felt embarrassed about how things ended between us the night before, or assumed that I'd discovered something incriminating at Coop's. Thanks to my big mouth, she already knew we had the car.

I watched Nicole drive away, then left a message for Bill McCutchen to call me. I heard noise in the kitchen and found Mama setting a pan on the stove.

"What are you doing?"

"Good morning to you, too, Dillon," she said over her shoulder, then turned around. "Someone has to make breakfast."

"Are you sure you feel up to it?"

"I'm fine." She looked at me curiously. "Where's Nicole?"

"Uh... she had to leave."

"When will she be back?"

"She's not coming back, Mama. We don't need her anymore."

"Oh. That's too bad. I like her." A faint smile crossed her face. "Remember when the two of you—"

"That was a long time ago."

Mama nodded, avoiding my eyes. She turned her attention back to the stove.

Nicole had told me to keep an eye on Mama, so after breakfast, I followed her around from room to room.

"You think I might be able to take a shower by myself?" she asked.

I left her alone and sat on the porch swing. Keeping an eye on Mama had been about as exciting as watching paint dry. I felt like there were things I should do, but I wasn't quite sure what. I closed my eyes. My stomach did a lazy barrel roll as I wrestled with the idea that Nicole knew something about Luke's disappearance. In all the years I'd known her, we'd never lied to each other. At least, that's what I'd believed.

Nicole had helped me through some difficult times after Mama left. We were only twelve years old, but she had the patience and compassion of someone much older. She never made me feel embarrassed, even when I cried in her arms. And that happened more times than I cared to admit.

We'd spent a lot of time down by the creek that ran behind our house. A large flat rock hung out over the water beneath a cypress tree. It became *our spot*, the first place we'd go when we needed to get away. Our first kiss had happened on that rock.

By sophomore year, I hadn't gotten over losing Mama, and it'd become clear that school and I weren't going to get along. At home, Pop drank himself stupid by suppertime, and Luke and I had to fend for ourselves.

One September afternoon, I came home from school and went straight to the rock to sulk. I don't remember exactly what had happened that day, but whatever it was had me feeling sorry for myself. Again.

Nicole showed up half an hour later and put her arm around my shoulders as I held my knees and stared into the water. The katydids sang while we sat in silence, as we often did. Eventually, Nicole spoke. She had a knack for bringing me back to life. She'd said something that made me smile, and I turned to her. I looked into the same sparkling green eyes that I'd looked into a thousand times before, but this time, I saw something different. I felt something different. Our faces, only inches apart, weren't close enough. I'd fallen in love like you fall asleep, slowly at first, then all at once.

I leaned in, then hesitated, worried about what this might mean. Was I about to screw up the only good thing I had going for me? Nicole closed her eyes, and I pressed my lips against hers. Apparently, she liked it because we did it again. And again.

It became something of a ritual after that. We'd meet on the rock and make out for hours. My life had new meaning. I'd wake up with Nicole on my mind and couldn't wait to see her again. I sailed through the school year on that high.

Junior year brought big changes, and once again, I'd learned the hard way that hearts are meant to be broken. Nicole made the varsity cheerleading squad, and I had to stand in line—a very long line. All that attention went to her head, and I spent most of my time on our rock alone after that.

Nicole wasn't there for me when Luke disappeared, and I had a sick feeling that I was about to find out why.

My phone rang, and I opened my eyes. When it rang again, I pulled it from my pocket. I told Bill McCutchen we'd found new evidence in Luke's missing-person case, but didn't want to take it to the police. He agreed to meet me at Coop's garage in the morning.

"Whatever you do, don't tell anyone about this," he said, and hung up the phone.

CHAPTER 16

I walked through the front door to find the living room empty. "C'mon, Mama," I called. "Let's go for a ride."

Mama appeared in the kitchen doorway. "Where?"

"To the police station. We need to report what happened to you." I'd decided to face this head-on. Someone had tried to paint Mama as a junkie who killed her husband. We needed to tell her side of the story.

Mama stared.

"Grab your purse. We'll take my car."

We pulled into the parking lot and sat for a moment. Two officers walked through the front door and down the steps. I thought I recognized one of them from school. A patrol car pulled in and parked a few spaces over.

"I'm nervous, Dillon."

I put my hand on hers. "You'll be fine. Just tell the truth about what happened."

Mama grabbed my arm with her free hand. Her nails dug into my skin.

"Ouch! What the—?"

The color had drained from her face. "That's him," she said, her voice brittle.

She stared through the windshield, and I followed her gaze. A policeman in his mid-forties walked up the steps and through the front door. "That's *who*?"

"The man who attacked me."

"The police officer?" Until now, George Bush was the only suspect, so I wouldn't be jumping to any conclusions right away. "Are you sure?"

She nodded slowly. "You don't forget something like that."

"Mama. You can let go now." She released her grip, and I inspected the damage.

"Don't make me go in there."

I watched her warm eyes turn cold and lifeless. "Sure, Mama. You can stay in the car. Keep the doors locked."

She gave me a quick nod, and I headed into the station.

I stopped at the front desk. "Excuse me. I'd like to talk to someone about—"

"Dillon Bishop." The voice from behind me sounded like truck tires on a gravel road. "I heard you were back in town."

I turned. "Yes, sir."

Harley Wilkerson had put on a few pounds since I'd last seen him. Jowls hung on either side of his mouth like a bulldog. I felt his cold black eyes size me up as he flashed his big tobacco-stained teeth. He motioned to a door behind him. "We can talk in my office."

I followed him in and sat.

"I'm sorry to hear about your daddy," he said.

I'll bet you are. "Thank you. I understand that you were friends."

He moved a coffee mug from the middle of his desk and rested on his elbows. "Y'all in town to settle his affairs?"

"That's right."

"You wouldn't be planning on moving back home now, would you?"

"No, sir. I'm on my way to Colorado with a friend."

"I hear it's nice country up there."

I sensed relief in his voice. "That's what she tells me."

He leaned back in his chair. "How's Bonnie?"

First-name basis? I had a strange feeling that he already knew. "She's fine."

"Shame about what happened."

"You heard about that?"

He seemed rattled for just a moment before he leaned forward and folded his heavy hands. "Not much goes on in this town that I don't hear about." A smug grin completed the recovery.

"I'll remember that."

"So, what is it you came down here for?"

I hesitated. "To report a break-in."

"A break-in? When did this happen?"

"You just said you knew about it." I scratched my temple.

"I was referring to the time Bonnie spent in the homeless shelter in Amarillo."

"Oh, that." I couldn't tell if he was backpedaling. I shouldn't be here. I needed to cut my losses and get the hell out. "On second thought, Mama hasn't been herself lately. I should probably talk to her and make sure she's not hallucinating again."

"I thought you said she was fine."

My collar felt like it had shrunk two sizes. I hooked a finger inside and gave it a tug. "That's what you say to be polite, right? People don't really want to know the truth."

He chuckled. "I reckon they don't."

"Good to see you again, Chief." I stood and nodded as I lied.

Harley leaned back in his chair. "Be sure to give my best to Bonnie. And y'all come back and see me if you need anything while you're in town. Anything at all, ya hear?"

"Yes, sir." I turned and left the building as fast as I could without running.

The relief that washed over me when I stepped outside quickly turned to panic. I ran down the stairs toward my empty car. Maybe Mama slid down in her seat or crawled in the back to lie down. I reached the passenger door and looked inside. No such luck.

I scanned the parking lot, but saw nothing unusual, then slapped the top of the car and cursed myself for having left her alone.

I'd gotten out of a few jams overseas by keeping my wits. I took a deep breath. There's no way she would have gone inside. I widened my initial scan radius to include the busy intersection as well as the shops across the street.

I stood at ground zero and initiated a slow, clockwise pivot. First quadrant—clear. Second—clear. I blew out a heavy breath when I spotted her through the window of the donut shop across the street.

Mama sat in the corner and stared at her empty table. A bell jingled when I opened the door. She didn't bother to look up.

I slid into the seat across from her. "Mama. I told you to stay in the car."

She looked at me, her eyes shrouded in fear. "I saw him again. I had to leave."

"Did he see you?"

"I'm not sure."

"Let's go." I helped her up. "I won't let him hurt you again."

After I dropped Mama off at home, I drove to Mort's office for an update. I approached the door and saw Chief Wilkerson and Mort in the waiting room. The Chief stabbed a finger into Mort's chest. Wilkerson towered over Mort, and the lawyer shrunk as he nodded his head.

I ducked out of sight before Harley stormed out the door and walked down the street toward the police station. Mort regained his composure before I walked in.

"Hello, Dillon." He glanced at the door, then back to me.

"The Chief looked pretty mad." I grinned. "What did you do?"

"You saw that?" He made a dismissing motion with his hand. "The Chief's always getting steamed up about something. He'll cool off eventually."

"Is he a client?"

"Harley? No. I agreed to work part-time as the Town Attorney when I realized there's no such thing as a private practice in a small town. If someone needs that kind of service, they go to Dallas or Fort Worth." He forced a smile. "A man's got to make a living."

"What was he so upset about?"

"The town is being sued by..." He paused. "I'm afraid I've already said too much." He smiled and waved me into his office.

I sat. "Have you heard anything?"

"Nothing yet."

"You know Mama. What do you think of all this?"

He pulled at his tie and unbuttoned the top button of his shirt. "Well, now... that was years ago."

"Yes, but you knew her pretty well back then."

He shuffled the papers on his desk, and I could have sworn he blushed a little. "Your mama was a good woman. I'd like to think that's still true."

"Do you think she killed Pop?"

"I'd rather not believe it, but it's hard to argue with the evidence."

"That's how I feel." I met his gaze. "Why haven't the police arrested her yet?"

"The DA doesn't like to lose. He wants to make sure he's got all his ducks in a row."

"Will you represent her if they do?"

"I would if she asked."

If I were ever on trial, I'd want a pit bull to represent me. Mort struck me as more of a basset hound. I nodded politely. "What can you tell me about Bill McCutchen?"

He gave me a wary glance, then shuffled more papers. "Bill? What does he have to do with any of this?"

"Wild Bill. Isn't that what they called him?"

"They did." Mort looked as nervous as a whore in church. "Bill did a lot of crazy things when he was young, took a lot of chances."

"And now?"

"I think he's retired. I hope he's mellowed out a bit."

"You and Bill and Pop were pretty tight, weren't you?"

"Years ago."

"What happened?"

"I guess we all got busy with different things."

"You ever see Bill?"

"We spoke at Eli's funeral." Mort shifted in his chair. "Why the sudden interest in Bill?"

"He's offered to help look into Luke's disappearance. I think it's somehow related to Pop's death."

Mort looked like he'd just swallowed a bug. "Why would you want to put yourself through that again?"

"Like you said, I'd rather not believe Mama did it."

Mort glanced at the clock and stood. "I'm sorry, Dillon. I just remembered that I have an appointment over at the courthouse."

"Wait a minute." I stood. "Where does this leave us?"

"Too soon to tell." He grabbed his briefcase and stood by the door, signaling the end of our conversation.

I walked into the waiting room, and he followed. Outside, I watched him lock the door, walk to the courthouse, and disappear inside.

CHAPTER 17

I lay in bed that night, anxious to meet Bill in the morning, and wondered how much he knew about the events surrounding Pop's death, or why the police let Mama go after he died. The ink on the insurance policy barely had time to dry, and the autopsy report and security video seemed pretty convincing. Did they not have all the evidence they needed? Was it still being manufactured? Someone went to great lengths to make Mama look guilty. But who? Perhaps the same person who attempted to kill her with a heroin overdose.

Could this be a vendetta against the Bishop family? First Luke, then Pop, then an attempt on Mama's life. *Am I next?* Thoughts bounced around inside my head like ricocheting bullets.

Shortly after sleep finally arrived, my phone rang and chased its sweet numbness away. I sat up and looked at the clock on the nightstand. 0215. Coop's picture stared up at me from the screen.

"What the hell do you want at this hour?"

"I'm at the garage. Get down here. *Now.*" His urgency cut through the cobwebs.

"Why? What's going on?"

Silence.

"Coop?"

I threw on some clothes, checked on Mama, and left in a hurry. Blue lights lit up the street in front of Coop's place. I skidded to a stop behind the emergency vehicles, jumped out of the truck, and ran toward the building. Thick black smoke disappeared against the night sky, but the flames cast an unnatural light over the chaos on the ground.

I choked on the acrid smell of burning rubber as I watched firefighters spray water on the garage behind Coop's place. Where's the goddamn rain when you need it?

Coop talked to Josh next to a police cruiser, and I walked toward them. Josh nodded when I arrived, then answered a call on the radio clipped to his shoulder strap and excused himself.

I looked at Coop. "What the hell happened?"

"Nobody knows yet. Someone driving by called 911." He turned toward the blaze and his shoulders dropped. "Look at it. The Road Runner is toast. So is the evidence."

I put my hand on his shoulder. "What else you got in there?"

"I saved two customer's cars. Two other bays were empty."

"That's not so bad," I said.

He stared at the flames as he continued. "I had a '69 Charger that I just bought in the bay next to yours."

An explosion shook the ground and created a fireball that rolled slowly up into the sky. The orange light reflected off a tear in the corner of Coop's eye.

An hour later, the water stopped flowing from the hoses. Puddles mirrored the pulse of lights from the emergency vehicles. I stared at the smoldering black mess. We'd have to wait for the police and fire investigators to determine the cause of the blaze. Losing that car was a setback, but I had bigger problems on my hands. This was no accident.

The next thought blew in like a December wind and sent a chill up my spine. Besides me and Coop, Nicole was the only other soul who knew about that car. I wished I'd kept my mouth shut, but I had no reason not to trust her at the time. I wanted to believe that an electrical problem or a gasoline-soaked rag had been the culprit. The fact that Nicole had been in that car the night Luke disappeared and had something to lose if it went public wasn't enough to sway this jury of one.

Josh returned and tapped Coop on the shoulder. "I'll need you to stop down to the station in the morning to answer a few questions." He glanced at me, then back to Coop. "Fire investigators will be here soon. There's nothing else we can do tonight. Why don't you go home and get some sleep?"

We both nodded. I couldn't tell whether Josh was a good actor, or he had no idea that his beloved douche-mobile had just been barbecued.

"Yeah. Thanks, Josh," Coop said, then waited until Josh was out of earshot. He turned to me with a puzzled look. "This whole thing's got me a little spooked. That car sat untouched for three years. Then, the night after we discover new evidence, everything goes up in flames. That's a whole lotta coincidence, wouldn't you say?" He shook his head and looked at the ground.

"You think it was intentional?"

"That's the confusing part. You and I are the only ones who knew the car was there." Coop looked at me and I shifted my weight to the other foot. "And I certainly didn't torch it."

"Well, don't look at *me*," I said a little too loudly.

I couldn't sleep when I returned home, so I flopped down in Pop's chair and picked up the remote. Not much to watch at four in the morning, unless you need laser hair removal or a weight-loss miracle. My mind slipped back to Nicole and the night Luke disappeared, the fire at Coop's garage, and the fact that Pop died on her watch. I told myself they weren't related. I didn't believe it the first time, so I told myself again.

I put on a pot of coffee when the sun came up.

Mama shuffled into the kitchen around 0600. "What are you doing up so early?"

"It's not early, it's late."

She gave me a curious look. "You've been up all night?"

"Coop's garage caught fire last night."

"Oh, no. Was anyone hurt?"

"No. Just a few cars." I couldn't remember if I'd mentioned anything to Mama about Josh's old car.

The coffee pot belched a final puff of steam. I poured Mama a cup and set it on the table.

"Maybe you should get some sleep," she said as I picked up the pot to pour myself a cup.

"Can't. I'm meeting Bill McCutchen in a couple of hours." I turned around just in time to see Mama, eyes wide, nearly spit her coffee across the table.

"What's the matter?" I asked.

She swallowed and wiped the corner of her mouth. "Bill McCutchen?"

"Yeah, he's an old friend of Pop's."

"I know who he is."

"How well do you know him?"

She traced the rim of her cup with her finger. "It's complicated."

I pulled a chair from the table and sat. "I'd like to know before I see him."

Mama smiled and nodded, a distant look in her eyes. "Bill dated my sister Betsy when we were in high school. But I had a crush on him. I could see in his eyes that he had feelings for me, too. I used to pray that they'd break up so Bill and I could be together."

I'd seen photos of Mama when she was young and understood why men would want to be with her. The past few years had taken their toll, but at fifty-one, Mama was still a good-looking woman by anyone's standards.

I sipped my coffee. "Were your prayers ever answered?" I asked after I swallowed.

"Not before I met Eli. Your daddy and Bill became best friends. That didn't change when Betsy broke it off eight months later. Bill still had feelings for me, but he was a loyal friend."

I avoided her eyes. "What about you? Did you have feelings for *him*?"

"I was loyal, too."

Yeah, until Wade what's-his-name came along. I drank more coffee. "Do you have any regrets?"

She smiled. "I have many regrets. They're part of life, but I won't dwell on them or let them keep me from moving forward."

"Did you ever see him again after you and Pop..." The question went unfinished, but the words hung in the air for a moment.

"He called on me shortly after I returned to Bradley." Her cheeks flared.

I sensed her discomfort, but I pressed on. "What happened?"

"We pretty much just picked up where we'd left off." She looked away for a moment. "He took me to dinner a couple of times."

"You're dating Bill McCutchen?"

"Don't be silly," she said with a dismissive wave. "We're just getting re-acquainted."

I didn't know much about Bill McCutchen, so I'm not sure why this bothered me. I raked my hands back through my hair. "Are you gonna see him again?"

Mama stood and walked her empty cup to the sink. "Probably."

"Why didn't you tell me?"

She turned. "I'm telling you now."

For a moment, neither of us spoke, and I looked at the clock. "I should go if I want to make that meeting."

An odd, twisted smile crossed Mama's lips. "Say hi to Bill for me."

I nodded. "Sure thing, Mama."

After a quick shower, I poured myself more coffee and drove to Coop's garage. I parked and checked the time on my phone. With a half-hour to kill, I walked toward what was once a six-bay garage. I surveyed the smoldering rubble from beyond the police tape until Coop pulled into the lot. We sat on his tailgate and waited for Bill.

Coop looked at me sideways. "You do realize the only piece of evidence we had is gone."

I tilted my head. "Gee, Coop. Thanks for bringing me up to speed."

His mouth went slack for a moment. "Don't be such an asshat. This isn't my fault."

I inhaled and slowly blew out my breath. "I know. I'm sorry."

"What's eatin' you?"

The mere mention of Nicole's name would have set him off, and I was too tired to argue. "It's nothing." I lowered my head. "I thought we were getting somewhere. Now, we're back to square one."

Coop put his hand on my shoulder. "We'll find something else."

CHAPTER 18

A large, black SUV pulled in and parked a couple of spaces over from where we sat. We watched a tall, tree-trunk-of-a-man step out and quickly survey the scene as if committing it to memory. He tucked his long white hair behind his ears and set a straw cowboy hat atop his head. His bronze skin and Hawaiian shirt gave the impression that he'd just stepped off a plane from a long Pacific vacation. I recognized the lopsided swagger as he walked toward us. Bill McCutchen had a larger-than-life persona that you didn't easily forget.

"Howdy, boys," he said as he balanced half a cigar in the corner of his mouth. "You must be Dillon. I'm sorry to hear about your daddy. We were good friends."

I nodded and shook his meaty hand. His laser-sharp eyes and strong chin contrasted his otherwise casual appearance.

"It's good to see you again, Mr. McCutchen."

"Bill," he said as he gave Coop's hand a quick shake. He removed the cigar from his mouth and flicked the ash, then waved it in the direction of the rubble. "Is that why I'm here?"

"Yes." I hesitated. "And no."

He shot me a curious glance.

"The garage was still standing when I called you."

I told him everything I knew about the fire and the events that led up to our discovery of the new evidence. Everything, that is, except the part where I'd told Nicole.

Bill held up the police tape with one hand and gestured for us to step inside the perimeter. "I reckon you boys think this wasn't an accident."

Coop and I ducked under, and Bill followed.

"We hoped maybe you could help us figure that out," I said.

Bill looked at Coop. "Is this your place?"

"Yes, sir. The garage is only five years old."

"I hope you've got insurance."

"I do."

"Contact them right away. They'll send an investigator." He crushed out his cigar on the wet pavement. "You don't want to rely on Harley's boys for the truth about anything."

"I see you two have met," I said, not hiding the sarcasm in my voice.

He smiled. "Harley Wilkerson and I go way back. He started at the police academy at the same time I joined the Rangers. We were going to clean up the state of Texas." He lit another cigar and exhaled a column of smoke.

"That didn't happen, did it?"

"I like to think that I did my part." He rolled the cigar in his mouth. "Harley never really cleaned up anything. He just moved the dirt around."

The fire had burned itself out. Bill found a long stick and poked around in the ashes. "Tell me, Cooper. What exactly did you find?"

Coop explained his theory about the car's headlights, and how he dismantled the front end and found the blood spatter inside the light assembly.

"We planned to ask you if you could have it tested for us," I said, "but I guess it's a little late for that."

"Certainly looks that way."

"What can you tell us that wasn't in Pop's journal?"

Bill paused for a moment to scratch the whiskers on his chin. "Last time I saw that thing was about eight months ago. Haven't thought about it much since." He tossed the stick into the ashes and turned. "You have it with you?"

"Sure do." I pulled it from my back pocket and handed it to him.

Bill flipped through the pages. He stopped several times to read a passage. "Would you mind if I held on to this for a few days to give it a good read?"

I hesitated. "No disrespect, sir, but I can't let that out of my sight."

"It's Bill... and I understand." He nodded and pointed his cigar tip in our direction. "You boys best be careful. Ol' Harley runs a tight ship. Crooked, but tight. And I don't have to tell you how fast news travels in a small town."

Coop and I nodded in unison as I slipped the journal into my back pocket.

Bill pulled two business cards from his shirt pocket and handed one to each of us. He pointed the cigar again. "If there's anything you need, you boys just give me a call. That's my cell. It's with me 24/7."

"What do we do next?" Coop asked while I studied the card.

"We wait and see what the investigator turns up." He took a few steps toward his vehicle, then stopped and turned around. "Tell you what. I'll send somebody over. Somebody I can trust. He'll get to the bottom of this."

"By the way," I said, "Mama says hi."

Bill stopped and removed his cigar. His eyes drifted. "Bonnie Bishop." He said the name slowly, as if savoring a fond memory.

"She said you two were friends."

"Through thick and thin, son. Wish we'd kept in touch." He replaced the cigar and nodded. "You'll give her my best, won't you?"

"When's the last time you saw her?"

"Too many years to count." He turned again to leave, then stopped. He motioned toward the journal in my pocket. "You sure I can't borrow that for a little while?"

"I'm sorry."

He wrinkled his brow. "How 'bout you fellas follow me down to the Parkway, and I'll buy you breakfast? I can have a look at that journal while you eat. It'll never leave your sight."

I looked at Coop, who gave a quick nod. "Sure, Mister—uh, Bill. That sounds like a plan."

Bill offered up a wave that looked more like a salute, then climbed into his big, black SUV. I watched him drive off and wondered why he'd lied about seeing Mama.

Coop and I followed in my car. I wanted to come clean to Coop, tell him that Nicole knew about Josh's car, but I decided to wait until the investigator's report came back. If the fire turned out to be an accident, I'd have no reason to poke that turd.

CHAPTER 19

After breakfast, I dropped Coop off and headed to the hospital. I dialed Nicole's cell on the way. No answer. My phone rang as soon as I set it down. Unknown number, so I let it go to voice mail. In the parking lot behind the hospital, I listened to a message from Sam Granger.

I returned his call, and he told me a third party had requested additional tests be run on blood samples taken at the hospital after Pop's death. The new results, which he received today, differed from the autopsy report. They didn't find methamphetamines.

"Why would the autopsy say there was meth?" I asked.

"That's a good question."

"Who requested the tests?"

"I'm not at liberty to say."

"Can you tell me when the request was made?"

"A week ago."

"Is it unusual to second-guess an autopsy?"

"I've only seen it done once before."

"Please, I need to know." I paused. "This is my mama's life we're talking about here."

A long silence followed. "You didn't hear it from me. His name is Bill McCutchen."

"*Bill* requested the tests?"

"You know him?"

"He's a friend of the family." I took a deep breath and wondered why Bill had also failed to mention that he'd been looking into Pop's death. "So, now you don't think Mama did it?"

"I'm not saying that. Don't forget, there's still the security video and the one-hundred-thousand-dollar payday."

"Do you think the medical examiner is lying?"

"It wouldn't be the first time."

I took a moment to let it all sink in. "Okay, you told me what you didn't find. Now tell me what you did find."

"Everything was pretty consistent with his age and medical condition, except for an unusually high level of adrenaline."

"What would cause that?"

"His numbers were off the chart. My guess is intravenous injection."

"And what would that do to him?"

"His heart would beat so fast it would explode."

"How could Mama have gotten her hands on something like that? I don't imagine you can walk into Walgreen's and buy it over the counter."

"No, you can't." He cleared his throat. "But it's available with a prescription. Like those do-it-yourself shots people carry for bee stings."

"Can you find it in a hospital?"

"Of course."

After I hung up with Granger, I found a shady bench in the park and texted Nicole. Five minutes later, she walked out the back door.

"What are you doing here?" she asked as she sat next to me.

"We need to talk."

She shifted in her seat. "About what?"

"Did you hear about Coop's garage?"

She fired off a couple of rapid blinks before she looked away. "Yes. Did anyone get hurt?"

"No. Just the car I told you about."

"That's good." She turned her head quickly. "I mean that nobody got hurt."

"How did you hear about it?"

She looked down at her lap. "On the police scanner."

"Why do you have a police scanner?"

"I… I don't know. I guess I just like to know what's happening in town."

Or maybe you just like to keep tabs on Josh. "Oh."

I watched her for a moment. She appeared to have trouble keeping her hands still.

"Did you tell anyone about the car?"

She twisted a few strands of hair around her finger. "Why would I do that?"

I shrugged. "I don't know." Nicole looked as nervous as a prize turkey in November, and I wanted to throw up.

"Dillon, what's going on?"

"How much do you know about adrenaline?"

She gave me a wary glance. "What?"

I studied her reaction. "What if someone was given a shot of adrenaline?"

"You mean like an EpiPen?"

"No. I mean like a big syringe full of it, injected into a vein."

She shook her head. "You wouldn't do that. epinephrine administered like that could cause extreme tachycardia, hypertension, even stroke."

"What if they gave it to someone in, say, Pop's condition?"

"It would be lethal."

"How long would it take?"

"He'd crash almost immediately."

That didn't fit with my theory. The killer wouldn't have had time to get away before the monitors squealed. I suppose she could have turned them off prior to the injection, but that would likely raise suspicion once they found him. I studied Nicole in the silence. She'd seemed more nervous when I told her about the fire than when I asked her about the epinephrine.

"Why do you want to know?"

"Is there any way to stretch out that time interval? The time between the injection and death."

"Are we still talking about your daddy?"

"Think. Is there any way to slow it down?"

She looked down and traced something on the back of her hand. "I suppose if you injected the epi into the IV and lowered the rate on the infusion pump, it might take ten minutes before he coded."

Bingo.

Nicole grabbed my arm. "Wait. You don't think I had anything to do with his death, do you? Why would I want to kill him?"

I lost my nerve. I couldn't make eye contact, let alone speak.

"Dillon?"

My own tachycardia rattled my chest. I took a deep breath. "Let's talk about the night Luke disappeared."

A wave of terror swept across those pretty green eyes. "Why? What... what does that have to do with anything?"

"I think you know."

Her eyes flashed, and she stood. "This was a mistake. I have to go."

"Wait."

She ignored me.

"Nicole!"

She stopped and turned slowly.

"You said Mama visited him after he died."

She wiped a tear from her cheek and nodded.

"Do you think anyone else would remember seeing her?"

Nicole hesitated. "She talked to Doctor Miller." The wind blew her hair across her face. She brushed it away, turned, and ran back inside the hospital.

I watched the door close behind her and wondered if I'd been the one who'd made the mistake, tipping my hand too soon.

CHAPTER 20

My phone rang. I didn't recognize the number.

"Hello," I said, still staring at the back door of the hospital.

"Dillon, we need to talk."

"Who's this?"

"Not on the phone. And not in Bradley." She paused. "There's a diner in Keene, The Stage Stop. It's on 174, near the high school. Can you meet me there in an hour?"

"What's this about?"

"See you in an hour."

I fired up the Mustang and headed for Keene, a fifteen-minute drive. I hadn't eaten lunch yet, so I planned to get there early and have a bite while I waited. I thought being the first to arrive might give me an advantage, even though I wasn't sure exactly what that would be.

The Stage Stop looked like the stage hadn't stopped there for some time. The empty parking lot at 1230 was not a good sign. A middle-aged waitress offered a friendly greeting from behind the counter. I ordered a turkey club with extra bacon and a Dr. Pepper, then sat in a red leather booth with a view of the parking lot.

The sandwich tasted better than I'd expected, and I ordered a slice of pecan pie and a cup of coffee when I finished. I set my fork down and pushed my plate away as a blue sedan pulled into the space next to mine. The driver's door opened, and Amanda Hughes stepped out. I resisted the urge to jump up and get the door.

"Hello, Dillon," she said softly once she arrived at my table. She slid into the seat across from me and set her purse on the edge of the table. The purse fell to the floor, spilling its contents.

I rose quickly, shoved everything back inside, and returned the purse to the table.

"Thank you."

"I'd be lying if I said I wasn't surprised to see you," I said as I sat.

She smiled a nervous smile. "Now you know how I felt. I almost lost my lunch when you walked into the gym."

"I noticed. Am I here to find out why?"

She nodded. "But first, I need you to promise me you won't tell anyone that we met. I'm taking a huge risk talking to you, but I can't keep this a secret any longer. I should have spoken up a long time ago."

The waitress came over and held a coffee pot above my empty cup. I nodded. She looked at Amanda. "What can I get you, honey?"

"Just coffee."

I added a little sugar, stirred, and tapped the spoon on the edge of my cup. "Is this about Luke?"

"How did you know?"

"I didn't. Do you know something about the night he disappeared?"

"Dillon, I'm sorry. I've always liked you. Even when Nicole—"

"It's okay. Just tell me."

"Josh, Nicole, Bobby, and I left the dance together in Josh's car."

Amanda paused while the waitress set a cup of coffee on the table. "It was still early," she said after the waitress left, "so Josh suggested we go up to the quarry for a while." She lowered her gaze. "You know…"

I nodded.

"The car skidded on the wet pavement as we turned onto Quarry Road. I couldn't see anything, but I felt the car hit something. Nicole screamed."

I closed my eyes and waited. I had a pretty good idea what she was about to say. I didn't want to hear it, but I knew I had to.

"Bobby and I stayed in the car while Josh and Nicole went to check it out. She came back all wet and hysterical. I couldn't understand her at first. I've never been so scared in my life—well, until now." She glanced out the window. "I calmed her down a little. That's when she told me it was Luke."

I squeezed my eyes shut and grabbed my head with both hands. I bit my tongue so I wouldn't scream. More than anything in my life, I wanted this to be a bad dream. I wanted to wake up in my bed in Dallas. No, that wasn't good enough. I wanted to wake up in my old room in Bradley on April 23, 2009, and stop feeling so goddamn sorry for myself because Nicole would be at the dance that night with Josh instead of me. I'd give Luke a ride that night, instead of cussin' at him and making him walk.

"I'm sorry, Dillon."

I put my hands on the table and took a deep breath. "It's okay. Please finish."

"Josh came back a couple of minutes later. I'd never seen Josh scared, but he sobered up in a matter of minutes. He told everyone to shut up so he could think."

"How drunk was he when you left the dance?"

She turned her cup on the table, avoiding my eyes. "He was really wasted."

"Damn it! Why didn't somebody take his keys?"

Amanda looked up, her eyes wide. "Dillon..." She hesitated. "Nicole drove."

I felt my lunch in the back of my throat and I covered my mouth. *Luke was dead, and Nicole killed him.*

"Are you okay?"

I took a deep breath and nodded. "What happened next?"

"Nicole took out her phone to call 911, but Josh grabbed it. They fought for a minute before Josh stepped outside. When he came back inside, he told us he'd called the police. Nicole went outside and stayed with Luke. I don't think anyone said another word until Josh's daddy showed up in a patrol car."

"Let me guess. He told you he'd take care of everything and sent you home."

Amanda leaned in, eyes wide. "That's exactly what he did. He said as far as anyone else was concerned, we weren't there. And if we told anyone, we'd be in so much trouble that even Jesus himself couldn't save us. Josh can be a real asshole sometimes, but nothin' like his daddy. That guy creeps me out."

I closed my eyes and shook my head.

"Dillon. He was the Police Chief. What was I supposed to do?"

I sighed. "I know. You didn't have much choice."

"We suspected something was wrong when we went to the hospital to see Luke the next day. No one had heard about the accident, and Luke had never been never admitted."

"What do you think happened?"

"I don't know for sure, but Josh freaked out when he heard we'd gone to the hospital. After that, he checked up on us and threatened us if we ever mentioned it again to anybody."

"Were the threats specific?"

"No. He just said that bad things would happen, but it was the way he said it. He scared the hell out of me." Her left hand trembled, and she placed it in her lap. "I hate to think about what would happen if anyone finds out I talked to you today."

"I won't tell."

"You better not, or we'll both end up like your daddy."

I blinked a few times. "What do you know about that?"

"C'mon, Dillon." She raised her eyebrows impatiently. "Do the math. Your daddy starts shootin' his mouth off about that night, sayin' he's got evidence that Luke had been murdered. Then he mysteriously dies. Someone involved in this mess killed him. Maybe Josh… maybe even Nicole."

"Josh, maybe. Not Nicole. She couldn't." I raised my cup. When I realized it was empty, I set it down quickly and pushed it away.

"You've been away for ten years."

"It doesn't make sense," I said. "Okay, she drove, but she got sent home with you and Bobby. Whatever happened to Luke after that couldn't have been on her."

"What if she's protecting someone?"

"Who? Josh?"

"Did you know they have a kid?"

I met her gaze with narrowed eyes. "I'm aware."

"They were engaged for a while. Maybe Josh told her something he wasn't supposed to." She stared into her empty cup. "He's had some kind of mysterious control over her for the longest time."

As much as I hated the thought, I guess I had to at least consider the possibility. "And now?"

"I don't know. She's been different since you've been back."

I felt no need to discuss my relationship with Nicole any further. "So, Amanda, why am I here? Is there something you need from me? Something you want me to do?"

She frowned and opened her mouth, but no words came out.

I stood and picked up the check. "Then I guess we're done."

"Dillon. Wait." She grabbed my wrist. "I thought you should know what happened. You need to be careful."

I shook my arm free. "Oh, so you're here for *me*. I don't see it that way, Amanda. I think your motives are a little more selfish."

I sat back down on the edge of the seat and leaned across the table. "I think you just went to confession, and now you're looking for absolution. Well, you've come to the wrong place."

I paid the bill and left without another word. I stared at Amanda through my windshield, head in her hands, still seated at the table. I felt like an asshole. I accused her of selfish intentions, but I'd been the selfish one. I let the talk about Nicole and Josh get under my skin, and I took it out on her. Sure, she wanted to get all that off her chest, but thanks to her call, I knew more about what happened that night, and I was grateful. She didn't deserve to be treated that way.

I wanted to go back inside and apologize, but Amanda stood and walked toward the exit before I could open my door. I watched her get into her car and knew something was wrong when she didn't leave right away. I walked to her car and stood by her door. She looked at me and held up her palms.

I opened the door. "Won't start?"

"It's dead. No lights or anything."

"Let me take a look."

She stepped out, and I sat in the driver's seat. I turned the key. Nothing. I checked the shifter, then removed and reinserted the key into the ignition. Still nothing. When I lifted the hood, I could barely see the battery terminals underneath the corrosion.

"This should only take a couple of minutes," I said. "I'll be right back." I went inside the diner and returned with napkins, pliers, and a glass of Coke. I cleaned the terminals and told Amanda to give it another try. It started right up.

"Thank you, Dillon," she called from the driver's seat.

All I could do was shrug.

Amanda got out of the car and gave me a hug. "I'm really sorry about all this."

"Me too."

I closed the hood, watched her drive away, then returned the pliers and the empty glass. I felt a little better as I drove home. But only a little.

CHAPTER 21

Coop had always been a good friend, and now he'd put himself and his business at risk to help me. I had to tell him about Nicole. I owed him that much.

I walked into Coop's office and sat. He held up a finger as he spoke into the phone. I stared at a four-barrel carburetor on the corner of his desk and considered what I would say and what his reaction might be. I had a feeling it wouldn't be pretty.

He hung up the phone and shuffled a few papers on his desk. "What's up?"

"There's no easy way to do this, so I'll just say it." I had his attention. "Nicole knew about the car. I told her a couple of days ago."

At first, he said nothing, his expression unreadable. He closed his eyes, and I waited. When he opened them again, he leaned forward and rested his elbows on his desk.

"I don't think you should be here right now," he said calmly.

I held up my hands in defense. "I know it looks bad, but I don't think she did it."

"You're damn right it looks bad."

If I was Coop, I probably wouldn't believe me either. I wasn't thinking straight, but I'd never let that stop me before.

Coop leaned back in his chair and shook his head. "I told you she was trouble."

"I know her. She wouldn't do something like that."

"Oh yeah, you know her SO well." Coop's eyes narrowed. "You have no idea what she's been up to for the past ten years, but somehow, you're an expert on Nicole Garcia. You think because you had a crush on her a dozen years ago, you know her? You don't know shit about her."

"I know she didn't do this."

"Oh. In that case, we can just forget about the whole thing."

"You mean it?"

He glared at me and picked up the phone.

"What are you doing?"

"Calling the police."

I jumped up. "Wait."

"She burned down my goddamn garage."

I felt like a matador waving a red cape in front of an angry bull. "You don't know that."

"Open your eyes, will you? She's the only other person who knew the car was in there."

"That doesn't mean she did it." My back stiffened. "Maybe she told Josh."

"Interesting theory, Columbo, but either way, she's the enemy. If you don't put some distance between you and that—"

"Watch it, Coop." The tables had just turned, and I saw red. "You don't want to force me to choose sides."

He raised his eyebrows, as well as his voice. "Are you saying that you'd choose *her* over *me*?"

A few seconds of silence passed.

"Shit!" He rolled his eyes and his head rocked backward. "You're sleeping with her."

"I didn't say that."

"Dammit, Bish. Don't make me watch you screw up your life." He shook his head slowly. "I don't think I can do that again."

"It's my life. I get to do whatever I want with it." I stood.

"Maybe you should join the Army. See the world. Get your other foot blown off. Maybe I'll see you in another ten years." He pointed a finger at me that felt like a bayonet. "On second thought, if you ever decide to come back to Bradley, do me a favor and don't look me up."

I turned and walked out the door. I expected him to stop me, to say something else, to take it back. He didn't. The air wrench hammered again, and I ducked my head.

I rested my elbows on the bar at Shady's, nursing a tall, cold one when Josh walked in. He stood at the bar next to me. I didn't look up.

"A call came into the station from your friend Cooper. He accused Nicole of burning down his garage." He folded his arms across his chest. "You know anything about that, Bishop?"

Dammit, Coop. I turned my head. "I might."

"Where would he get a crazy idea like that?"

"Let's see." I put my finger up to my chin. "It might be because something in that garage scared the crap out of her, and she's the only other person who knew it was there."

Josh glared at me as he bit his lower lip.

I pushed my stool away from the bar. "Maybe behind door number three, there was a special surprise. A car, perhaps."

His nostrils flared and a vein twitched above his left eye.

We stood face to face again; a place I'd hoped to avoid. "But this wasn't just any car, Josh. This was the car that killed my little brother." As soon as I said it, I realized I'd made a terrible mistake.

Something flashed in Josh's eyes, but he made a quick recovery. "I always knew you had shit for brains," he said with a sneer, "but now they're really starting to stink."

"Oh, yeah?" I should have kept my big mouth shut, but I let the bastard get to me. "Somehow those shitty brains figured out how to find blood spatter inside the front end of a repainted 1970 Road Runner and send it off to the crime lab in Austin." Okay, so I stretched the truth a little to watch him squirm.

Josh's face turned red, and he clenched his teeth. "You better think long and hard about what you say or do next." He shoved an index finger in my face. "Tread lightly, Mr. Bishop. I guarantee you do not want to have this conversation again."

I pushed his hand away.

"Did you just assault a police officer?"

I sat back down at the bar and took a long draw on my beer. Josh hovered for a moment, then turned and left.

I checked my phone. Quarter to four. I finished my beer and ordered another. It had already been at least a two-beer day. Maybe three or four. I'd alienated my best friend and trusted partner. I felt a little like Sherlock without Watson, Butch without Sundance, Starsky without Hutch. If that wasn't bad enough, I'd just kicked a big ol' hornet's nest, and I could hear them buzzing all around me, ready to attack.

I picked up my Lone Star and took it with me to the table in the back where I'd sat with Jenn a week ago. She could take care of herself, I knew that, but I couldn't allow her to follow me into harm's way, which is pretty much where I sat at the moment. I just wished that she'd left on better terms.

Jenn had become a positive force in my life when I'd needed it most. She once told me she knew before we met that I would come into her life, and I would need her help. She called it a cosmic connection and said that we'd known each other in a past life. If I ever needed her for anything, all I had to do was think about her and she would *hear* me. That's what she said. I told her she was wacky, but she proved me wrong on more than one occasion.

My phone vibrated on the table. Coop's name appeared on the screen.

"Hello."

"Bill's guy just left. Your *girlfriend* is an arsonist."

CHAPTER 22

I pushed my food around my plate at breakfast the next morning. I hadn't slept much, and my appetite suffered as well.

"Do you plan to eat that or just play with it?" Mama said from across the table.

I shrugged but didn't bother to look up.

"What's wrong, Dillon?"

I set my fork down and slowly raised my head. "Do you know a Doctor Miller?"

"I do." She tilted her head to the side. "Why do you ask?"

"Did you see him the day Pop died?"

She nodded, and her gaze muddied. She looked down at her hands. "He was the one who told me Eli passed."

"I'm sorry, but I have to ask." I waited for her to look up. "Did you see Pop at all that day before you spoke with Doctor Miller?"

Her face tightened as if she knew why I'd asked, then her shoulders dropped. "No," she said in a small voice. "He met me in the hall outside Eli's room."

"Do you think he'll remember seeing you there?"

"I'm pretty sure he will. I dropped a vase of flowers on the floor when he told me."

I studied her for a moment, convinced that she'd been honest with me, but reluctant to accept the implications of her innocence. However, if the doctor's recollection lined up with hers, I'd no longer have a good reason to view her as a suspect.

I scraped my plate into the basket under the sink, then set it on the counter.

"Good morning, Cooper," Mama said from behind me. "How nice to see you."

Coop had let himself in and stood in the kitchen doorway. I didn't think it was so nice, and nodded without words.

"Would you like something to eat?" she asked.

"I'm sure Coop has eaten breakfast, Mama."

Coop stared at me. "I reckon a cup of coffee would be nice," he said, then turned to Mama with a smile.

He pulled out a chair while Mama removed a cup that hung from a hook underneath one of the upper cabinets.

"What brings you around this morning?" she asked as she poured.

"I need to talk to Dillon about a few things." He glanced at me as she placed the steaming cup on the table. He picked it up and took a sip. "Good coffee, Mrs. B."

Mama smiled.

"I hope I didn't interrupt anything." Coop shot another glance my way before he focused his attention on Mama.

"Not at all. Dillon was just asking me about the day his daddy died."

"Coop's not interested in hearing about that."

He reached for his cup. "You were saying…"

"Well, I told Dillon how I dropped a vase of fresh flowers on the floor when Doctor Miller told me that Eli had died."

"You found out on your way to visit him?"

"Yes, I'd stopped at the florist first to pick up fresh flowers. Eli used to think flowers were for sissies, but I thought they would brighten up that dreary room." Mama's voice cracked.

"Nice work, Coop." I put a hand on Mama's shoulder.

"No, no, that's okay," she said. She wiped her cheek.

"It's not okay, Mama." I stood next to Coop's chair. "Coop needs to go. I'll walk him out."

Coop stood, pushed in his chair, and thanked Mama for the coffee. I followed him into the living room. He stopped near the front door. "Looks like you can scratch your mama from the top of the *Ten Most Wanted List.*"

"Is that what you came all the way over here to tell me?"

"Pretty much. And to see the look on your face when you realize Nicole is number two."

"How do you figure?"

"Nicole had to be in Josh's car that night. You cried yourself to sleep because she went to the dance with him instead of you. She knows something about that night. At the very least, she covered up a crime."

"So, you think she killed Pop because he was about to expose her, then made it look like Mama did it?"

"She had the means, the motive, and the opportunity."

"Now you're a lawyer?"

Coop rolled his eyes.

I couldn't believe this was Coop, my best friend since forever. "You used to be my friend."

"I still am. You just don't want to admit that you're sleeping with the woman who killed your daddy."

"I told you, I'm not sleeping with her." I dragged my hands back through my hair. "And even if I was, she's not like that. She could never kill Pop."

"Oh yeah, I forgot." More eye rolling. "You're the Nicole expert."

"Why would she admit that Mama visited the hospital *after* Pop died? Someone went to a lot of trouble to make it look like Mama was there just before he died. Why would she say that, huh?"

"I don't know, Bish. Maybe she's stupid, too."

Coop stepped over the line, and I got up in his face. "You better take that back."

"You're choosing sides again." He held his ground. "It's obvious that nothing I say is gonna get through that thick skull of yours."

"You used to be my friend."

Coop shook his head. "Nicole killed your daddy, and you know it." He walked backward toward the door and pointed a finger at me. "The question is, what are you gonna do about it?"

I wondered the same thing as I watched Coop leave. Mama stood in the kitchen doorway. Our eyes met briefly, but no one spoke. I walked down the hall and slammed the bedroom door.

Coop's case against Nicole had just gained serious traction, but I still chose to ignore the evidence. I knew firsthand that Nicole could break a heart, but I refused to believe she could kill anyone. I'd spent more time defending Nicole than Mama, even as the evidence seemed to shift the blame in Nicole's direction. It bothered me that it didn't bother me.

I continued to move forward with my investigation, speaking with Dr. Miller later that day. He explained that he'd been making rounds at the hospital the afternoon Pop died. When Pop coded, he had tried unsuccessfully to resuscitate him. He spoke to Mama when she arrived at the hospital fifteen minutes later. He even remembered calling maintenance to clean up the vase that had shattered on the floor.

Two witnesses corroborated Mama's story, which contradicted the video. I pulled Bill's card from my pocket and dialed his number. I explained my concerns and asked him to look into it. Once again, he was a step ahead of me. He told me that a friend in the Ranger's forensics lab has agreed to testify that the video had been doctored.

Without that video, they didn't have much of a case against Mama. Perhaps I'd been too hard on Coop.

CHAPTER 23

"I've had enough," I said aloud and threw my duffel bag on the bed. I wished I'd never opened that goddamn letter. Jenn said she didn't think it was a good idea to come back here. *When will I listen to the people who care about me?* It shouldn't be too hard. There aren't that many.

It had been a long day that began with an argument with my best friend at breakfast, and it went downhill from there. After lunch, I took a couple of pills and slept through the afternoon and into the evening. Something had to give.

I emptied the top dresser drawer and threw everything in my bag. Mama answered a loud knock at the front door. I opened the bedroom door a crack to listen. She sounded upset, so I stepped into the hall. Josh's voice froze me in my tracks.

"You can't come in here without a warrant," Mama fired back.

She appeared to have it under control, so I thought it best to stay out of sight. I returned to my room and continued to pack while I waited for her to fill me in.

"Dillon?" A soft knock on the bedroom door accompanied Mama's voice.

"Come in."

She stepped into the room and stopped. "Going somewhere?"

"I can't stay here."

"What did you do, Dillon?"

"I didn't do anything. I never should have come back."

She folded her arms across her chest. "Don't you want to know who was at the door?"

"It sounded like Josh." I zipped my bag and noticed Luke's badge pinned to the outside. *Now might be a good time to help me out, little brother.*

"He wanted to arrest you for the murder of Amanda Hughes."

"What?" I sat on the edge of the bed. "Amanda's dead?"

"Apparently. Do you know anything about it?"

"Why would I know anything?"

"I guess I forgot to mention that Amanda stopped by the house yesterday."

Words escaped me, or perhaps they couldn't get past my stomach, which had lodged itself in my throat.

"Dillon. I just lied to the police. You'd better tell me what's going on."

"Did Amanda say what she wanted?"

"No."

Mama studied me for a few seconds. "Talk to me, Dillon."

"I told you, I don't know anything."

She sat on the bed next to me. "What should we do?"

"You don't have to do anything." I picked up my bag and grabbed the pill bottle from the nightstand. "I'm leaving."

Mama followed me into the living room. "Where will you go?"

"I don't know. I didn't kill anybody, but it looks like I'm going to have to find a way to prove it. I need time to think." I set my bag down and walked to the gun cabinet.

"Dillon. Don't."

"It's for protection." I opened the door and picked up a 45-caliber pistol and an extra clip. "I won't use it unless I have to."

"I can't let you do this." Her voice cracked as she spoke.

"You don't understand. I have no choice. And neither do you." I reached behind my back and tucked the gun inside my belt. "Josh and his daddy don't want me in jail. They want me dead."

Mama cried.

"I think Josh killed Pop, with help from Nicole. And I think Harley knew about it." I stood beside one of the front windows and moved the curtain away from the wall with my finger. The end of a cigarette glowed from inside a car parked across the street. "Now they've killed Amanda and somehow made it look like I did it."

"Why are they killing these people?"

"I think it has to do with Luke."

"With Luke? I don't understand."

"Look, Mama. The less you know, the better. At least for now." I wrapped my arms around her and held on for at least a minute while ancient memories swirled around in my head like a Texas twister. I pulled back, hesitated for a second, then kissed her forehead. "I love you, Mama."

She looked at me through tears. "You have no idea how much that means to me."

I brushed her cheeks with my thumbs. "I better go."

"Please be careful. I can't lose you again." She wiped her eyes with the backs of her hands. "They're watching the house. You won't be able to drive out of here."

"I'll walk. Pop's truck is over at Coop's. I'll sneak out the back and pick it up."

"Let me help," she said.

"Can you distract the guy out front?"

She smiled. "I'll go see if he'd like some coffee."

"Thanks, Mama." I picked up my bag. "And don't worry. I'll be fine."

Mama waited until I walked into the kitchen before she opened the front door. I slipped out the back into the night. The full moon that hung in a cloudless sky lighted my way but offered little as far as cover. Coop's shop was near the high school, so I knew the route by heart.

I stopped under the cypress tree for a moment and looked back at our house. Pop used to say: *Don't dig up more snakes than you can kill.* I wished I'd remembered that before I shot off my mouth to Josh the last time I saw him. I pulled a tiny white pill from the bottle in my pocket and swallowed it.

I continued my trek through back yards and open fields, away from the main roads. I found Pop's truck in Coop's parking lot, opened the driver's door, and threw my bag across the cab to the passenger seat. All I had to do was climb in, start it up, and get the hell out of Dodge. But as much as I tried to resist the temptation, I had to know the truth, and I had to hear it from *her*, face to face. If that meant extracting a confession at gunpoint, so be it. I slammed the door and set off on foot.

The street in front of Nicole's house was empty, but I didn't want to take any chances. I knocked on her back door just before 2230. Her face appeared on the other side of the glass after the second knock. In the fleeting moment that she held my gaze, I saw surprise, confusion, desire, and a healthy dose of regret. She unlocked the door and pulled it open.

Nicole stood barefoot in the doorway, dressed in a flimsy pink robe that was dangerously short. "Dillon. What are you doing here?"

I took a deep breath to regain control after the surge in my chest and points south. "Go put some clothes on. We need to talk."

She led me into the living room, disappeared for a few minutes, then returned wearing denim cut-offs and a Dallas Mavericks t-shirt.

"Better?"

Only a little. I forced a smile.

"Why are you here?" she asked. She sat on the sofa and pulled her legs up alongside her.

"Amanda's dead, and Josh thinks I killed her."

"What?" Nicole covered her mouth with her hand.

I studied her reaction. She seemed genuinely surprised.

"When? What happened?"

"I don't know. I wasn't there."

"Why does Josh think you killed her?" she asked between tears.

"That's what I'd like to know. You got any ideas?"

"Me? No." She became defensive. "I don't know what you may have heard about me and Josh, but we're done. He's Annabelle's father. That's it."

"Oh, good. Because I thought maybe you called him and told him about the car Pop had stored at Coop's garage." I tried to maintain eye contact, but she looked away. "The day after I told you about it, the garage burned down. Investigators say it was arson."

Nicole stared at her feet.

"Look at me!"

She flinched and met my gaze.

"You may not have burned down Coop's garage, but your hands are dirty. There's something you haven't told me." I stood. "But that's gonna change tonight."

I walked to the sofa and looked down at her. She looked away. I reached my right hand behind my back and closed my fingers around the gun handle.

CHAPTER 24

Nicole looked up at me as tears rolled down her cheeks. "Dillon, I can't."

I grabbed her arm and pulled her to her feet. "I need to know what happened, and I need to hear it from you."

"Ow!" She struggled. "If I say anything, he'll take Annabelle."

"Who? Josh?"

Nicole didn't respond.

"I know you were in the car with him that night."

"He wasn't driving. I was." She glared at me. "Now, will you please let go?"

I released my grip, closed my eyes, and squeezed the bridge of my nose. Her admission crushed my heart like a cigarette put out on a sidewalk.

"I'm sorry, Dillon." She sat and tears spilled into her lap. "I wanted to tell you so many times, but I couldn't. Then you left town. I cried for months." She drew in a ragged breath. "I would have done anything to go back in time to before it happened."

I struggled to suppress the nausea. I'd seen and done things in Afghanistan that would turn a serial killer's stomach, but this... this was family. This was ten years of agony and frustration. This was betrayal by someone whose bed I nearly crawled into.

"Just tell me what happened," I said as calmly as I could.

She pulled in a long breath. "Josh was too drunk to drive, so I took his keys. Amanda and Bobby sat in the back seat."

She paused for a moment to wipe her eyes, and I waited.

"Josh didn't want to go right home, so we drove up to the quarry. The roads were wet from the rain. The car skidded as we turned onto Quarry Road. I swear to God, Dillon, I never saw him. He was still alive when I knelt over his body. He opened his eyes and squeezed my hand."

She paused, and I felt her eyes on me, but I stared at the ground.

"I wanted to call 911, but Josh wouldn't let me. He said we needed to think about how to handle this. That it could ruin all our lives. He was worried about his football scholarship. He called his daddy, and ten minutes later, Harley showed up in a patrol car." She stared for a moment, as she chewed her bottom lip.

"And?"

"They talked for a few minutes. Harley told us that as far as the rest of the world was concerned, we weren't there. He would handle it. Then Josh drove us home."

"Did Josh go back there?"

She shrugged. "I think so."

"What did you do when you got home?"

"What could I do? I tried to sleep. I watched the news the next morning but found nothing about the accident. Not a word. Amanda and I went to the hospital to see Luke, but he wasn't there. I felt stupid and naïve to think that Josh would have taken the rap alone and jeopardize his goddamn scholarship. For what? For me?"

"And you never mentioned this to anyone?"

"This is the first time."

"And Amanda?"

"As far as I know, she's never told anyone."

"She told me."

Nicole blinked back surprise. "When?"

"Last Saturday."

"So, this whole time, you knew what happened?"

"Like I said, I wanted to hear it from you."

Her eyes narrowed. "You bastard!"

"Me? I'm the bastard? That's funny coming from the person who killed half my family."

She stood and paced back and forth in front of the sofa. I noticed her steal a glance at the clock before she spoke. "You still believe I killed your daddy?"

"I don't want to. I fought it all the way. Ask Coop. He'll probably never speak to me again. But you had a lot to lose if Pop didn't drop his investigation into Luke's disappearance."

She stopped to glare at me.

Our eyes locked. "He had a bad liver and would've died soon, anyway. Is that how you justified it?"

"Stop it."

"I guess you didn't count on me coming back around after he died and picking up where he left off, did you? When you think about killing me, I hope it's a little harder than when you thought about Pop."

"Stop it, Dillon. I didn't kill anybody."

"You sure about that?"

"I didn't kill your daddy." She sat down again. "And I didn't kill Luke. I told you, he was alive when I left."

"But you felt guilty. That's why you avoided me after he died. After all we'd been through, I thought you loved me, but it was pity." My shoulders fell.

"No, Dillon." Her eyes begged for forgiveness. "I loved you... I still do."

"I don't know what to believe anymore." I shook my head. "Now Amanda's dead because she opened her mouth about that night. If you didn't kill her, maybe you're next."

Nicole slid to the edge of the sofa, her back stiff. "Why are you here, Dillon?"

I hesitated. "I guess I came to find out if you killed Pop."

"I'm sorry for my part in what happened to Luke, but I swear to you, I had nothing to do with your daddy's death."

"Whoever killed him went to a lot of trouble to frame Mama."

"Dillon, I'm not trying to frame anyone."

I wanted to believe her almost as much as I'd wanted to believe Mama.

"What do you plan to do?" she asked as she rubbed the back of her hand.

"I don't know." I snorted. "I can't call the police."

"What if *Josh* is trying to frame *me*?"

I considered that possibility for a moment. "It doesn't matter anymore. I'm leaving Bradley for good." I took a deep breath to release the tightness in my chest. "I guess the other reason I'm here tonight is to say goodbye."

She glanced at the clock again. "You don't have to leave. Whatever is going on, we can figure it out together. Please stay."

"I've made up my mind."

Nicole stood. "Please, Dillon."

Before I responded, the front door burst open and three police officers rushed in, guns drawn.

Josh turned his gun on me. "Hands on your head, Bishop."

Reluctantly, I obliged. One of the other officers patted me down, and I wished I'd listened to Mama. He pulled the pistol from my belt and held it up between two fingers.

"Bag it." Josh made no attempt to hid a smug grin.

The other officer removed my hands from my head one at a time and snapped the cuffs on behind my back.

"Am I under arrest?"

"We'll figure that out down at the station."

Josh looked at Nicole. "Thanks for the tip."

I turned my head in her direction. Her eyes grew wide. "No. He's lying. I didn't—"

"Shut up, Nicole." Josh scolded. "You did your job. Now let us do ours."

"Dillon, please. I would never—"

An officer grabbed Nicole and threw her on the sofa.

I turned my head and our eyes met as Josh pulled me through the door. I watched her until the last one out closed the door behind us.

CHAPTER 25

By the time we reached the station, I looked like Rocky Balboa after a few rounds with Apollo Creed. Blood flowed from a busted lip, and my left eye was nearly swollen shut. Three against one would have been a fair fight if I hadn't been in handcuffs. I think I broke one of Josh's ribs, and the other two thugs would be plenty sore in the morning.

The chief didn't try to hide his shit-eatin' grin when Josh paraded me past his office door. Josh deposited me in a small interrogation room on the first floor. I leaned over the table so the blood wouldn't drip onto my jeans.

A nurse entered the room, cleaned me up, and put a couple of stitches in my lip. I thanked her and asked if she could give me something for my headache. She put three ibuprofen in my mouth and held a glass of water while I drank.

Josh returned five minutes later with an older, female officer. Her silver name tag read *Harris*. My guess is that she had to be there to make sure he didn't cross the line again with the recorder running. I already had a case for police brutality, but instead, they'd probably add *resisting arrest* to my list of trumped-up charges. He sat down slowly, unable to hide his physical discomfort.

"I'll get right to it," Josh said. "Where were you Monday night?"

I had to think. I'd spent the late afternoon and early evening at Shady's, feeling sorry for myself over a few too many drinks. "Any particular time?"

"Between ten and midnight."

Dammit! I'd gone home around nine and crashed. I had no alibi. "I was home in bed."

"Were you alone?"

He held his breath as he waited for my answer. I hesitated for a few seconds. I wanted to lie and tell him that Nicole had been with me, but nodded instead.

"Can anyone verify that?"

"I talked to Mama for a few minutes when I got home."

"You mean Bonnie Bishop? The mama that abandoned her family, became a meth head, then returned to kill her husband for the insurance money?" He leaned over the table. "Is that the mama you're referring to?"

My skin burned, and I glanced at Harris before glaring at Josh. I wanted to reach across the table and slam his head down on it, but that would only be a temporary fix. "You say something like that again about Mama and I'll break the rest of those ribs."

Josh had a shit-eatin' grin like his old man, and he flashed it. "Let the record show that Mr. Bishop admitted to assaulting a police officer and has made additional threats."

"I want a lawyer."

Josh turned his head a little to the left. "I'm sorry, did you say something?"

"I said I want my lawyer."

"I can see your mouth moving, but I can't seem to make out what you're tryin' to say." He looked at Harris. "Did you catch that?"

She shrugged and shook her head.

So much for the chaperone.

"You must know why we brought you in here."

I shook my head, unsure whether I should say anything else.

"A mutual friend was murdered Monday night."

"I'm sorry to hear that. Shouldn't you be out trying to catch her killer?"

The grin was back. "I never said it was a woman."

As long as I had to spend time with this asshole, I figured information can go both ways. "Lucky guess. How did she die?"

Josh tilted his head. "Why don't you tell me?"

"I would if I knew."

"Drug overdose." He leaned back and folded his arms across his chest. "Seems to be a lot of that going around lately."

"Sounds like a suicide to me."

"It appeared that way until we found your fingerprints on the pill bottle."

I didn't see that coming. How was that even possible? He had to be bluffing.

"Yeah. We found your prints all over the place—in her car, on her purse. Nothing in the bedroom, though. Weren't you hittin' that?"

What a douchebag. Our eyes locked. "No, Josh. I had my hands full with Nicole."

Josh showed his teeth, and his nostrils flared, but he didn't move. He took a deep breath, presumably counting to ten to avoid an eruption. I hoped he remembered how to count that high.

"You think you're funny," he said calmly. "Let's see how funny you are when you're cuddlin' up with some big, sweaty hillbilly in a cell at Huntsville."

My butt cheeks clenched involuntarily as a wave of panic washed over me. I still hadn't learned when to keep my mouth shut. *Any time now, little brother.*

We went at it like that for what felt like hours until Josh finally stood. "Dillon Bishop, you're under arrest for the murder of Amanda Hughes." He cracked a smug smile. "Too bad they did away with lynchings in the town square," he added, then nodded to Harris.

Josh read me my rights while she pulled me up by the arm. He left the room quickly, and Officer Harris escorted me downstairs to an 8'x10' cell. I watched her lock the door and leave. A small, gray-haired man slept in the only other cell.

My shoulders drooped as my arms became heavy and pulled them toward the floor. I flopped down on the cot, squeezed my eyes shut, and cursed myself for ever setting foot in this crappy little town again. Sleep did not come easy.

I awoke to a clanging noise. With no windows, I couldn't tell if it was day or night. I raised my head and saw an officer rap the bars with his nightstick.

"You got a visitor," he said with a twisted smile.

I rubbed the sleep from my good eye and raked my hands back through my hair. "Let me guess. Long black hair, green eyes. A real looker." My eyes met his.

He raised an envious eyebrow. "That's her."

"Tell her I'm not home."

"You're kidding."

I stood and glared. "Do I look like I'm kidding?"

He studied me for a moment, then scratched his head. "That all adds up to zero to me." He turned to leave.

"I'd like to make a phone call."

"What?" he said with his hand on the doorknob.

"I didn't get my phone call last night."

"I'll see what I can do."

He returned ten minutes later without a phone. "You have another visitor. Says she's your mama."

I stood. "I'll see her."

He unlocked the cage and led me to a small, windowless room that looked a lot like the interrogation room where I'd spent a lifetime last night. I sat in one of the two chairs and rested my elbows on the table between them. A camera watched me from the ceiling.

An officer opened the door and let Mama in. "Dillon. What happened?" She hurried to the table and sat down.

"A few of Bradley's finest tuned me up on the way to the station."

"You look terrible."

"You should see the other three guys." I tried to smile.

"That's not right. They can't do that."

"I'm afraid they can do pretty much whatever they want."

She reached for my hand.

A warning came from a speaker on the ceiling. "Please do not touch the prisoner. Physical contact is prohibited."

Mama looked around the room. I pointed to the camera. "How long will they keep you?"

I leaned forward and lowered my voice. "Call Bill McCutchen and let him know that I'm here. I might need him to bail me out." I leaned back. "And I need to talk to Mort ASAP. My arraignment is tomorrow morning."

Mama nodded. "I saw Nicole outside. Did she visit you?"

"She tried." I leaned forward again. "I don't want to talk about her. She's the reason I'm in here."

"What?" Her eyes widened. "She's the one who called to tell me you were in trouble."

She would know. "I said I don't want to talk about it. You need to stay away from her. She's poison."

Mama's expression gave no indication whether she would heed my warning.

CHAPTER 26

Mort never showed, and I felt sick as a guard walked me over to the courthouse for my arraignment. Relief washed over me when I spotted him at the defendant's table.

"How come you didn't stop by yesterday?"

He looked up. "Hi, Dillon. I… uh… couldn't get away." He pulled a legal pad from his briefcase. "We've got a few minutes. Tell me what happened."

We've got a few minutes? I'm seeing scenes from the movie *Deliverance* in my dreams, and he can only spare a few minutes to prepare my defense? I may have to find a new lawyer.

I explained my side of the story as he wrote. He never asked about my battered face, like he knew what to expect. The judge arrived, and the proceedings began. Mort seemed a bit timid in court, and I wondered whose side he was on. More than once, I wanted to stand up and object to something the District Attorney said as Mort sat there like he had cotton in his ears.

The judge denied bail. Mort, who was about as useless as tits on a bull, shrugged his shoulders and slipped his pad back into his briefcase.

"I'm sorry, Dillon," he said as a guard snapped the cuffs on my wrists. "I'll come by tomorrow to discuss our next step."

"Don't bother, Mort. You're fired."

"I'm sorry, Dillon."

As the guard walked me toward the door, I saw Bill McCutchen in the back row. He stepped into our path, and we stopped a few feet away.

Bill removed his hat when he saw my face. "Sweet Georgia Brown! Somebody sure cleaned your plow."

I shot a glance at the guard but said nothing.

Somehow, Bill convinced him to give us a minute to talk in private. He put his arm around my shoulder while the guard waited impatiently by the door.

"Did you see that?" I asked.

"That's not like Mort. Harley musta got to him."

"What can I do?"

"You're in a heap o' trouble here, boy."

"Tell me something I *don't* know." Well aware of the problem, what I needed was a solution.

Bill pulled a cigar from his shirt pocket.

"I need your help," I said.

He rolled the unlit cigar in his mouth with his free hand. "These boys are playin' hardball. They're scared, and I think I know why."

"This has to do with Luke's accident," I said.

"Okay, son, you sit tight. Don't go makin' any trouble just yet." He smiled. "You can do plenty of that after I get you out."

"So, what's the plan?"

"Harley might rule this pissant little town, but I've got some powerful friends who'd like to see him dethroned." He slapped my back. "I'll call in a few favors and we'll get to the bottom of this."

I felt a little better when I returned to my cell, but only a little. It's obvious now that I should have blown town two nights ago, like I'd planned. I could have been holding Jenn right now instead of holding my breath in this stinkin' cell. I sat on the hard cot and remembered the first time she told me about Colorado.

Jenn spent many childhood summers on her uncle's horse ranch near Colorado Springs with her cousin, Seth. She'd learned to ride and to love care for the majestic animals. She called it a magical place and dreamed of moving there someday. *Good country living*, she said, *and a nice place to raise a family.*

Uncle Roy never married. He lived alone and spent all his time working the ranch. When he died, he left it to Jenny Lee and Seth, the only two people in the family who showed an interest in the ranch, or in Roy, for that matter. Jenn told me she was moving to Colorado to keep the ranch going with Seth's help. I assumed it meant the end for us. Fortunately, Jenn had other ideas.

A nightstick crashed against the bars. "Hey Zero, you got a visitor."

I shook my head to clear it. "What?"

"The hottie's back," he said through his twisted smile. "If you don't see her, maybe I will."

"Good luck with that, Peckerwood."

He shook his head slowly. "I don't know what you're doin' in jail, 'cause y'all belong in the nut house."

Nicole was the last person I wanted to see after she'd sold me out. *What's takin' Bill so long?* Despite my anxiety, I almost laughed. It'd been less than an hour since I'd seen him in court. Even if he could spring me, I reckoned I'd have to put up with this place for another day or two.

Not much happened over the weekend. Nicole tried to visit two more times, and Peckerwood muttered to himself in disbelief each time I refused to see her. Mama came by again. She baked a file into a cake, but it didn't get past the metal detector. I'm kidding, of course. However, she did agree to help me find a real lawyer in Dallas—even offered to pay for it with Pop's insurance money that had just been released. Sam Granger must have conceded that Mama had nothing to do with Pop's murder after all.

On Tuesday, Bill came by with good news. A powerful friend had convinced the local judge to reverse his ruling and set bail at $100,000, or $10,000 bond. Bill posted the bond. He walked me past Harley's office on our way out of the station. I shoved my hands in my pockets to keep from flipping off the fat bastard. I wasn't about to take this lying down, but I realized now that I had to choose my battles wisely.

CHAPTER 27

I plugged in my dead cell phone when I got home and dumped the envelope with the rest of my personal effects onto the table. Wallet, truck keys, pill bottle, and some loose change. The police had returned everything except Pop's gun when they released me. Said they needed to keep it for evidence, even though Amanda hadn't been shot.

I hadn't been able to take my medication since my arrest. I picked up the bottle. *Empty.* I'd always been a little compulsive and counted them every time I took one, afraid that I'd run out and have to return to the VA in Dallas to get another script. I'd had eleven pills left in that bottle the last time I left the house.

Bill sat in the living room with Mama while I checked my messages. I deleted several voice mails from Nicole without listening to them. A text from Jenn, sent two days ago, indicated that she'd arrived safely in Colorado. I dialed her number. She answered on the second ring.

"Hey, Jenn. It's Dillon."

"Dillon? Dillon who?"

"*Ouch!* I guess I deserve that."

"I expected a call."

"I'm sorry, but I was tied up."

"Hmm… I didn't realize Nicole was into that kind of thing."

"Very funny." I hesitated while I considered how much to tell her, but after her last remark, I went for shock and awe. "Actually, I was in jail for the murder of an old high school friend, Amanda Hughes. I don't think the two of you have met."

"Cut it out, Dillon. I'm sorry for the crack about Nicole."

"Apology accepted. I wish I could tell you I was kidding. I'm out on bail thanks to Pop's friend, Bill. The cops just gave me my phone back."

"You're serious?"

"That's not the kind of thing you joke about."

"Oh my God, Dillon. What happened?"

"I hope you believe me when I say that I didn't kill anyone."

"Of course I believe you."

"Someone killed Pop, and I'm pretty sure it's the same person that killed Luke. I think I'm being framed for Amanda's murder because I've become a threat to whoever is responsible."

"Do you think the same person killed Amanda?"

"It's beginning to look that way."

"Dillon, you need to get out of there."

"I can't."

"What do you mean, you can't?"

"The judge says I can't leave before the trial."

"Trial?" she squeaked. "When is the trial?"

"Well..." I tried to think of a way to make this easier to swallow but couldn't come up with anything. "In about a month."

"You're stuck in Bradley for another month?"

"Depending on which way the trial goes, it could be twenty to life."

"I never should have let you stay there."

"That wasn't your call. I needed to see this through. I still do."

"I had a dream a couple of nights ago that you got into a terrible fight."

"I'm fine," I assured her, grateful that this was a phone call and not one of those video chats.

"Please, Dillon, if y'all need anything, call me. I can be there in twelve hours."

"Roger that."

An awkward silence hung in the air.

"How's everything in Colorado?" I asked.

"Nobody's been arrested for murder yet."

Funny. "How's the ranch?"

"Dillon, it's so beautiful here. You're gonna love it."

"I already do. You sound so happy."

"I'll be happier when you're here."

"I'm gonna fix this."

I underestimated how good it felt to hear her voice and found it difficult to hang up. Neither of us wanted to give in and let go. It reminded me of those middle school phone calls with your first girlfriend. *You hang up. No, you hang up. No, you hang up.* And on and on until someone fell asleep.

Eventually, she made an excuse about needing to help Seth, and I let her go. I walked into the living room where Mama and Bill talked over a glass of iced tea.

"Who was that?"

I forgot how Mama used to have to know every detail about my life. "Jenn."

"Oh. I haven't seen her around lately."

"That's because she's in Colorado."

"What's she doing there?"

"She lives there now, Mama. She owns a ranch with her cousin. I plan to move there when the trial's over and we're done with this whole stupid mess."

"You don't plan to stay in Bradley?"

I shook my head. "Mama, please."

Bill leaned forward to pick up his glass from the coffee table. "With any luck, there won't be a trial."

I lifted an eyebrow. "What do you mean?"

He took a long drink and licked his lips, then rubbed the cold glass across his forehead. "All we have to do to get you off the hook is find the real killer."

"Oh. Is that all?" He'd raised my hopes, then dashed them in less than ten seconds.

"How do you plan to do that?" Mama asked.

Bill acknowledged her question with a nod, then turned to me. "First, I need to know how your fingerprints got on that pill bottle."

"I couldn't understand it myself at first, but then I remembered that Amanda dropped her purse the day we met at the diner. It spilled on the floor, and I picked it up for her. I must have touched everything in there, including a couple of pill bottles."

He pulled a cigar from his shirt pocket and dragged it under his nose. I waited for a response.

"When were you inside her car?" He stuck the end of the unlit cigar in his mouth.

"Same day. After our meeting, her car wouldn't start, so naturally, I helped her out. I touched her keys, the shifter, the steering wheel. I'm sure you'll find my prints all over her battery cables, as well."

"I knew there had to be a simple explanation," Bill said before he removed the cigar for another sip of tea.

"I think Josh is responsible for all this," I said. "Perhaps with help from Nicole."

The heat from Mama's stare burned the side of my face. I avoided eye contact, and she said nothing.

Bill set his glass down and leaned back like he was settling in to tell us a story. "I'm afraid Bradley is your stereotypical Southern town," he said. "The kind those Yankees love to write about. A bunch of good-'ol-boy rednecks runnin' things the way they see fit. They love their guns, an' their fishin' poles, an', of course, their whiskey. Probably have a sky box at Cowboy Stadium where they get together to hoot an' holler for every home game."

Unfortunately, that sounded about right.

He took the unlit cigar from his mouth and pointed the wrinkled, wet tip at me. "Once those boys circle their wagons, you got a real fight on your hands."

"So, what can we do?"

"This ain't my first rodeo, son." He returned the cigar, then flashed a grin so wide he nearly lost it. "Hell, they don't call me Wild Bill for nothin'."

Mama smiled, and I breathed in a little relief, glad to have Bill on my side.

"Can you do me a favor?" I asked.

"Name it."

"That insurance investigator, Granger, said Pop died from an adrenaline overdose. What if Amanda died the same way?"

Bill nodded as though deep in thought. "Are you thinkin' what I'm thinkin'?"

"If you're thinkin' that we should get our hands on a copy of Amanda's autopsy report, then yes, I am."

"Let's keep this between us."

"What about Mort?"

Instead of responding, Bill shook his head slowly.

"What?"

"I think Harley's got him by the balls for somethin' or other, an' he's playin' him like a fiddle." Bill let out a sigh. "Your daddy an' Mort an' me, we've always been like kin. I reckoned that's why it hurts me to have to say this, but right now, I wouldn't trust Mort any farther than I can throw him."

I glanced at Mama, then nodded in agreement. "That's not far."

Bill grinned. "What can I say? The man loves his barbecue."

"Now, you boys be kind. Mort's a good man," Mama scolded.

Bill removed his cigar and pointed it in my direction. "I'll get you those results in a couple of days."

CHAPTER 28

I watched the big blue numbers on the clock beside the bed, a constant reminder that I needed my medication. A parade of memories, both good and bad, marched through my mind, punctuated by the occasional flashback to my childhood or my time in Afghanistan. Exhaustion overwhelmed me, but not enough to snuff out the endless barrage of thoughts.

My arrest had been an unwelcome distraction to my investigation into Pop's and Luke's murders. However, my gut told me they were connected. While Amanda's death and my resulting legal predicament required more immediate attention, I believed if we solved one of these murders, we'd solve them all.

Luke appeared to be the common denominator. I believe Pop's theories about Luke's death are what got him killed. Three of the four people in the car that night were somehow entangled in the events of the past two months. The fourth, Bobby Perez, was unaccounted for. Maybe he got away in time, or maybe his bones were lying in a shallow grave somewhere. Maybe next to Luke's.

I needed to patch things up with Coop. We'd always made a good team, and now that my relationship with Nicole was circling the drain, we no longer had anything to fight about. After all, he'd been right. I'd chosen sides and bet on the wrong horse. He deserved an apology.

I picked up my phone from the nightstand and dialed Coop's number. He answered on the fifth ring.

"I'm sorry, Coop," I blurted out before he answered.

"Dillon?"

"Yeah. You were right. I've been a real asshat, and I just wanted to say I'm sorry."

"What time is it?" he asked in a ragged whisper.

"0315."

"Jeezus, Bish. You couldn't wait 'til morning?"

"Are we good?"

"We're good." He snorted. "Unless you call me again tonight."

I woke early, despite having slept only an hour or two, and drove to Coop's house. Jolene answered the door.

"Hey, Dillon." Her smile led me to believe that Coop hadn't mentioned our falling-out. "C'mon in. Cooper's in the shower. I'll tell him you're here."

"Wait." I removed my hat and held it in my hands. "Can we talk?"

"Sure," she said with a curious expression. "Is something going on with you and Cooper? He hasn't been himself lately. He came home all pissed off at you about a week ago and hasn't mentioned your name since."

I hung my head. "I'm afraid that's my fault."

"What happened?"

"You know how he feels about Nicole." I watched her roll her eyes. "I stuck up for her and he accused me of choosing Nicole over him like it was a best friend contest."

Jolene put her hand on my arm. "I think he's just afraid to lose you again. He'll come around." She smiled. "Now, what did you want to talk about?"

"The prodigal friend returns," Coop interjected from the living room doorway.

Jolene shot him a look. "Cooper. You behave."

"Sorry about the call last night. The cops took my meds, and I've had trouble sleeping. I plan to drive up to Dallas today and renew my script."

Jolene's expression fell. "You think that's a good idea?"

"I don't have much choice."

"If I didn't have to work, I'd drive you there myself."

"What brings you around this morning?" Coop asked.

"I miss my best friend."

"She's not here." He stared at me for a few seconds, then shrugged. "Too soon?"

I nodded as Jolene picked up a dish towel and threw it in Coop's direction. "I told you I was sorry."

"At three in the morning? I thought it was a dream." The remark earned him another glare from Jolene. "Okay. Apology accepted. Now what's for breakfast?"

Jo smiled at me. "I made biscuits and gravy. Would you like to join us?"

She didn't have to ask twice. The three of us ate while their girls, Katey Jo and Carrie Beth, slept in. I recounted the events that led up to my arrest, including Nicole's betrayal. I could tell Coop struggled to hold back a stinging comment. He settled for an *I-told-you-so* look.

Jo nodded. "I never believed you had anything to do with that poor girl's death."

"Thank you."

"For the record," Coop said, "neither did I."

"I still don't believe that Nicole blew you in like that," Jo said with a frown.

"She denied it at the time."

Coop raised an eyebrow as he held a forkful over his plate. "Have you talked to her since then?"

I shook my head. "She tried to visit me in jail a few times, but I refused."

"Attaboy," he said before he emptied the contents into his mouth.

Jo looked at me. "At the very least, you owe her a chance to explain her side... dontcha think?"

"Jeezus, Jo," Coop said with his mouth full. He swallowed hard. "Let the man make his own decisions, will ya?"

"I'm just sayin'..."

"Well, it sounds to me like he's finally come to his senses. So don't—"

I cleared my throat. "I'm in the room..."

Jolene glanced at Coop, and then me. "I'm sorry, Dillon."

Coop nodded, and we finished our meal with nothing more than small talk.

"Thanks for breakfast." I stood, picked up my hat from the corner of the chair, and headed for the door.

"Dillon, wait," Coop said as he stood.

I stopped at the door. "It's okay. We're good."

I drove straight home and found Mama on the front porch with a cup of coffee. When I mentioned my plan to drive to the VA hospital, she balked.

"You're not supposed to leave town."

"I have to go. If I don't get my meds, I'll be in a different kind of trouble."

"But—"

"They don't have to know I'm gone."

Her brow furrowed before she let out a sigh. "I have an appointment with an attorney in Dallas at one o'clock. We can go together."

Mama drove. I suggested she drop me off on the way to the lawyer's, then pick me up on the way home, but she wouldn't have it.

"This is your lawyer, not mine, so you should be there."

"Can't you just talk to him? I trust you." I paused for a moment, surprised by what I'd just said. "I mean, if you like him and he's willing to take the case, then I'll meet with him."

"Dillon, please…"

"I don't even know how long I'll be at the hospital. You can drop me off on your way, and I'll call you when I'm done."

She looked at me for a moment, then sighed. "Fine. On one condition."

"What do you want?"

"I want you to tell me everything."

CHAPTER 29

I stared out the passenger window of the Silverado, the bag that I'd packed a week ago still stowed behind my seat. A freight train rolled down the tracks that paralleled the highway. I'd be long gone if I hadn't stopped that night to see Nicole.

"Time to make good on our deal," Mama said.

"I found Pop's journal." My eyes never left the train, even as I felt the truck drift onto the shoulder.

"Where?"

"At the cabin."

"What did it say?"

As promised, I told her what I knew.

Her tears flowed freely. "This is all my fault."

Unsure how to respond, I said nothing. I guess it wasn't fair to blame her for everything that's happened, but she destroyed our family, and I struggled to let her off the hook for that.

"I'm so sorry, Dillon."

"I still have nightmares, and not just about the war. Sometimes, I dream that we're driving to Fort Worth to see a rodeo. I count telephone poles out the window until I see you hanging from one of them. Sometimes you swing limp in the breeze and other times you call my name. I'm frightened, but I know it can't be real because you're driving. When the truck begins to weave from lane to lane,

I turn my head to find the driver's seat empty. I try to grab the wheel, but my seatbelt holds me just out of reach. I push the button to release it, but it's jammed."

She watched the road through tears. I handed her a napkin from the glove box, and she wiped her eyes. "This medicine. Does it help?"

"It helps." I turned toward the window. "I've only had one dream about you since I've been back."

An awkward silence descended between us for several miles.

"I noticed you favor your left leg," she finally said. "What happened?"

I hesitated, then removed my hat and ran my hand back through my hair. "How well did Pop know Bill McCutchen?"

"They were good friends." She turned. "Why do you ask?"

"I saw a picture of them on Pop's desk at the cabin. They stood in a field together, all smiles and big cigars."

"I imagine it had something to do with a piece of land they bought before we were married."

"What kind of land?"

"The worthless kind, it turns out." She shook her head. "They wanted to become oil barons."

"Obviously, that didn't happen."

"No. It did not."

"Would it have made a difference?" I asked, not expecting her to answer.

She glanced in the rearview mirror, then back to the road.

"What happened to the land after he died?"

She shrugged. "Honestly, I'd forgotten about it until you brought it up."

I rubbed the stubble on my chin. "Strange that Mort never mentioned it."

Mama said nothing.

"Why would Bill say that he hasn't seen you in years?"

"I don't know. When did he say that?"

"When I met him at Coop's last week. I asked him straight-up when he saw you last. He told me it'd been too many years."

She turned to me. "Why would he lie?"

"Is he?"

"You don't believe me?"

"I don't believe somebody."

The highway widened and traffic thickened after we crossed I-20. Ten minutes later, we pulled into the VA parking lot. I made sure Mama had directions to the lawyer's office and told her I'd call when I finished with the doctor.

My appointment with Doc Griffin went pretty much as expected. He asked a lot of questions and performed a quick exam before handing out another script. I mentioned my plans to move to Colorado, and he said he could transfer my records to the Vet Center there.

I walked the four blocks to my apartment. I hadn't been back there in nearly a month. When I opened the door, I thought I had the wrong building. The place looked cleaner than I'd left it, and the air didn't smell like something had died in there. A stack of broken-down cardboard boxes leaned against the wall in the living room with a roll of packing tape on the floor in front of them.

In the kitchen, I found a note on the table.

Dillon,

Yes, this really is your place. I couldn't leave without tidying up a bit. I had to rent a hazmat suit to clean the fridge. I left you a few beers.

I love you, Dillon. We don't say it a lot, but I know in my heart, we both feel it. We're just two lost souls looking for love, but afraid to find it. Maybe we can work on that when we see each other again.

By the time you read this, I'll probably be in Colorado. I hate the way we left things, but please try to understand that I need all of you. I pray that you'll be able to let go of whatever is holding you back there and finally get to where we both know you should be. I miss you, Dillon.

Always, Jenn

I missed her, too. More than I realized. I set the note down, walked to the fridge, and grabbed a beer. Jenn had removed her things from the apartment, but her energy remained. We didn't go out much, splitting our time between her place and mine, so technically we weren't dating, just hanging out together.

After I packed up a few things, including some CDs to listen to on the ride home, I called Mama and gave her directions to the apartment. Fifteen minutes later, I opened the door and invited her in.

Mama glanced around the room, a combination eat-in kitchen and living room. "This isn't so bad."

"What did you expect?"

She smiled. "It's cleaner than I'd imagined."

"Would you like something to drink? I have water and beer."

"Nothing, thank you." Her expression dropped as we sat on the sofa. "I have bad news."

"The lawyer?"

She nodded. "He won't take the case unless we can get it moved to Dallas. Actually, he said anywhere but Bradley. Said there's no such thing as a fair trial in Bradley."

I chuckled. "I guess he knows Harley and the boys."

"This is serious, Dillon." She stood and walked to the window above the kitchen sink. She looked outside for a moment, then turned. "What are we going to do?"

"Like Bill said, find the real killer."

She walked over to the table and picked up the paper. "What's this?"

"It's a note from Jenn."

She held it out between us. "May I?"

"I guess," I said with a shrug, as though I had a choice.

"It sounds serious," she said after she read it.

"We're just..." I stopped myself. "Yes, Mama. It's serious."

She set the paper down on the table. "I like her..."

"But?"

"Well, I guess I always thought that you and Nicole would—"

"It's not gonna happen. Nicole and I are friends. We'll always be friends." At the moment, I wasn't so sure.

"Don't tell me you never wanted it to be more."

"Maybe." I stood. "But you don't get to do this. You weren't around when she dragged my heart through a mile of broken glass."

Mama had nothing to say.

"I'm not in love with Nicole, so please stop acting like you know what's best for me."

She picked up Jenn's note again and studied it. "You're right. I'm sorry." She set it down and walked into the living room. "I understand now."

"Understand what?"

"You were looking for validation."

"That's not true."

"I'm afraid it's my fault." She sat on the sofa and patted the cushion next to her. "I abandoned you. Failed you as a mother. You must have felt unworthy of my love, but that's the furthest thing from the truth."

I said nothing as I sat next to her. A few seconds passed.

"You never learned to love yourself. How could you?" She ran the edge of her finger under one eye. "Nicole was a good friend to you after I left. Perhaps she filled part of the void that I created."

"Are you saying I should forget about Nicole?"

"No, honey, that would be impossible. But you need to let her go."

I looked at Mama through squinted eyes. "A minute ago, you said—"

"I need to let her go, too. I can do that now." She put her hand on mine. "People come into our lives for a reason. We need to accept that and not try to make it more than it's intended to be."

She gazed into my eyes and combed through my hair with her fingers like she did when I was a child. I didn't stop her.

"When you let go," she said. "You create space in your life for someone else."

"You mean like Jenn?"

She smiled.

"Is that what you did when you left? Did you let go of me?"

"Never," she whispered, then paused to catch her breath. "I missed you so much, it hurt."

"Then why did you stay away so long?"

She closed her eyes and shook her head slowly. "I was stupid... and selfish."

"I just figured you forgot about me."

"When you walked into the kitchen with that shotgun," she said, eyes open and locked on mine, "you could have blown me away right then and there, and I'd have died happy, seeing your face again."

"Mama..." I whispered.

She wrapped me in her arms.

Forgiveness may be difficult to give, but it can be downright painful to withhold. Tears spilled from my eyes, and I welcomed the release like a soaking rain after a long Texas drought.

CHAPTER 30

I don't recall how long Bonnie Bishop held her son on that sofa. Eventually, I raised my head and looked into her swollen eyes. No words passed between us as she smiled a hopeful smile.

I sat back and stared at nothing in particular. "It happened in a little village outside Kandahar."

Mama leaned forward to make eye contact. "What?"

"On the way here, you asked about my leg." I made no attempt to move.

"Dillon... you don't have to—"

"There'd been a lot of insurgent activity and an air strike had just blasted the shit out of the village. We came in to mop up. Door-to-door. Secure the area, then move on to the next target."

"Did you get shot?"

"No." I took a deep breath. "As we cleared one of the last houses, I found a boy, maybe seven years old, in an upstairs room. He sat alone on the floor next to his dead mother. I held up my hands, so he knew I wouldn't hurt him, then scanned the room. In the corner, a man lay pinned under a jagged slab of concrete. His lifeless eyes stared up through a hole in the ceiling."

Mama's eyes widened, and her hand covered her mouth.

I remembered it like it was yesterday.

In that moment, I'd seen myself in his frightened eyes. My mama didn't die, but she might as well have. All those memories I tried so hard to erase flooded back.

"This one's clear. Let's move out." The voice came from somewhere behind me.

I continued to stare at the boy. As bad as I thought my childhood had been, this kid had it worse. I hadn't lived in a war-torn village. I still had a father, at least for a few more years.

The voice barked again from behind me. "Sarge!"

I turned. Captain Driscoll stood in the doorway.

"Sir?"

"I said we're clear. Let's move out."

"What about the kid?" I asked.

"What *about* him?"

"I can't leave him here."

"You can. And you will. Now, move it!"

I hesitated.

"That's an order."

"Roger that," I said.

He disappeared down the stairs. I knelt in front of the boy and my chest tightened. I didn't know what to say, or if he would even understand me. After a few moments of silence, I forced a smile. "You heard the man. We need to move." I grabbed him up and carried him out like a lost puppy.

Captain Driscoll waited by the door of our Humvee and held up his hands as I approached. He glared at me for a moment, then opened the door and stuck his head inside. "Make some room," he said in a snarky voice. "GI Joe's got an extra passenger."

As we got underway, the boy looked up at me from my lap. "GI Joe?"

I grinned. "Yeah, that's me, kid. GI Joe."

He noticed the tattoo on my arm and traced it with his finger. I never got the chance to ask his name. Our Humvee took a hit from an RPG, no doubt because I'd held our convoy up. I covered the boy as best I could. The explosion ripped off my boot and took a couple of toes with it. We're all lucky to be alive.

I opened my eyes when I heard Mama cry.

"It's okay," I whispered. "That was a long time ago."

Mama nodded.

"Anyway, they put me on a chopper, and that's the last time I saw the boy." I looked at Mama and shook my head. "I don't know what I thought, but I couldn't walk away and leave him there. Maybe if I brought him back to the base, Uncle Sam would find him a home."

"You did the right thing, Dillon."

"Did I? Maybe he would have been better off dead. That's how I felt after you ran away."

Mama avoided my eyes.

"I'm... Mama, I'm sorry."

"Don't be. I deserve it." She blinked a few times, and I thought she might cry again. "You may never forgive me for what I've done, and there's probably nothing I can do to make it up to you, but as long as I live, I'll never stop trying."

I'd sifted through enough emotional wreckage for one day. I nodded, then drained my beer. "We should go."

Mama put her hand on my knee when I attempted to stand. "There's someone I want you to meet."

"Mama, I don't need any more women in my life."

"She's a woman," Mama smiled, "but not like that."

I waited.

"She's the medicine woman I told you about. She helped me turn my life around and to… to find myself. Actually, I found more than that."

"I don't need to be found."

"I think you do."

"Any help I need, I can get from Jenny Lee. We have a special connection."

"I'm afraid Jenny Lee can't fix what's broken inside you."

"And this witch doctor can?"

"No. Only you can do that, but Leotie can show you the way."

Her eyes held a sincerity that felt like a mother's love.

"She lives here in Dallas?" I asked.

"No. Muskogee."

"Oklahoma? How do you know her?"

"Wade met her on the rodeo circuit when he became friends with her son. We visited her after Wade's first heart attack. He'd looked death in the eye and didn't like what he saw."

"So, what did this woman do for him?"

"It's hard to explain. I guess you could say she helped him to restore balance and find meaning in his life." Mama paused and her expression fell. "By the time the second heart attack took him, he was at peace with himself."

"You were in love with him."

"I was." She cleared her throat. "I'll admit, at first, I enjoyed the thrill. But it wasn't until after his heart attack, after he spent time with Leotie, that I got to know the real man. That's the one I fell in love with."

"So, you want to change me?"

"A mother's love is unconditional, Dillon. I'll always love you just the way you are."

"Then what are you saying? I'm not good enough for Jenn?"

She looked at me for a moment, then sighed. "Wade and I ran out of time. I want you and Jenny Lee to be as happy as we were while you still have many years to look forward to."

My voice softened. "I'm sorry for your loss."

"Thank you, dear. That means a lot." A flicker of a smile crossed her lips. "Looking back, I'd have to say that I gained more than I lost."

While our field trip had not been productive in terms of a legal solution, I felt relieved to be on my medication again. But more importantly, I had my mama back.

CHAPTER 31

I spotted Nicole's car in our driveway when we turned the corner, and the dinner I'd eaten on the way home nearly made another appearance.

"Isn't that Nicole's car?" Mama asked.

"It sure looks like it," I said as calmly as I could.

"Do you know why she's here?"

"I have a pretty good idea. Keep driving."

She ignored my request and pulled into the driveway.

"Mama!"

She turned the car off and looked at me. "Whatever this is, you've got to face it eventually. She's your friend. Let her say her piece. If you want to tell her to go to hell after that, you have my blessing."

I studied her for a moment, then nodded. "Deal."

Nicole sat on the front porch. She stood as we made our way toward the house.

"Hi, Nicole," Mama said. "How nice to see you again."

Maybe for you. I said nothing.

Nicole smiled. "You certainly look better than the last time I saw you."

"It wouldn't take much, would it?" Mama let out a nervous laugh as she reached the front door. "Can I get you something to drink?"

"No, thank you, Mrs. Bishop."

"Well, then, I'll let you two have a little privacy," she said and stepped inside.

I leaned against the post. "You'd better just say what you came here to say, and then leave."

"Dillon, please, just sit."

I didn't want to get that close, but if I sat, it would be easier to avoid those eyes. I felt their stare as I perched on the opposite end of the swing.

"I didn't rat you out to the police. Josh lied to turn you against me." She sighed. "Apparently, it worked."

I continued to stare out over the porch railing at the street. I felt no need to reply.

"Look at me!"

I turned.

"I would never do that."

I looked back at the street.

"What can I do to make you believe me?"

"Maybe I should talk to someone else who was there."

"Where?"

"In the car."

"I thought we were talking about the other night at my house."

"It's all connected. Isn't it?"

She sighed. "You talked to Amanda."

"What about Bobby?"

"No," she said, her tone as stern as it was quiet. "You can't talk to him."

"Why? Because he'll end up dead like Amanda?"

"I didn't mean it like that."

I met her gaze. "Do you think I killed her?"

"No." She paused. "Do you think *I* did?"

Instead of answering, I looked away again.

"Seriously, Dillon? You think I killed Amanda? And framed *you*?"

"You certainly had motive."

"I didn't kill anyone," she said as she struggled to stay calm. "Luke was alive when I left him. You can ask—"

"Who? Amanda?" I snorted. "I guess that brings us back to Bobby."

A silence descended between us. She hesitated, then gave a quick nod. "Okay. I'll call him."

"No. I don't want you to spook him. Just tell me where he is."

"Dillon…"

"You asked me what you can do to make me believe you." I stood. "This will go a long way toward that."

Her eyes turned to green glass when she looked up at me.

"Text me his address and anything else I should know."

"Wait." She stood and took a step toward me.

I stepped back.

"Let me go with you."

"Absolutely not."

"He's scared, Dillon. He won't talk to you. Would *you*, if you were him?"

She had a point. "How far away is he?"

"Two hours."

Four hours in a car with Nicole? I didn't like it. "Can we take separate cars?"

"Stop it." She put her hands on her hips. "We don't have to talk, if that will make it easier for you."

"Okay. When do you want to do this?"

"I'm off tomorrow. I'll pick you up at ten."
"Roger that."

CHAPTER 32

I waited in the hospital parking lot with two large coffees in the cup holders. I hoped Jolene would be early so we could talk before she went inside. Her car pulled in at 0635. I grabbed the coffee and walked across the lot. She tilted her head and watched with curiosity.

"Dillon? What are you doing here?"

I handed her a coffee and pointed to a picnic table at the edge of the lot. "Can I steal you for a few minutes before you go in?"

"Sure, but—"

"We never got a chance to talk yesterday."

"Yeah, I wondered about that." She took a sip as we sat. "Cooper would pitch a fit if he knew I told you this, but you made his day when you stopped by."

"The food alone was worth the trip."

"I'm serious, Dillon. This thing with Nicole, he's just trying to protect you. He really wants to be your friend."

"That's what I want to talk to you about."

"Nicole?"

I nodded. "I think she had something to do with Pop's death."

"Oh, Dillon, I don't see how that's possible." She frowned as she spoke. "Why? What could possibly be her motive?"

"How much has Coop told you about Luke's death?"

She blinked back surprise. "You know for sure that he's dead?"

"He didn't tell you what we found out since I've been back?"

"Are you kidding? With you and Coop and Jimmy, it was always like a secret club. He never told me anything."

I blew out a long breath. "Okay, but please don't share this with anyone. Not even Coop. He knows everything, but I'm sure he doesn't want to involve you, and I don't think he'd appreciate me dragging you into it."

She rubbed the back of her hand. "You're scaring me."

"I'm sorry, but I need to understand some things about Nicole, and I figured because you work with her, maybe you could help."

"I'll try." She bit down on her lower lip.

"Thank you." I hoped Coop could forgive me if he ever found out. "Luke was the victim of a hit-and-run accident out on Quarry Road. There were four people in the car— Josh, Nicole, Amanda, and Bobby. Nicole drove Josh's car because he was wasted."

"How do you know that?"

"Nicole told me." I paused. "So did Amanda, a couple of days before she died."

Jolene's eyes widened.

"Josh called his daddy, who sent everyone home and threatened them if they ever mentioned that night to anyone. I'm not sure what happened after that."

"Do you think Nicole's in danger?"

"She could be… unless she's the one behind all this."

"Why would she kill your daddy?"

"Apparently, he wouldn't let the Luke thing go. He blabbed about evidence that he'd found, then died mysteriously in the hospital. Amanda died two days after talking to me about the accident." I looked into Jolene's eyes. "Do you see a pattern here?"

"So, you think Nicole killed them to protect herself?"

"I thought she might have been involved, but I wasn't convinced until the fire."

"Our fire? The one at the garage?"

"Yep. Pop tracked down Josh's old car. He bought it at an auction and stored it in Coop's garage. Coop discovered blood spatter behind one of the headlights. We planned to have it tested. Unfortunately, I told Nicole about it the next day, and twenty-four hours later, it burned."

"C'mon, Dillon. She didn't burn down the garage."

"I'd like to think she didn't, but she was the only other person who knew what we had and where we hid it."

Jolene had no response.

I checked my phone. "Nicole and I are going to see Bobby at ten."

"Bobby?" She leaned forward. "Where?"

"She wouldn't tell me."

"Does Cooper know you're going?"

"Are you kidding?" I snorted. "And you can't tell him."

"I don't like it. What do you hope to accomplish?"

"Bobby was in the car. He's the only one who left town. Maybe he knows more than the others." I ran my hands through my hair. "I don't know, Jo, but I can't just sit around and wait to be thrown in prison."

"So, why are you here?"

"I need to know if Nicole had access to epinephrine in the hospital."

"Most of the nurses do. Why?"

"I believe that's what killed Pop."

She grabbed my arm and our eyes met. "You really believe Nicole killed him?"

I looked down at my coffee. "Sometimes it's the person you least expect. Like the little barefoot kid walking on the side of the road. You feel sorry for him until he chucks a grenade under your Humvee."

"Dillon. You're home now." She released my arm. "No one is chucking grenades."

My eyes met hers. "Maybe not, but people are getting killed."

"Besides the fact that she'd never do anything like that, there's a lot of security."

"What kind of security?"

"About a year ago, the hospital installed a machine to dispense high-alert medications. It requires a fingerprint and a patient barcode."

"What happens when the machine runs out? Who refills it?"

"Someone from the pharmacy."

"So, they keep a supply in the pharmacy?"

"Yes, but—"

"Could she have gotten it directly from there?"

"It's not like Walgreen's, Dillon."

"Maybe she had help."

Jolene sighed. "I don't think Nicole is the bad guy here." Her expression softened, and she looked at me with sympathetic eyes. "I wish I could be more help."

"You've helped plenty, Jo. Thanks."

She offered a hopeful smile before a few seconds of silence. "How's Jenny Lee?"

"She's in Colorado now. She seems happy."

"I bet you miss her."

"I sure do."

"I think you two make a cute couple."

"Well, I just hope I'm as lucky as Coop when it comes to finding someone."

"Why, thank you, Dillon. That's sweet." Her cheeks flared. "You have something special between you. I saw it the night we went out to dinner."

I looked down at the tattoo on my arm and remembered the day I told Jenn what it meant. She'd invited me to dinner shortly after we'd met. I cut up a salad while she tended to something on the stove. She reached over and picked up a cucumber slice that I'd just cut and took a bite.

She pointed to my arm. "Nice ink. What's it mean?"

"Why does it have to mean something?"

"Everything means something."

I set the knife down and picked up a tomato. "Really? What does this tomato mean?"

"Y'all gonna tell me or not?"

I studied her for a moment, then smiled. "Okay. You got me." I held up my arm. "It's me. I'm a lone wolf, driven from the pack."

"I know what a lone wolf is."

"You do?"

She unbuttoned her shirt, pulled it down below her shoulders, and turned around. She had a tattoo in the middle of her back, just below her neck. I stared in silent surprise.

"You like it?"

How could I not like it? It was nearly identical to mine. "I sure do."

"Animal spirit guide."

"What?"

She turned and buttoned her shirt. "I'm part Cherokee."

"You don't look it."

"It's a small part." She smiled. "It's more about spirit than looks."

"Spirit, huh?"

"In case y'all are thinkin' that I ripped off your idea, I've had this tatt since I was sixteen."

Jolene finally brought me back. "Dillon?"

I looked up. "I'm sorry, what?"

Jolene smiled. "You were thinking about her, weren't you?"

I shrugged. "I reckon I was."

"I'll miss you when you go, but Colorado is where you need to be."

"I have to get to the bottom of this mess, or the only place I'm going is prison."

"Thanks for the coffee." Jolene stood. "I need to get inside." She pulled me into a hug and whispered in my ear. "Please be careful. I don't want you to end up like your daddy."

I nodded. Unfortunately, no one ever got to the bottom of anything by being careful.

CHAPTER 33

I grabbed a quick breakfast and waited for Nicole on the front porch swing. Mama sat down next to me with a cup of coffee. I told her my plans for the day. Rather than reply, she simply nodded and sipped her coffee.

"I talked to another lawyer in Dallas," she said.

"I don't want to waste any more time driving to—"

"We don't have to. He turned down your case over the phone."

"Same reason?"

"Afraid so," she said, an ominous futility in her voice.

"I guess I'll have to represent myself."

"Don't be silly. What about Mort?"

Nicole's car pulled in the driveway. I leaned over and gave Mama a kiss on the cheek.

"Be careful," she said as I walked down the steps.

After a quick greeting, we drove the first few miles in silence. Apparently, Nicole was prepared to honor my request that we don't talk. I realized how uncomfortable that would be for the next two hours.

"Okay, maybe I overreacted," I finally said.

"Ya think?"

"I'm sorry." I took a deep breath. "So, where are we going?"

She stared at me like she didn't want to tell me.

"Unless you plan to put a bag over my head, I'll figure it out anyway."

"Wichita Falls."

"What's he do up there?"

"Assistant football coach at MSU."

"Sounds like a nice gig."

"I set up a meeting on campus."

"What?" I straightened up until the seatbelt grabbed my shoulder. "He knows we're coming?"

"He knows *I'm* coming. I didn't mention that I was bringing a friend."

Nicole had a plan. We would meet Bobby at Bolin Fountain on the campus quad. The football team had begun practice, and with tours and orientation, there would be a fair number of people milling around. We'd show up late so he wouldn't see us waiting and abort at the last minute.

The rest of the trip went by quicker than I'd expected. Conversation was light, and I turned on the radio to fill the silence. We arrived on campus at 1215 and walked around for a bit. We avoided the fountain until after our designated meeting time of 1230. Bobby Perez sat on the edge of the fountain, wearing a red Mustangs cap, red golf shirt, and khakis.

The trees that surrounded the fountain area provided a good deal of shade and created the impression of an oasis amid the dry grass, brick buildings, and paved parking lots. I dropped back a couple of steps as we approached. Bobby walked toward us when he saw Nicole, then stopped dead in his tracks when he realized she wasn't alone. He looked around like he wanted to make a hasty retreat.

Nicole held up her hands. "It's okay, Bobby."

Bobby blew out a breath. "Who is he?"

I glanced at Nicole, then extended my hand. "Dillon Bishop."

His eyes grew wide. Instead of shaking my hand, he grabbed Nicole by the arm and pulled her aside. I folded my arms across my chest and waited.

Bobby held out his hand when they returned. "I'm sorry, Dillon, but it was quite a shock to see you again."

Nicole flashed an uneasy smile. My heart whispered *trust her.* "I can imagine." I shook his hand.

"Let's sit." He directed us to one of two shaded patios that contained several picnic tables. Bobby folded his hands on the table and looked at me. "What is it you want?"

"I need you to tell me what you know about the night my brother died."

He glanced at Nicole before he spoke. "I was gettin' busy with Amanda in the backseat, so I didn't see him get hit. He looked awful, but he was alive."

He told me that Josh called his father, and a heated discussion ensued when he arrived. At one point, Harley hit Josh upside the head and knocked him to the ground. Josh took everyone home after he told them in no uncertain terms they were never there and the accident never happened.

Bobby assumed there'd be a cover-up, that they'd fabricate a story about why Luke was in the hospital that didn't include a drunken Josh in the car that hit him. He panicked when the girls told him that Luke had never been admitted. Josh refused to tell him what transpired after they went home, only that bad things would happen if he ever spoke a word to anyone about that night.

"When Josh dropped me off, he seemed more angry than afraid. He hated that he had to call his father to bail him out and swore that if Harley ever hit him like that again, he'd kill him." Bobby paused. "At first, I thought it was the alcohol talking, but Josh was scared sober by then."

"You guys had been friends for a while. Did he ever talk like that before?"

He frowned, lost in thought. "I don't think he ever said that he wanted to kill him, but he had it rough growing up. Harley's always been a real asshole."

"What about Amanda?" I asked.

Nicole gave me a wary glance. "Dillon thinks I killed her."

"I never said that."

Bobby looked at me sideways. "I heard they tried to pin it on *you*."

"Still trying. What do *you* think happened?"

"At first it sounded like a suicide, but I refuse to believe Amanda could do that." He shot a sideways glance at Nicole. "I think it has something to do with that night."

"So do I," Nicole added. "That's what scares me. What if one of us is next?"

"They'd better leave me alone," Bobby said as he shook his head. "Josh offered me a deal I couldn't refuse, and I agreed to leave town and never look back." His eyes narrowed. "I've held up my end."

"What kind of deal?"

He raised his hands. "Look around. Dream job, money to move and start over. I saw it as an opportunity to put the past behind me."

I turned to Nicole. "What about you?"

"Amanda and I felt less intimidated and chose to stay." She sighed. "Maybe that wasn't such a good idea."

I turned back to Bobby. "And Josh did all this?"

"He's the one who approached me and said he had connections that could set it all up."

I didn't think Josh was that smart or that connected. I turned to Nicole. "What is he holding over *your* head?"

She stared at me, and I thought she might burst into tears. "Annabelle," she said with a shaky voice.

I felt bad for what I was about to say, but I needed to believe her. I needed to know the truth. "It sounds like Josh can make you do anything he wants." I paused. "Like kill Amanda because she talked to me."

Bobby put his hand on Nicole's as she hung her head. "Nicole didn't kill anyone."

"Thank you," she said to Bobby, then glared at me.

I locked eyes with Bobby. "Prove it."

"Why don't *you?*"

"I'm a little busy trying to prove *I* didn't do it."

"Oh, I get it." He rested his elbows on the table. "Reasonable doubt, is that it? Point the finger at someone else to confuse the jury?"

"That's not what I'm doing here."

After a few moments of silence, Bobby asked, "What time did Amanda die?"

"I'm not on trial here."

He held up his hands. "Calm down. I'm trying to establish an alibi for Nicole, so maybe you'll stop your ridiculous accusations."

I stood and paced in a tight pattern. "I don't know for sure."

"Take your time. Think."

I stopped. "Wait a minute." I sat back down. "Josh asked me where I'd been between ten and midnight. That must be when she died. Monday the 27th, between ten and midnight."

"Good." He turned to Nicole, who was deep in thought.

"Oh my God!" she said, her eyes wide. "I worked a double that day. I was at the hospital from three in the afternoon until seven the next morning."

Bobby nodded triumphantly.

"Are you satisfied now?" Nicole said with a bit of righteous indignation.

"I'm sorry. I'm just trying to get to the truth."

"Look, Dillon," Bobby said. "I sympathize with your situation, but I haven't set foot in Bradley in six years, and I have no intention of doing so now."

"You'll always be looking over your shoulder," I said. "Is that how you want to live?"

My words hung there in the silence that followed.

"If I found a way to get us all out from under this that didn't involve you going back to Bradley, would you help me?"

Bobby hesitated. "If you could do that," he said with a reluctant nod, "I'd consider it."

CHAPTER 34

Nicole shifted her car into park in the driveway, waved to Mama on the front porch, then turned to me. "Thank you."

"For what?"

"For not being a jerk."

"It doesn't mean you're off the hook." I paused. "I'd still like to know how Josh knew I was at your house that night."

"I told you, Dillon. I don't know. He made it look like I contacted him, but I swear, I didn't."

"I want to believe you. I really do."

"So, what now?"

I opened the door. "I'll be in touch."

As I walked toward the house, Mama ran down the steps and met me halfway. Fear flashed in her eyes, and she grabbed my arm.

"What's wrong?" I asked.

"I found something in the house."

"Something of Pop's?"

"I wish." She bit down on her lower lip. "I'll show you, but don't say a word."

Mama pulled me toward the house, and I had no choice but to follow. I wondered if she might be high again. We went inside and stood in front of the fireplace. She pointed to a framed photo on the mantle with one hand and raised a finger to her lips with the other.

I stared at the photo of Pop and his two boys, then looked at Mama. She gave a nervous nod. I picked up the photo, and she pointed to the back. A thin, black plastic box had been attached to the upper left corner. It appeared to be some type of electronic listening device. Apparently, Mama thought the same.

I gently placed the photo back on the mantle and took Mama outside. I exhaled when we reached the porch, as if the air inside had been unbreathable. My brain went into rewind mode, and I tried to remember things that had been said in that room. Was that the only bug, or had someone listened to our private conversations in other rooms, as well?

"How did you find it?" I asked.

"Cleaning."

"How long do you think it's been there?"

She shrugged.

"Someone had to have been inside to plant it. Who's been in the house besides you and me?"

She thought for a moment. "Bill was the last one. Your friend, Cooper, was here before that. Nicole—"

"I mean strangers." Someone could have broken in, but Mama hardly ever left the house, and there'd been no signs of forced entry. "Have you let anyone in to fix anything, or to read the meter?"

Mama shook her head.

"How about any..." My question went unfinished as I suddenly remembered Mama's overdose two weeks ago. Her attacker had been inside the house.

"Any what?"

"Never mind." I pulled my cell phone from my pocket.

"Are you calling Bill?"

"No."

"Why not? I'm sure he can figure out what's going on. It's what he does."

"I need to call someone I can trust."

"You don't trust Bill after all the help he's given us?"

"It's not that I don't trust him…"

Mama put her hand on my arm as I dialed Coop's number. "Do you trust me?"

I hesitated, looking into her anxious eyes. God help me. "Yes, Mama. I trust you."

She nodded and removed her hand.

Coop answered on the second ring.

"I've got a problem," I said.

"Do I know her?"

"I'm serious. Can you get over here right now?"

"First, tell me what's going on."

"I'll tell you when you get here."

"Have it your way, but you're gonna owe me."

I ended the call and looked at Mama. "We need to stay out here and wait for Coop."

"What will he do?"

"I don't know."

"This is serious, Bish," Coop said after I showed him the bug and we were safely outside. "Whoever's got it in for your mama isn't fooling around."

"Do you think they're after Mama, or me?"

"Flip a coin."

"What about Jimmy? He works with this stuff. He might be able to tell us what it is, and maybe even who put it there."

Coop nodded. "It's worth a shot."

Jimmy pulled into the driveway an hour later, all smiles and high-fives. After he inspected the device, we gathered outside, and he confirmed our suspicions.

"What you've got here is a high-end, voice-activated listening device. It transmits a signal to a cell phone or recorder, or both. Depending on the battery life, this had to set someone back five or six hundred dollars."

"Can you tell what number it's calling?" I asked.

Jimmy shook his head. "Not without removing the SIM card."

"Let's do it."

"Hold on," he said, raising his hands. "If I do that, the person on the other end will know that we're on to them."

"I saw a movie once," Coop said, "where the person who discovered the bug left it alone, then used it to his advantage by feeding the listener false information."

Jimmy put a hand on my shoulder. "Coop's got a point. Let's not rush into anything."

"Can you check the rest of the house?"

"I thought you'd never ask," Jimmy said with a grin. He opened the case that he'd brought and pulled out something that resembled a large smartphone. "If there's more in the house, this will find 'em."

After Jimmy checked our phones, we turned them off and followed him inside. He found another bug on the underside of the kitchen table. The rest of the house was clean.

We left them alone for now. Mama and I would have to act as normal as possible without saying anything in the house that we didn't want overheard.

I pointed to the device in his hand. "I'll feel a little safer if you let me hang on to that for a few days."

"Sure, Bish. I'll come back this weekend and pick it up."

After they both left, I walked to my car. I noticed the detector in my shirt pocket light up as I reached for the door handle. I walked around the car, paying attention to the strength of the signal.

The rear wheel well on the passenger side seemed to be the hot spot. I ran my hand inside the opening and found what I assumed to be a GPS tracker. On the way to Nicole's house, I took a detour to the bus station. I removed the device from my car and stuck it underneath one of the buses.

Nicole's car wasn't in the driveway, and she didn't answer her bell. I walked around back and found an open window. I forced the screen up and climbed in.

"Sorry, Nicole," I whispered under my breath, "but this can't wait." Inside, the detector lights flashed. Our spy wasn't very creative. Two bugs—one in the living room, the other under the kitchen table.

Perhaps Nicole hadn't tipped off Josh the night I was arrested.

CHAPTER 35

The next day, I went through Pop's room again. I didn't know what to look for, just that I would be more thorough this time.

I checked the pockets of all the clothes that hung in his closet. Nothing important turned up until I reached the only suit he'd owned. He stopped going to church after Mama left and probably hadn't worn it since. I always figured the next time I'd see him in it, they'd be closing the lid of his casket and covering it with dirt.

When Mama told me that Pop had been cremated, I was at first suspicious. But then I remembered how he used to tell anyone who'd listen, "I don't want to be laid out like a side of beef on a buffet table so the whole town can gawk at my dead carcass." A few glasses of whiskey usually preceded such comments, but I'm sure there had been some truth to it. Ashes to ashes, and all that.

I pulled a small, odd-shaped key from the inside pocket. Pop didn't care much for banks, otherwise I would have assumed it opened a safe deposit box. I slipped it into my pocket and continued my search.

Two pairs of Levis hung from a hook on the side wall. When I checked the pockets, I noticed a small door in the wall behind where they'd hung. Inside, I found a locked strongbox.

I reached into my pocket and retrieved the key I'd found in Pop's suit. It fit into the lock, and the top let go when I turned the key. I removed a savings passbook, the title to his truck, two legal documents, and the keys and storage receipt from Coop's garage. Paid two years in advance.

Some old photographs and a ten-page report that Luke wrote in eighth grade remained at the bottom of the box. I examined the report. The cover page read *Native American Healers, by Luke Bishop.*

Luke had always been interested in Native American culture, and I remembered how proud he'd been when his teacher gave him an *A* and told him it was the best in the class. He deserved it. He interviewed local tribal leaders and spent many hours doing research at the library.

I flipped through the pages, reading passages and looking at the pictures. One in particular caught my attention. The photo, taken in 1981, showed an attractive Cherokee woman who'd just begun her journey as a shaman. She appeared to be in her early thirties with long black braids, perfect skin, and a pair of black onyx eyes that looked into your soul. A chill ran up my arms and out through the top of my head. Her name was Leotie, which meant *flower of the prairie.* I set it down, trying to recall where I'd heard that name before.

I unfolded one of the other documents to find the deed to Pop's house. The next one appeared to be a contract between Pop and Bill McCutchen, drawn up by Mort in June 1975. I scanned both pages, paying particular attention to a rather lengthy clause outlining the disposition of the subject land in the event of the death of one of the parties.

I folded the contract, grabbed Luke's report, and hurried downstairs. Mama stood at the kitchen counter, making lunch. I sat at the table.

"I found the contract for the—"

Mama spun around, eyes wild. She drew her hand across her neck, then pointed at the table.

I nodded in silent recognition.

"The plumber, I hope," she said, an obvious attempt at damage control.

"Yeah." I played along. "The thief who took Pop's money and never finished the bathroom."

"I've been fixin' to give that man a piece of my mind, but I haven't been able to locate that damn contract."

"Well, here it is." I forced a smile.

Mama picked up her plate and a glass of iced tea. "I think I'd like to eat lunch out on the porch. Will you sit with me?"

"Sure," I said and followed her outside.

I let the screen door slam behind me. We both exhaled and sat on the swing.

"Thanks for stopping me," I said. "That was a close one."

"Dillon, you've got to be more careful. Whatever it is you found, I don't think we should broadcast it to the sons of bitches who are listening."

"I'm sorry, Mama." I nodded. "We need to get those damn things out of there."

"Be patient." She patted my knee. "So, what did you find?"

"The contract for the land that Pop bought with Bill. There's some interesting shit in there."

"Dillon."

"Sorry, Mama. It's just that they had this arrangement for what would happen to the land if one of them died."

I tried to explain it to Mama, at least as much as I understood of it.

"You should talk to Mort," she said.

"Should I?" I held up the contact. "How come he never mentioned it? It's not like he didn't know about it. He's the one who drew it up."

"I know you and Bill don't trust him, but I do. He helped me when I came back. He didn't have to do that."

"That's true, but—"

"Whether you trust him or not, you need to confront him about this. See what he has to say." She closed her eyes and shook her head. "I think Mort would be the last one to do anything to hurt this family."

"Until he chucks a grenade."

"What?"

"Nothing."

We sat in silence for a few minutes while Mama finished her lunch.

"What was the name of that medicine woman you met in Oklahoma?" I asked.

"Will you go see her?"

"I don't know. What was her name?"

"Her name was Leotie." Mama smiled. "I can go with you."

I pulled Luke's report from my back pocket and handed it to her.

She read the cover. "Where'd you find this?"

"Look at page seven."

Mama flipped through the pages, then stopped. I tapped Leotie's picture. She pulled the paper closer to her face, then turned to me with wide eyes.

"He wrote that twelve years ago," I said.

"Don't you see, Dillon? This is a sign."

CHAPTER 36

"What can I do for you, Dillon?" Mort asked from behind his desk.

"I need a lawyer."

"Bonnie said she planned to look for someone in Dallas."

"No one will take the case without a change of venue."

Mort leaned on his elbows and touched his lips with his steepled fingers. He took a few moments, as if weighing both sides of a difficult decision.

"Dillon, I'd like to help, but—"

"Look. I'm sorry about firing you and all that."

"Don't be. I would have done the same thing." He shifted in his chair. "I could get into trouble for telling you this, but I was under a great deal of pressure to ensure a conviction."

"You're being blackmailed?"

Mort sighed. "It's not blackmail when it's your job."

"Mama's desperate," I said.

Mama was my ace in the hole, but it still felt a little underhanded to use her like that. Clearly, Mort was sweet on Mama and wasn't too happy with the way Bill had been sniffing around lately.

"She said she'd be forever in your debt if you took my case."

"She said that?"

"Sure as I'm sittin' here." I reached into my pocket. "In fact, she gave me this check to give you as a down payment."

Mort studied the check, then smiled. "Son, you just hired yourself a lawyer."

"Thank you. But what about your blackmailer?"

"I'll figure something out."

Mort seemed willing to go to bat for me, or perhaps Mama, at the risk of his own peril. This unexpected turn of events made me second-guess what I was about to do. But only for a minute. I got up to leave, then hesitated.

"One more thing," I said as I held up the contract.

"What's that?" Mort asked.

"Why don't *you* tell *me*?" I handed him the papers across the desk.

Mort scanned the first page, then flipped to the second.

"That's your name there as attorney of record, isn't it?"

"It is." He set it down. "But this contract is forty years old. My memory's not what it used to—"

"Cut the crap, Mort. Why didn't you tell me about this?"

"Those boys never found any oil, so I didn't think it was relevant."

I leaned over his desk. "You best clear your calendar, Mort, 'cause we're about to go over this contract line by line. Then you and I will take a little ride. I want to see this worthless piece of land."

"Calm down now, Dillon." Mort pulled a handkerchief from his pocket and dabbed his forehead. He glanced at his watch. "I think that can be arranged."

Mort explained the contract details over the next hour.

"So, the whole thing was set up to protect their families?"

"That was the intent."

"And it all hinges on whether they find any oil?"

"Correct." Mort stood and walked over to a potted cactus plant in front of the window. "Let's say your daddy and Bill run up a big debt looking for oil that they never find. If your daddy died, you wouldn't want to be stuck with that bill, would you?"

"I sure wouldn't."

He picked up a water bottle and poured a little into the pot. "Of course not."

"What if they find oil and one of them gets greedy?"

Mort walked back to his desk, flipped to the second page of the contract, and pointed to a paragraph near the bottom. "This reversionary clause states that if one of the parties dies as a result of foul play, the entire property and all the associated rights revert to the dead man's heirs."

"They thought of everything, didn't they?"

Mort had a worried look in his eyes that made me wonder if he was holding something back.

"You can't tell anyone that I know about this contract." I leaned over the desk. "Attorney-client privilege and all."

Mort's expression fell. "Do you still want to go see it?" he asked in a flat voice as he handed me the papers.

"Roger that." I nodded. "I'll drive."

We turned off Route 67 just outside Alvarado and followed an old service road for a couple of miles.

"Stop!" Mort said.

I pulled over.

He stared out the passenger window. "I think this is it."

"You *think*?"

"It's difficult to tell without the survey and a GPS."

No landmarks to speak of, just dirt roads and prairie grass. "When's the last time you were here?"

Mort took a deep breath.

"Damn it, Mort. I want the truth."

"Last week."

"So you should know where it is."

"I know the general area, but it's hard to tell one scruffy patch of grass from the other. There's a survey stake up ahead. Maybe that can tell us for sure."

I pulled the photo of Pop and Bill from above the visor and showed it to Mort. "Recognize this?"

He studied it for a moment. "I should. I was the one holding the camera." He handed it back to me. "Where'd you get this?"

"Pop's cabin."

I pointed to a small rock outcropping in the photo, then through the windshield at a similar feature up ahead, about a hundred yards from the road.

Mort nodded.

I drove along the shoulder until we reached the rock. I shut off the engine and turned to Mort. "Why did you come out here last week?"

"Look, Dillon, I did what you asked. I went over the contract with you and showed you the land." He sighed. "Can you please take me back to the office?"

"Did Bill come to see you?"

Mort sighed. "A couple of weeks ago. He wanted the deed changed to his name only."

"Did you do it?"

Mort frowned, then gave a sarcastic smile. "If I did, I wouldn't be able to tell you about it, would I?"

"Why didn't you do it?"

"I told him he needed to get an official copy of Eli's death certificate." He shifted in his seat. "Frankly, the police investigation left a lot of unanswered questions about Eli's death."

"You think Bill had something to do with Pop's death?"

"I didn't say that."

"Why would he?" I pointed out the window. "Clearly, there isn't any oil comin' up."

"I know. That's why I was out here a week ago."

"Bill said he didn't trust you." I turned the key in the ignition. "Maybe that's why."

"I'm not sure Bill trusts anyone but himself."

I drove to Coop's shop after I dropped Mort off at his office. Bill called before I entered the building, and I stood in the parking lot to talk. He told me Amanda died from an adrenaline overdose. He also told me she left a suicide note.

"The police never mentioned anything about a note," I said.

"Sounds like someone set you up, son."

My foot tingled like it had fallen asleep, and I paced the lot. "What did it say?"

"I didn't actually see it, but I heard she fessed up to killing your daddy."

I stopped. "Amanda?"

"Said Josh put her up to it to cover up Luke's murder."

"We need to find that note."

"Good luck with that." He paused. "We need to find another way to get the truth out of that snake."

"We could squeeze its head until it talks."

"If Amanda's death is ruled a suicide, there's no need for a trial."

"Thanks, Bill. I gotta go."

I slipped the phone into my pocket, then turned and walked back to my car. The last thing I needed was one of Coop's lectures. I rolled down the window and sat for a few minutes. The clock continued to tick away the hours before I would have to stand in a courtroom and fight for my life.

I needed a shot of Jenny Lee. I dialed her number. Voicemail.

"Hi. You were right. I miss the crap out of you." I paused. "Amanda's death might have been a suicide. Looks like Josh set me up to take the fall. I need to figure out why and find a way to prove it. The good news is I've got more to go on than I had yesterday." I sighed. "I know... be careful. Talk to you soon."

I hadn't seen Nicole since we visited Bobby, so I never mentioned the bugs I'd found in her house. The fact that someone is also listening to her seems to suggest that she had nothing to do with Pop's or Amanda's deaths. I'm not sure why I never told her about the bugs. Maybe I didn't want her to know I broke into her house. Or maybe I just wanted to avoid her.

I drove home to find that Mama had made dinner. I didn't feel much like eating, and I pushed my food around on my plate while Mama cleaned hers.

"What's the matter, Dillon?"

"Not hungry tonight."

"Anything you want to talk about?"

"No." I pointed under the table.

Most of what Mama and I talked about in the house was benign. However, from time to time, we made shit up to confuse our electronic interlopers, or throw in something juicy so they wouldn't suspect we were on to them. I wasn't in the mood to play games tonight.

Mama walked her plate over to the sink, then took my hand and led me outside. "What is it, Dillon?"

I told her I met with Mort earlier, and he agreed to take my case.

"That's good news, isn't it?"

Then I told her about the contract and our road trip to Alvarado. When I told her about Bill's phone call, she stood and paced in front of the swing.

"Sit down, Mama. You're making me nervous."

She stopped. Her eyes darted back and forth before they found mine.

"I'm gonna take care of it," I assured her.

"How?"

"First, I'm gonna go find the son-of-a-bitch and rattle his cage."

"I don't think that's a good idea."

The more I thought about Josh and his underhanded scheme to ruin my life, the more my blood boiled. I stood just as Mama sat. "Sorry, Mama, but I gotta go."

"Dillon." Mama stood. "Come back here."

"Don't wait up."

"Please don't do something you're gonna regret."

Like one more thing is going to matter.

CHAPTER 37

I found Josh at Shady's, sitting with a woman I didn't recognize. "Hey, asshole."

He looked up like it wasn't the first time he'd been addressed that way. When he saw me, he rolled his eyes and took a long draw on his beer. "What is it now?"

"Where's the note?"

I had his attention. He set the bottle down and stood. His eyes darted around the room. "What note?"

"The suicide note? The one you found at Amanda's house?"

Josh's eyes became slits, and he showed his teeth. "I don't know what you're talking about."

"I think you do."

"Maybe we should take this outside."

I glanced around the bar. "I like it in here."

He flexed his fingers and clenched his hands into fists. "I'm warning you, Bishop. You'd better leave now before you get hurt."

I snorted. "That's a good one."

Josh threw the first punch. I blocked it, grabbed his forearm, and twisted it behind his back. The couple at the table next to us stood and took a few steps backward. Every eye in the bar watched us.

"You're setting me up." I applied more pressure to his arm, and he winced. "I don't like being set up."

"You'd better let go. I'm a police officer, and I can have you—"

"You're an off-duty cop, and not a very good one at that." I pushed a little harder on his arm.

Josh attempted to grab my head with his free hand, but I pulled back out of reach.

"What'd you do with the note?"

"I... I don't know anything about a note." Josh struggled as he tried to break loose.

I wrapped my other arm around his neck and squeezed. I leaned in and whispered in his ear. "This is a little tougher when one of us isn't in handcuffs, dontcha think?"

I smelled the venom on his breath as I waited for a response. None came.

"Amanda Hughes left a suicide note." I squeezed a little tighter. "But you thought it would be more fun to destroy the note and set up your old friend, Dillon Bishop, for murder."

He kicked at my legs, and I took a half-step backward. I turned to face the other side of the room so everyone had a chance to see his face. "Any of this ring a bell?"

Josh jerked his head backward and caught me in the jaw. I recovered quickly and tightened my grip on his neck. He clawed harder at my arm, gasping for air. I could almost hear his eyes bulge out of his head.

Someone yelled, "Stop. You're going to kill him."

I planted one foot in front of Josh and pushed him hard toward the empty table. He broke a chair on his way to the ground.

Everyone and everything in the bar stood still. I stared down at Josh and waited for him to get up so I could put him on the floor again. Someone grabbed my shoulder from behind. Fortunately, I recognized Coop's voice before I reacted.

"Time to get the hell outta here, Rambo."

I didn't argue. When we turned, one of Josh's friends came after us. I noticed he was carrying. He entered the circle of death—a four-foot radius around my body in which I could kill or disarm any attacker. I let him get close enough to reach for me, then sidestepped quickly. After I wrenched his arm behind his back with one hand and removed the pistol from his belt with the other, I jammed the barrel against his head.

"Anybody else wanna try?" I asked as I glanced around the room.

Coop stood slack-jawed by the door. No one dared speak. I pushed my would-be assailant back into the room, then released the clip and shoved it in my pocket. I checked the chamber, then tossed his gun on the floor. The bartender picked up a bat from behind the bar and made a move in our direction. Coop held up his hands to let him know we were done.

"Are you crazy?" Coop said after we stepped outside.

"That felt good." I held my hand up for a high-five. Coop did not reciprocate. "C'mon, Coop." I waited a few more seconds before I pulled it down.

"It's Josh, for chrissake," Coop said. "You're gonna have to watch your back and sleep with one eye open."

"Been there."

"You embarrassed the shit out of him. He's never gonna let it go."

"I'm not afraid of Josh."

"You should be." Coop shook his head. "You need to be smarter than that, Dillon. You're lucky he was off duty, or your ass would be back in jail."

"The son-of-a-bitch had it coming."

"Maybe so, but—"

"How did you know I was here?"

"Your mama called. She's worried about you. She said something about Luke, but she was talking nonsense, like after her attack. Do you think—"

"Mama's clean."

We walked to the parking lot and stopped next to my car.

"Haven't you ever read *The Art of War?*" Coop asked.

"No, I just fought in one."

"It's a book about military strategy and tactics written by a Chinese General, Sun Tzu, like fifteen-hundred years ago. He was all about creativity and timing instead of brute force."

"Why the hell would a grease monkey read a book like that?"

"I had to read it for a business class I took at the community college." Coop glared. "Where did *you* go to college, jarhead?"

"College? I don't need no stinkin' college."

"Really? Maybe if you went to college, you'd know better than to pull a bonehead stunt like that."

"Don't you see what's going on here, Coop? Josh framed me for Amanda's death. Bill told me she left a suicide note, but the cops buried it."

"By cops, you mean Josh?"

I nodded.

"How does Bill know about the note?"

"He's connected. He knows shit. Same way he knew about Pop's autopsy report and the doctored surveillance video."

"I still don't think you should go around tuning Josh up in public."

"You got any better ideas?"

"Maybe you can kill Nicole and make it look like Josh did it."

"Very funny. Maybe I'll kill *you*."

"Relax. I'm kidding." He held up his hands like I might be serious. "Okay, here's something to think about. *He who is prudent and lies in wait for an enemy who is not, will be victorious.*"

"What?"

"It's my favorite quote from the book. It means you need to be smarter and more patient than Josh. Don't *you* screw up. Wait until *he* does."

"In case you forgot, I don't have a lot of time."

"Meet the enemy on your terms, not his."

I looked at him sideways. "Sun Tzu?"

He smiled. "No, Cooper Hill." His expression turned serious. "You've made it difficult lately, Bish, but you're still my best friend." He sighed. "I don't want to see you go to prison or end up like your daddy."

"Thanks. Neither do I."

"You sure can handle yourself. I'll give you that."

"I did some Special Forces training after boot camp."

"C'mon." He put his hand on my shoulder. "Let's go down to the DQ. Butterfinger Blizzards. My treat."

Walking into that old Dairy Queen felt like a walk back in time. We took two Blizzards to our old table in the back that probably still had a few pieces of my gum stuck to the underside.

Coop shoved a big spoonful of ice cream in his mouth and stared at me. After a few seconds, he squinted, and I thought it might be a brain freeze.

"What?"

He swallowed. "You were like a ninja in there."

I grinned. "They used to call me *Teenage Mutant Ninja Texan*."

Coop flashed a quick smile and held up his hand. I slapped it.

"So what's next, Raphael?"

Instead of answering, I told Coop about the contract.

CHAPTER 38

I lay in bed the next morning, thinking that Coop had been right about one thing—Josh wouldn't go down without a fight. I wasn't afraid of Josh, just a little concerned about what his warped mind might be capable of.

In combat, my biggest fear had been to step on a land mine. You can't fight what you can't see. The last thing you hear before you find yourself at heaven's door, or in a hospital bed with no legs, is the *click* under your boot. Sometimes, you don't even hear that. My instincts told me to tread lightly.

Unfortunately, I don't always listen to my instincts, particularly when they border on common sense. I had just declared war on Josh, and I'd never been one to back down from a fight. Well, almost never. I'd run away from Bradley ten years earlier. That wouldn't happen again.

Life had dealt Pop a bad hand, and he hadn't taken it well. Some people said that he deserved what he got. But Luke, he was just a kid.

"Dillon? Are you up?" Mama called from the other side of the door.

"Come in."

"You didn't sleep much last night. Is everything all right?"

I nodded, then changed my mind. "No, it's not. I don't get much sleep anymore. I tried doubling my meds, but that doesn't seem to help."

Mama sat on the edge of the bed. "I talked to Leotie yesterday."

"The Indian?"

She smiled. "The Cherokee medicine woman."

"What did you talk about?"

"You."

"Mama…"

"Hush." She placed her hand on mine. "I think she can help you."

My curiosity trumped my annoyance. "What makes you think that?"

"She gave me a gift—a chance to get to know my son." A tear fell on the sheet as another rolled down her cheek. "She's the reason I'm alive."

I straightened up. "What happened?"

"I'd hit rock bottom; I couldn't go on. In one last desperate attempt to save what was left of my life, I went to see Leotie. She remembered me from the few visits when I'd accompanied Wade."

"She talked you out of killing yourself?"

Mama nodded. "I felt worthless until Leotie told me that the spirit inside me, inside every living thing, is the Creator's spirit. She taught me that I was an integral part of the entire universe, and that I helped maintain a delicate balance in our world. I stopped feeling sorry for myself and honored my position. The Cherokee people, our people, took me in and taught me to restore the balance I'd lost."

"What do you mean, *our people?*"

Mama hesitated. "Your great-grandmother was born on the Cherokee reservation in Oklahoma."

I glared at Mama. "And you didn't think that I might want to know something like that?"

"Dillon, I'm sorry," she whispered. "For many years, I wanted to keep it a secret. No more. I'm proud of my Native American blood, and you should be, too."

"I'm pretty sure I would have been if I'd known."

"I spent a month on the reservation. After that, it seemed that the world around me changed, but I was the one who had changed. I no longer needed drugs to escape. I knew I could come home again."

"Did Pop know about this?"

"I told him everything."

I closed my eyes and lay back on my pillow.

"Please, Dillon. I know I wasn't there for you all those years, but I'm here now. I love you. Let me help you."

Mama just said the only thing I'd ever wanted to hear. The reason I'd cried myself to sleep all those nights. I'd done a lot of stupid things in my life, but turning Mama away now wouldn't be one of them. I opened one eye. "When do we leave?"

She leaned in and hugged my neck. The tears came swiftly and silently.

We stopped in front of a small house on a narrow road whose pavement ended a quarter of a mile behind us. A few patches of brown grass dotted the dusty front yard, but the house appeared neat and well-maintained. I'd half-expected to find this woman living in a teepee.

Wind chimes hung silently from the corner of her front porch, the air still and hot under a cloudless sky. A sign on the door directed us to the rear entrance.

"How much does she charge?" I asked Mama as we made our way around back.

Mama frowned at me like I was a child who'd spoken out of turn. "Her medicine is not for sale. This isn't a doctor's office."

An old Indian woman appeared behind the screen at the back door. "Welcome."

I held the door for Mama. She entered, but I found myself frozen in place, studying the woman's face. When I detected the resemblance to the woman in Luke's report, she smiled and nodded as if she knew. Leotie recognized Mama, and the two hugged.

Inside, a large owl perched on a branch that appeared to grow out of one of the walls drew my attention. I watched intently, certain that its enormous eyes had blinked when we entered the room.

"You've traveled a long way. Please sit."

Her voice released me from my distraction.

Two chairs faced each other in the middle of the room, separated by a small table that resembled a tree stump. A third chair sat a few feet away along an empty wall. Leotie took a seat in one of the facing chairs. I looked at Mama, who nudged me toward the other one before she took a seat against the wall.

Behind Leotie, feathers and animal skulls adorned the wall above a table filled with all manner of uniquely shaped bottles, pipes, and small bowls that contained tobacco or herbs. Mama had been right about one thing—this was no doctor's office.

Leotie wore her long, gray hair in tight braids on either side of her head. Two feathers hung from one side, woven in at the top of the braid. Turquoise earrings matched the larger stone in the middle of a handmade silver necklace that hung around her neck. Her onyx eyes, set deep within her dark skin, studied me as if reading my innermost thoughts.

After a few uncomfortable moments, she leaned over the stump, placed some dried sage leaves in a shallow bowl, and lit them. When a flame appeared, she quickly blew it out. She cupped her hands and pulled the small column of white smoke toward herself, then closed her eyes and spoke in her native tongue.

When she opened her eyes, they met mine.

"This medicine will help you let go of the things you don't need to be carrying around in your heart."

She gently wafted the smoke in my direction with a large feather. Leotie stood and walked slowly around my chair. She stopped three times at the remaining compass points to wave her feather, then returned to her seat and set the bowl down.

I watched a thin column of smoke drift upward. It swirled and danced before it dissipated and became one with the air in the room.

"Waya," she said.

"What?"

She pointed to my arm, and I held it out between us.

"Your name is Waya. The wolf."

I studied her weathered face as she traced the tattoo on my arm.

"You have a kindred spirit who wears the same sign."

It wasn't a question. "Uh... my friend Jenny Lee has one."

"More than friend. You share Cherokee blood."

I turned to Mama, and she smiled. I'd never known much about Mama's side of the family, but I suddenly wanted to learn more.

Leotie let go of my arm. "Your friend's Cherokee name is Ahyoka, one who brings happiness." She paused for a moment. "What you seek is seeking you."

"She lives in Colorado," I said as I hung my head.

"Spirit knows no distance."

"I plan to join her there."

"Signs from the Great Spirit will guide you on your journey."

"What kind of signs?"

"Only you will know. Trust your instincts, like the wolf."

"I hoped for something a little more... concrete."

She closed her eyes. "You have a brother."

"Where is he? Is he alive?"

"He is no longer with us on the Earth plane, but he is very much alive. He watches over you like Noquisi."

"Noquisi?"

"A star. He is the reason you are here."

Despite the heat, a chill ran up both arms. I pictured Lawman Luke's sheriff's star pinned to my duffel bag.

She opened her eyes. "You will return tomorrow."

"What for?"

"Your little white pills poison your body and your mind. I will prepare medicine from Mother Earth."

"But I need them."

"Then why are you here?"

"I..." I glanced at Mama. "It was her idea. She said you could help me."

"I can't help you." She paused, apparently looking into my soul again. "I can only give advice. You must choose to follow it."

I hesitated. "What kind of medicine?"

"Herbs that I will gather and bless."

"That's it?"

"Be careful," she whispered in a voice that triggered another round of chills. "Someone you trust speaks with a serpent's tongue."

"Who?"

Leotie shook her head. "You must go now and return tomorrow."

I looked at Mama for help, but she had nothing to say. Leotie sat as still as a stone, eyes closed once again.

Mama stood, and I followed her to the door. I looked back at the old medicine woman and her owl as I held the door for Mama.

"She needs to work on her people skills," I said when we reached the car.

Mama glared. "Sounds like you need to work on a few things yourself."

"What's that supposed to mean?"

She remained silent for a few moments. Perhaps she felt bad for criticizing me after the terrible things she'd done.

"Well?"

"Just because you might not understand something, doesn't mean you should disrespect the people who do, or disregard its importance."

Mama was right, her comment punctuated by the jolt I felt when the car left the dirt road and returned to the pavement. As desperate as it sounded, I went there for the woman's help. "I'm sorry."

"So am I." Her expression softened. "I'm still your mother."

"Will you come with me tomorrow?"

"I think you can handle it on your own."

A few moments of silence passed. "What's with the owl?" I asked.

A flicker of a smile crossed her face. "What do you mean?"

"I could have sworn I saw it blink, but he was dead, right?"

"Spirit never dies."

I wasn't sure how to respond. My usual inclination for sarcasm failed me.

"To the Cherokee, all animals are sacred, but the owl is believed to be a spiritual consultant to their shamans. Some believe that the appearance of an owl, a nocturnal creature, during the daytime signifies impending death."

"You believe this stuff?"

"I guess it's in my blood. It's in yours, too."

"About that..."

We had a long talk on the drive home.

CHAPTER 39

When I returned alone the next day to pick up my medicine, I entered the sacred space with more respect than the day before. I might have even bowed a little when I saw Leotie, which probably wasn't necessary, but Mama's comment had struck a nerve.

I sat in my previous spot, and Leotie handed me a cloth sack before she took a seat across from me. I opened the sack, looked inside, then back to Leotie.

"Custom blend," she said. "Only for you."

I smiled, feeling somewhat special.

"When your body is out of balance," she continued, "so is your life. I treat cause, not symptoms. The herbs will help restore your natural balance. You think you need chemicals, but nature provides everything you need."

I opened the sack again and looked inside. It reminded me of pot, but with a strange minty smell, aromatic like a menthol cigarette. "Do I smoke it?"

Leotie smiled for the first time since I'd met her. "You could… but I wouldn't recommend it. Make a cup of tea and drink it before bed."

"Will it help me sleep?"

She nodded. "Your dreams may become more vivid."

I closed the bag. "My dreams are vivid enough, thank you."

"Dreams are visions of your inner life."

"Then I'm in big trouble."

"No." Leotie shook her head. "Out of balance."

"You say tomato…"

"The Creator takes care of us like a mother takes care of her children. She sends abundance and good fortune at every opportunity. You would be wise to view life through the eyes of a child."

"How do I do that?"

She smiled. "When water falls from the sky to cleanse the Earth, don't curse the rain. Dance in it."

Her eyes held me captive.

"Life is a journey," she said, "and there are two ways to walk. We can choose to walk forward toward the light, or backward toward the darkness. Go now and choose your way wisely."

I nodded, avoiding her eyes. I didn't have the best track record for making good decisions.

Leotie's words stayed with me for the rest of the day and into the night. I drank a cup of her tea before bed.

Back in high school, Coop and I occasionally played hooky and spent the afternoon down at the swimming hole on Jamison Creek. Today felt like one of those days. Today I wanted to take a break from… life.

I'd had the best night's sleep since my return to Bradley, and I wanted to remember what it was like to have fun and linger in the thoughts of innocence that I'd long forgotten. I packed a cooler and drove to Coop's shop around eleven to convince him to take the afternoon off. He resisted until

I promised to buy him lunch at the little barbecue joint on the way.

We stopped at Coop's house and threw a few things in the back of the Silverado. I'm not sure Jolene would have approved of our little field trip. On second thought, she probably would have made us take her along. Coop came out of the house sportin' his Ray Bans and the straw hat he wore the crap out of in high school. I gave him shit about it when he climbed into the truck.

"Time to retire that ol' hat, dontcha think?"

Coop removed it from his head and eyed it affectionately. "Hell, Bish, this baby's just gettin' broken in."

"It's *your* head," I said with a shrug and backed out of his driveway.

A Bradley patrol car, with lights flashing, caught up with us near the edge of town. I pulled over and watched the officer step out of his car. I pounded the steering wheel. "Josh."

"How fast were you going?" Coop asked.

"Not fast enough to get pulled over." I kicked the bag of Leotie's herbs under the seat. I couldn't be sure if all of them were legal.

Coop pulled out his phone.

"Who are you calling?"

"Nobody. I'm gonna get this on video."

"Here he comes," I said. "Keep that thing out of sight."

I felt a thud from the back of the truck as glass shattered.

"Dude, he just broke your taillight," Coop whispered.

I wanted to get out of the car and kick his ass, but he was in uniform. The thought of spending more time with Peckerwood held me in my seat.

Josh stared down at me with a smug look. "One of your taillights is out."

"Yeah, I heard. You gonna pay for that?"

"No, but you're gonna pay for this." He pulled out his citation pad and a pen.

"Hey, Josh," Coop called from the passenger seat.

Josh leaned over to look in the window. The smug expression slid off his face when he saw the phone. "What are you doing?"

Coop smiled. "I'm filming a documentary on police misconduct. This clip here is for the section on bogus traffic stops. It's about a Texas cop who pulled over a law-abiding citizen for no reason, and then smashed his friggin' taillight. What a douchebag, huh?"

"Hand it over, Hill."

Coop turned the camera toward me. I smiled and waved. Then he turned it on himself.

"I can't do that, Officer Wilkerson," he said into the camera. "This is my phone, and I'm expecting an important call. The Attorney General is interested in this project."

Coop looked at me. "What time did he say he would call?"

Coop was a master at improv. I bit my tongue to stifle a laugh.

Josh straightened up. "Step out of the car."

I glanced at Coop and gave a quick nod. He leaned over to position his camera.

"Later, Josh," I said, then pushed the gas pedal to the floor.

Coop twisted and turned to hold the camera steady on Josh, frozen in the middle of the road like he'd just shit himself.

We started hootin' and hollerin' as I kept the pedal pinned to the floor.

I checked the rearview, and saw Josh walk back to his car, shaking his head. He hung a hard U-turn and sped off in the opposite direction.

Coop and I watched the video—three times—over ribs, salt potatoes, beans, and a couple of Lone Stars. Definitely a keeper. I missed the days when we used to get in trouble and laugh about it like we didn't have a care in the world. Things had changed since then, but I wouldn't let it bother me. Not today. Today, I took a break.

We hardly recognized the old swimmin' hole when we pulled off the road near Jamison Creek. Catclaw and trumpet vine grew wild and had taken over much of the riverbank. We followed a narrow path down to the water and found the tire swing that hung out over the creek from a big Cypress branch.

Coop yanked on it a couple of times. "Think this old rope will hold us?"

"Only one way to find out." I pointed in his direction. "You first."

The rope held until we'd had our fill of muddy creek water. We sat on the bank drying in the sun when Coop asked if I'd heard from Jenny Lee. I told him we'd only spoken once since she left. He narrowed his eyes, shook his head, and reminded me she was the best thing that had ever happened to me. Present company excluded, of course.

Despite our best efforts to forget about life for a while, our conversation circled around to the strategy for my trial. I told Coop I wasn't sure we had a strategy. Mort had reviewed the DA's case against me, and I saw through his efforts to minimize the hopelessness of beating the charges. The fact that I was innocent seemed to hold less sway with the local judicial system than I'd hoped.

CHAPTER 40

I felt better on the drive home than I had in a long time. Our little field trip had been therapeutic. Leotie had talked about feeling like a kid, and that's exactly how I felt all afternoon and into the evening. Sure, we occasionally slipped back into this world's reality, but it never lasted for more than a few minutes.

I dropped Coop off and drove directly home. I said good night to Mama, made myself a cup of tea, and hit the rack. Once again, sleep came easy. During the night, I had a dream.

I stood alone at the edge of a cliff, high above a narrow river that snaked its way between jagged red rock and rolling, evergreen-studded hills. Majestic snow-capped mountains guarded the land below on two sides, creating a breathtaking view worthy of a postcard.

A voice from behind startled me. "Waya."

I turned, squinting my eyes against the sun, to see a beautiful young Cherokee woman. I held my hand to my forehead and studied her. She looked as if she'd just stepped off the page of Luke's report, wearing the same traditional Native American regalia with the addition of a large turquoise medallion that hung around her neck. Her black eyes looked into my soul.

"Leotie?"

The innocence and sincerity in her smile made me catch my breath.

"What are you doing here?" I whispered.

"I've come to take your little white pills. You don't need them anymore."

"I don't have them."

She smiled a knowing smile.

I hung my head as I reached into my pocket and produced the pill bottle. I held it out in front of me. Instead of taking the bottle, she pointed to the canyon floor.

"I cannot do this for you."

I hesitated briefly before I heaved the bottle into the abyss. I turned to Leotie. "Are you satisfied?"

"There are things you must embrace and things you must let go. Wisdom is knowing the difference."

I had no words. She joined me, and we stood side by side at the edge.

"There is a battle that goes on inside people," she said. "The battle is between two wolves inside us all. One is evil. It is anger, jealousy, greed, resentment, lies, and ego. The other is good. It is joy, peace, love, kindness, empathy, and truth."

I thought about it for a moment. "Which one wins?"

"The one you feed."

Again, I had no words.

"I must go now," she said.

I turned. "Where?"

She pointed out over the canyon. "The Great Spirit is in the wind. May he bless you as I have been blessed. *Dodadagohvi*."

I didn't have to speak Cherokee to understand she was saying goodbye. "Leotie. No!"

She stepped off the edge of the cliff, and her human body morphed into an eagle. She only fell a couple of feet before her powerful wings opened and she floated out over the canyon. Leotie soared with such grace and majesty that I barely contained my emotion. A haunting Native American melody drifted in from a flute played somewhere just beyond my field of vision.

I watched the eagle climb effortlessly into the heavens. Rain fell from the cloudless sky as she disappeared into the sun. At first, the drops evaporated the instant they touched my hot skin. The rain fell faster and harder and brought comfort. The water ran in tiny rivulets, falling to the ground from my fingers and the tip of my nose.

The landscape softened and came to life. All manner of lush vegetation sprouted from the rock beneath my feet. I lay down and let the unstoppable life force envelop me.

The brilliant sunlight turned to blackness when I opened my eyes. My bed of thick green moss became a mattress. I sat up in bed, my hair and clothes soaking wet.

Leotie had sent me a message, and I made a mental note to ask her about it the next time I saw her. I rolled over and covered my head with my pillow. I remained in that position for only a few minutes before I remembered Coop had invited me for breakfast. Biscuits and gravy. The clock on the nightstand displayed 0750. I hope he remembered to mention it to Jolene. I threw on some clothes and told Mama I was going out.

A police cruiser sat in Coop's driveway, and I parked beside it. The number on the license plate identified it as Josh's. This couldn't be good.

I let myself in. Coop, Jolene, and Josh looked up from the kitchen table.

"Hi, Dillon," Jo said without her usual smile. Coop nodded.

Josh frowned but said nothing.

Coop excused himself and pulled me aside, out of Josh's earshot.

"What's going on?" I asked.

"Someone broke in last night."

"What did they take?"

"My phone."

"That's it?"

"No. They took Jo's phone and our laptop, but I think they only took them so it wouldn't be obvious that all they wanted was my phone."

I raised an eyebrow. "You think Josh did it?"

"Probably trying to sabotage my documentary."

"What a dumbass."

Coop returned to his seat next to Jolene, and I leaned against the counter behind them.

"Got any leads?" I asked.

"Not yet, but we've had a couple of similar incidents in the area."

I doubt that. I shifted my weight to the other foot.

"You think they're related?" Jo asked.

"It's too soon to tell, but that would be my guess."

Coop's girls walked into the kitchen looking like they'd just rolled out of bed. They paused when they saw a policeman at their table.

Josh stood. "Well, I've got everything I need for now."

Jo looked up at him. "Do you think we'll get our stuff back?"

"We'll do our best, but it's not likely."

I'd have bet money that we'd never see Coop's phone again.

"Thank you for your help." Jo sighed.

Yeah, thanks for nothin'.

Josh turned to Coop, his eyes narrow and cold. "You might want to think about installing a security system." He glanced at the girls. "You've got a beautiful family. I'd hate to see anything bad happen to them."

I think Jo saw through his thinly-veiled threat. "I'll show you out, Officer Wilkerson."

I sat at the table next to Coop.

Jolene closed the door, watched Josh get into his car, then turned around. "What just happened here?"

It sounded like more of an accusation than a question, and I looked away. She folded her arms across her chest. "Cooper?"

"It's my fault," I said.

The girls poured cereal into two bowls on the counter. I nodded toward the porch, and Coop and Jolene followed me. Outside, I told her about yesterday's traffic stop.

"Cooper Harrison Hill. What is the matter with you?" She glanced at me, then back to Coop. "I don't mind if you boys have a little fun now and then, but not when it puts our family at risk." She exhaled sharply. "You know what a prick Josh can be."

He was all that, and then some, in high school. Now it appeared he'd gotten worse, if that was possible. Perhaps it had something to do with the badge.

Coop gently touched his wife's arm. "I'm sorry. I'll keep my distance from Josh."

"It's not just you I'm worried about."

I didn't think this would be a good time to mention that I'd broken Josh's taillight on the way in. I looked at Coop with a sly smile. "Does this mean you won't finish the documentary?"

Four eyes glared at me.

"Too soon?"

I left quickly—with no biscuits or gravy—and made it home in time to have breakfast with Mama.

CHAPTER 41

Coop convinced Jimmy to drive down from Arlington and install a state-of-the-art security system in his home. My recklessness might have put his family in harm's way, but it strengthened my resolve to neutralize the threat.

I could kill Josh with my bare hands in a matter of seconds. After a few moments of serious consideration, I realized I'd be stooping to his level, which I'd done enough of lately. My chances of staying out of prison would be reduced to almost nil.

Clearly, I couldn't count on the local police for any help, which reminded me why I'd left Bradley ten years ago. The same crooked cop still ran the show, but this time, I would see justice prevail… or die trying.

Bill offered to help take Harley and his boys down. I hoped that a veteran outside consultant with strong ties to state law enforcement might make the difference this time. However, something Leotie said gnawed at me. Bill had lied to me about seeing Mama. Why? Was that the only time? Did he have a hidden agenda? Did it involve Mama? The land? Or perhaps something more nefarious.

Nicole could be the reason for Leotie's warning. Or Bobby. I needed to figure out what she meant. I shook my head to clear it.

Mama sat down next to me on the porch swing.

"I have sad news," she said.

I raised an eyebrow but said nothing.

"Leotie passed away."

"What?"

"Last night."

"How do you know that?"

"A friend called."

I waited for her to add something more. When she didn't, I told her about the dream.

"That's wonderful, Dillon. She must have been fond of you to say goodbye."

"She wanted my pills. Made me throw them off the edge of a cliff."

"She preferred natural remedies."

"She looked like the picture in Luke's report."

Mama smiled. "That's a beautiful way to remember her."

I pulled the pill bottle from my pocket and held it between us. "Take it."

"I thought you said you needed them to—"

"Maybe it's time to let go, try something different."

She removed the bottle from my hand and smiled. "Like the tea?"

"I thought so, but now that Leotie's gone, I won't be able to get more."

"I don't think you'll need it."

"Why do you say that?"

"Leotie knew exactly how much to give you. Nothing she does is left to chance. She never intended to replace one crutch with another. I believe she provided a way for your body to transition back to its natural state."

"She told me to dance in the rain."

Mama grinned. "You could use a little whimsy."

"Maybe so, but—"

"I'm proud of you, Dillon." She rested her hand on my knee. "You probably only went there to shut me up, but I'm glad that you got to meet Leotie, and you listened to what she had to say."

"I didn't go just to shut you up. I went because I believed what you said—that you love me and want the best for me." Her hand remained on my knee. "I didn't hear a lot of that growing up."

"Does this mean you forgive me?"

I'd resigned myself to the fact that I would never see my mama again. I'd thought I would take my anger and resentment to the grave. It never occurred to me that she might come back.

Our eyes met. "I reckon it does."

My phone vibrated. A text from Nicole.

We need to talk. I'm home. Please come over when you get a chance.

"Who was that?" Mama asked as I returned the phone to my pocket.

"Nicole." I rolled my eyes. "She wants to talk."

Mama shot me a curious glance. "Then why didn't she just call?"

I smiled and kissed her forehead. After a few seconds of silence, I stood to leave.

"Are you going to see her?"

"I haven't decided yet."

The screen door slapped against the wood frame, ending our conversation.

An hour later, I parked the Mustang in front of Nicole's house. I reached for the door handle, then stopped when I remembered I hadn't told Nicole about the bugs. Someone might be listening. She probably hadn't tipped off Josh the night of my arrest, so I didn't see any reason not to tell her.

Nicole opened her door after the first knock.

"You look surprised to see me," I said.

"A little. I thought… I thought I might never see…" She closed her eyes and shook her head. "I'm sorry. Come in."

I let her stay in this place for over a week, unaware that her every word had been monitored. I followed her into the living room where she sat on the sofa. I stood in front of her and extended my hand.

"Dillon, what's going on?"

My gesture became more insistent.

"Where are we going?"

"Your bedroom."

Her expression softened. She took my hand, and I pulled her up.

As we walked down the hall, I hoped to God that Josh had been listening.

I sat her down on the bed. I felt bad that I'd led her on this way, but we couldn't have this conversation in her living room.

"Someone bugged your house."

"What?"

"There's one in your living room and another in the kitchen. That's why we're in here."

A wave of disappointment splashed across her face, followed quickly by concern. "How do you know that?"

"They bugged my place, too."

"Who?"

"I'm not sure, but my guess is Josh, or maybe Harley. I'm pretty sure Josh destroyed a suicide note from Amanda. He's framing me to keep us apart."

"Can you keep him from getting away with it?"

"What… framing me, or keeping us apart?"

The flicker of a smile flashed across her lips before a quick recovery. "Both."

Time to change the subject. I paced in a tight pattern alongside the bed. "What did you want to talk to me about?"

"What do you mean?" Her eyes squinted her confusion.

"Your text. You said we needed to talk."

"I didn't text you."

I stopped, pulled my phone from my pocket, and shoved it in her face. "Really? What's this?"

She looked at the phone, then back to me. "I didn't send that."

"Well, it says here you did."

She stood and moved toward the door. "I'll show you."

She returned with her purse and dumped it on the bed. I watched her paw through the contents, slowly at first, her movements quickening as the seconds passed. Finally, she turned to me.

"My phone. It's not here."

"Where else could it be?"

"Nowhere," she said, her voice tight. She continued to push things around on the bed like she might have missed it. "It's always in my purse."

She straightened up, and we stood in silence. I glanced at the sliding glass door that led to a small outdoor balcony. A large owl stared at me from the railing.

My foot tingled. In my mind, I'd just heard a *click* under my boot.

CHAPTER 42

"We need to get outta here."

"What?"

"Quick. Follow me." I took a step toward the door.

"Dillon, wait." She collected the contents of her purse.

I grabbed her arm. "Now!"

The screen flew off the rails and landed on the deck as I ran through the back door, dragging Nicole behind me. She tripped and fell onto her knees.

"Are you insane?" she shouted.

I turned, bent down, and threw her over my shoulder. She made a fuss and pounded my back until I set her down fifty yards from the house. She pushed hard on my chest with both hands.

"What the hell do you think you're—"

She didn't have time to finish her sentence before the shock wave knocked us both to the ground. The big orange fireball that rolled slowly into the sky above her house reminded me of the night we lost the Road Runner. A cloud of black smoke pushed it higher until it dissolved into a thick haze.

Nicole watched with one hand over her mouth. Neither of us spoke until we gained our feet.

"You're welcome," I said.

Her eyes held equal parts of shock and terror. "Someone just tried to kill us."

"Someone?" I knew who was behind this attack. "I hate to have to break it to you like this, but your ex-fiance just tried to kill me, and apparently, he doesn't care if you're collateral damage."

Nicole glared. "Josh wouldn't do that." Her expression softened as she watched the flames consume what the blast had left of her house. "Would he?"

I nodded without words.

"Dillon, I'm sorry."

"Don't be. This is my fault, and I'm going to fix it."

We stared silently at the wreckage. If Josh had been listening to our conversation inside, he had to assume that he'd just blown us to bits while we were doing it in Nicole's bedroom. Talk about *coitus interruptus*. I laughed.

Nicole glared at me like I'd just farted in church. "It's not funny."

My serious face returned. "I know."

She shook her head slowly. "I should have left town like Bobby."

I put my hand on her shoulder. "You had Annabelle to think about."

"Oh my God! Annabelle. I have to let her know I'm okay."

"I'm sorry, Nicole, but I can't let you do that. No one can know we survived the blast."

"For how long?"

"Let's just take it one step at a time." I turned away to survey the rubble.

"Dillon. You're bleeding."

I took a quick visual inventory. "Where?"

"The back of your left arm."

I turned my arm around as far as I could. My shirt sleeve had become saturated. "How bad is it?"

"It's not good, but I can't tell for sure without taking a closer look."

Sirens wailed. "Right now, we need to get out of here."

"Where are we going?"

"We'll figure that out on the way."

As we walked, I turned for one last look. This wasn't over. Not by a long shot. The next time we did battle, it would be on my terms, not his.

Nicole and I wouldn't get far on foot. I'd parked the Silverado at Pop's house, but it was too risky to show up there. Besides, we needed to drive something that would make us invisible. We took the back way to Coop's garage and stopped near the charred remains of the building that once housed a 1970 Road Runner with blood spatter behind the headlight. I called the landline in his office, and he told me to come on up. I told him he needed to come down and to bring a shirt and some bandages.

We waited behind a bulldozer that belonged to the contractor Coop hired to clear the rubble. Coop arrived a few minutes later and rolled his eyes when he saw my female companion. He nodded in Nicole's direction, then turned to me and folded his arms across his chest.

"What's wrong with this picture?"

"Don't start."

He handed me a first-aid kit and a clean t-shirt.

"Did you hear the explosion?" I asked.

"No. What explosion?"

"The one that leveled my house and nearly killed us," Nicole said.

Coop's eyes never left mine. "What's she talking about?"

"Someone lured me over there, then *BOOM!*"

"How did you get out alive?" Coop asked.

"Apparently, I have friends in high places." *Like trees.* "No one knows we're alive. Well, except you. I'd like to keep it that way."

Coop fell silent as his eyes drifted to my bloody sleeve. I suspected images of Jolene and the girls had hijacked his attention.

"I need to get a message to Annabelle."

I turned to Nicole. "I told you we can't do that yet."

Coop returned to the conversation with fearful eyes. "You think Josh did this?"

I put my hand on his shoulder. "Coop, I'm the one he wants to hurt. I'm going to keep you out of this."

"Really? Somehow, I don't see how showing up here accomplishes that."

"I need a vehicle. Then we're gone."

Coop closed his eyes and squeezed the bridge of his nose. A few seconds passed. "There's an old Grand Cherokee on the lot," he said with some resignation. "I'll go put plates on it and bring it around."

"Thanks, buddy." I slapped his back. "I owe you one."

"One?"

I shrugged, and Coop headed back toward his office. Nicole helped me remove my shirt and noticed glass in my arm. I told her I'd let her clean it out when we reached our destination. She wrapped it in gauze from the first-aid kit, and I gingerly pulled the t-shirt over my head.

Coop returned five minutes later with a green '95 Jeep in better shape than I'd expected.

"Anything I should know about it?" I asked when he held the keys up in front of me.

"It's got new tires and a full tank of gas. It's a 4x4 in case you can't keep it on the road."

I reached for the keys.

He pulled them back. "One more thing. Try not to destroy it."

"It's insured, isn't it?"

"That's not the point."

I took the keys.

"Where you headed?"

I climbed in and closed the door. I looked at Nicole in the passenger seat, then back to Coop. "Pop's cabin," I said through the open window, "until I figure out what to do."

I only drove a few feet before I stopped. Coop caught up with us and leaned in the window.

"Forget something?"

"You got fifty bucks I can borrow?"

"Your killin' me, Bish," he said as he reached for his wallet. He held out the money. "You better live long enough to pay me back."

"Roger that."

"Call me when you get there."

"Did you ever get your phone back?"

He shook his head. "Had to buy a new one. Same number."

"I'll mention it to Josh the next time I see him."

"You better get going."

He didn't have to tell me twice.

We had a quiet and uneventful drive to Lake Whitney. I think we were both still in shock. I parked the Jeep in the driveway and wondered if Nicole had given any thought to the sleeping arrangements. A part of me hoped she wouldn't try to cash in her rain check.

Inside, Nicole removed the glass from my arm with a steak knife. We used a bottle of Pop's whiskey to sterilize it after I had a couple of quick shots. She said the cut needed stitches, but I found some super glue that would do the trick for now. She used the rest of the gauze to wrap it.

After dinner, I went out to the dock and called Jenn. Hearing her voice again centered me. It allowed me to remember what was at stake. I told her everything that had happened and assured her I was safe. I felt the need to be totally up-front, so I clarified where I was, and who I was with. I sensed her concern.

The call ended on a pleasant note. I promised to check in with her every day and looked forward to the time when we would be together again. I slipped the phone back into my pocket and turned to find Nicole walking down the dock toward me with two bottles of beer.

I didn't think alcohol was a good idea, but after a day like we'd had, I needed one… or maybe a couple. Besides, I'd left my tea in Bradley. Alcohol was a poor substitute, but it was all I had at the moment.

"How's the arm?" she asked as she handed me a bottle and sat beside me on the edge of the dock.

"Better. Thanks."

She smiled. "Guess if you're on the lam, it doesn't hurt to have a nurse along."

I tilted my bottle and tapped it against hers.

Nicole asked how Jenn and I had met. I watched the fireflies while I decided where to start. I told her as much as I felt comfortable talking about, which was most of it. She offered up similar information about her past.

Nicole went inside to get more beer. My thoughts turned to Mama and how worried she must be. I wondered how different things would have been if she hadn't left us. A dozen possible scenarios swirled around my head and eventually collided with each other. I realized it was an exercise in futility. I heard a small voice say, *Don't stumble over something behind you. It's not the direction you should be headed.*

Nicole returned, and we drank our last beer as we stared into the heavens. A billion stars looked down on us, and I had a feeling that we'd both silently realized that our names were not written there.

CHAPTER 43

I awoke early the next morning. Nicole's door was closed, so I made coffee and brought a cup with me to the dock. The water reflected the morning sun's brilliance like a sheet of blue glass. I felt an energy in the stillness that I couldn't explain. I set my cup down and sat motionless, feeling like an integral part of the beauty and serenity that surrounded me. I lost track of where my body ended and the landscape began. In that moment, I understood what Leotie had meant when she spoke of *being one with nature.*

The feeling didn't last long. My thoughts reached into this new space and dragged me back into the real world. How long before Josh realized we were alive? Who else knew about this cabin? How long would we be safe here?

I picked up my coffee and took a sip. Two hawks drew lazy circles in the sky above me. I told myself I was not a fugitive, but simply the victim of an attack. Unfortunately, the public servants who'd taken an oath to protect me were most likely the ones who had tried to kill me.

I pulled out my phone and dialed.

"Dillon. Thank God you're alive!"

"Mama, please tell me you're not in the house."

After a few seconds of silence, Mama responded. "I'm sorry. I'm on the porch now."

I had to assume that we'd just blown our cover. "I think we're safe for the moment."

"Is Nicole with you?"

"Yes."

"Chief Wilkerson was here," she said, her voice brittle. "He told me there'd been an accident, an explosion at Nicole's house. He thinks you're both dead."

"The explosion was no accident."

"What do you plan to do?"

"I wanted them to think we died, at least until they couldn't find any bodies."

"I'm sorry, Dillon."

"It's okay."

"Mort called to say that they moved the trial up a week to the twenty-fifth. He wants to meet with you tomorrow."

"That's not gonna happen. For now, don't tell anyone that you talked to me, including Mort."

"I won't."

"Does Harley know about Pop's cabin?"

"Not to my knowledge. I doubt that Eli had any reason to mention it. They weren't on very good terms."

"I think we'll hide out here for a while."

"Dillon… please be careful." Her voice echoed her fear.

"Don't worry, Mama. I'm working on a plan to put an end to this shit storm. I'll need your help, but first I have to verify something."

"I'll help any way I can."

"I know."

I'd spent the past ten years demanding that someone pay for what happened to Luke and that I'd have a front-row seat to watch them burn. But lately, the thirst for revenge gave way to a need for justice. I realized that I no longer required an eye for an eye—I needed the truth. I hoped Jenn would still be waiting for me when I found it.

I waited a few minutes, then dialed another number.

"Hey, Bill. It's Dillon."

"Dillon. I thought you were dead."

I detected a genuine element of surprise in his voice, but not much relief. "Did you?"

"I went over to the house to sniff around. Your car, what's left of it, was parked out front."

Losing my car pissed me off, but I had more important things to think about. "If I needed to wear a wire to collect evidence," I asked, "could you help me with that?"

"Sure, but who—"

"I'll tell you later." I ended the call.

Bill hadn't been the one listening to our conversations at the house, but I continued to suspect he knew more about what's been going on in Bradley than he'd let on.

"Morning," Nicole said as she sat beside me.

"How'd you sleep?" I asked.

She shrugged. "Could have been better."

I felt the same, but probably for different reasons.

"Who were you talking to?"

I held the phone out between us. "You can call Annabelle."

Her eyes flashed with surprise and a good measure of relief. "What about—?"

"I think they know we're alive. Just don't tell anyone where we are."

"I won't. Thank you, Dillon." She took the phone and walked toward the cabin.

I called over my shoulder. "The battery is low, so make it quick."

Nicole returned a few minutes later with my phone. When she headed back toward the cabin, I called Coop. I hesitated to involve him because of Josh's threats, but I needed a few things. One of them was Jimmy Arroyo.

I gave him a short list of the things I needed, which included a cell phone charger, a change of clothes, more first-aid supplies, and my tea. "Bring Jimmy when you come. Tell him it's a matter of life and death." I paused. "And make sure you're not followed."

"Did you forget who you're talking to? I can spot a tail."

A truck I'd never seen before pulled in around noon. Jimmy smiled through the driver's window as Coop stepped out of the passenger side. He slipped a backpack over one shoulder and grinned as he held up two paper sacks. "I brought lunch."

"Tell Jo I said thanks."

The expression slid off his face. "How do you know I didn't make lunch?"

"You don't really need me to answer that, do you?"

After a quick tour, we went out on the deck where Nicole had set out the food. I told Coop and Jimmy my suspicions about Josh, and I outlined a tentative plan to set a trap to snare him. We discussed various options and hammered out the strategy that we felt had the greatest probability of success.

We'd use the bugs at Pop's house to trick Josh into thinking that Nicole had died and that I'd set up a meeting with Bobby at the cabin to plan a retaliatory strike. What he didn't know, was that I'd be waiting for him and wearing a wire. Nicole would hide upstairs in case I needed her. Bill would record everything from outside and, when we had what we needed, charge in and make the arrest.

"Before we do anything else," Coop said, "give Jimmy your phone."

I handed it to him and watched him navigate through the options menu. He tapped the screen a few times and handed it back.

"I disabled the GPS."

"Jimmy used it to locate your phone," Coop said.

I looked at Jimmy. "You can do that?"

"Let's hope no one else has tried."

Coop put his hand on Jimmy's shoulder. "Jimmy here is as good at electronics as you are at kicking ass."

Jimmy grinned. "Coop told me you put on a show at Shady's the other night. Something about a Teenage Mutant Ninja Texan?"

"Everything except the teenage part, I guess."

"All right, let's talk about what equipment you'll need to pull off this little sting."

I told him that Bill had agreed to provide the wire, but I wanted to have my own audio and video surveillance inside the cabin. Bill's an unknown in this equation, a wild card, so I wanted backup.

Coop chewed his thumbnail like a dog with a piece of rawhide.

"Something bothering you, Coop?"

He hesitated for a second. "I don't like the fact that Bill is the cavalry. I think he might be a problem."

"You know something I don't?"

"After you told me about that land contract, I went out there to take a look. I spent the afternoon walking from one end of that goddamn property to the other. I found big tire tracks and neat little holes, like somebody had been drilling core samples."

"I can take care of Bill. If he had anything to do with Pop's death, and I suspect he did, then I want him here."

Nicole spoke for the first time since lunch. "Maybe this is too dangerous to do alone."

"I won't be alone." I turned to Nicole. "You'll be there."

"C'mon, Bish," Coop said. "She's got a point. Maybe I should—"

"I said I can handle Bill." I took a deep breath, then turned to Nicole. "You ever fire a pistol?"

"Of course," she said with a little indignation.

I looked at Coop and nodded my head in Nicole's direction. "There's my backup."

"Now I see it. You two deserve each other." Coop shook his head. "If you end up like Bonnie and Clyde, I swear I'll have *I told you so* written on your headstone."

"If that's how this plays out, I won't give a flyin'—"

"Stop it," Jimmy yelled. "What the hell's wrong with you two?"

"I'm sorry," I said to Coop. He looked away.

Jimmy promised to return with the equipment by noon on Sunday and install everything, but he needed to be home as soon as possible to prepare for an early flight to Washington in the morning.

CHAPTER 44

What started as a smattering of rain turned into the worst storm I'd seen in a decade. It began just after dark, which allowed it to roll in across the lake undetected. Lightning flashed, followed by thunder that rattled everything that wasn't nailed down. I counted the seconds between the two. The fury intensified as the interval decreased.

The lights dimmed and flickered just before the power went out. We sat in the dark on the sofa. Nicole lifted my good arm and slid underneath. She looked up at me for a moment. Lightning flashes illuminated the fear that clouded her pretty green eyes.

Wood splintered outside and rain pelted the windows like machine gun fire, driven sideways by the howling wind. Powerful gusts attempted to separate the cabin from its foundation. The walls moaned under the pressure. Nicole buried her head deeper in my chest.

I closed my eyes. *Luke, if you're really watching over me, help us make it through the night.* It didn't seem possible that my journey would end here, with Nicole of all people. What would be the point? I needed to finish what I'd started. I needed justice for my family. Ironically, I didn't want to leave Mama alone in the world.

I'm not sure how or when it happened, but I eventually fell asleep. Sunlight opened my eyes, and I found myself on the sofa with Nicole resting silently in my arms. I thanked my little brother for having my back. Nicole straightened as I stretched my arms. She rubbed her eyes and ran her fingers through her hair.

She stared into my eyes. "Thank you."

I nodded.

Outside, the lake looked peaceful under a clear blue sky. However, the rest of the landscape had been painted with a different brush. Last night's storm had marched through East Texas like Sherman had marched through Georgia.

The Jeep, covered in debris, had sustained only minor damage—the outbuilding hadn't been so lucky. The padlock held tight when I gave it a good pull, but the building needed a new roof.

I walked to the end of the driveway, stopping every few feet to drag fallen branches out of the way. I panicked when I reached the road. Three large trees had fallen across the hundred yards of road that I could see. There could be dozens more between here and the main road. It would most likely be days before they were cleared. I considered my options as I walked back to the cabin.

I'd set my plan in motion yesterday when I called Mama after Coop and Jimmy left. I couldn't wait around until Josh found me and had time to plan an attack. My story would inevitably be played out on this little piece of land, and I needed to control the narrative. Whatever happened here had to go down on my terms.

I'd explained my plan to Mama on the phone. She moved inside where her end of our staged conversation could be overheard. The eavesdropper would learn that we indeed escaped the blast and traveled to Pop's cabin on Lake Whitney. After Nicole died of injuries she sustained in the explosion, I'd contacted Bobby Perez and told him how Josh had killed her. Bobby agreed to meet me at the cabin at noon on Monday to discuss a plan to exact our revenge.

What he didn't hear, was that Bill would drive down Sunday night and test the wire. On Monday morning, he would set up surveillance on Josh and call me when he left town. He would follow Josh to the cabin and establish a post outside. I would know exactly when and where Josh attempted to overtake our position.

Nicole met me at the cabin door. "The power's out." She chewed her bottom lip and her eyes darted back and forth as they searched mine.

Strike two. I had to stay cool. "That happens a lot out here. It'll be back on in a couple of hours." I lied. "We're still good."

I fired up the gas grill and put on a pot of water for coffee. When it boiled, I had Nicole pour it through the coffee maker while I grilled some bacon and eggs. I hadn't mentioned anything to Nicole yet, but we'd need plenty of energy if we had any chance of clearing the road before Coop and Jimmy got there.

After we ate, I called Coop. He said Jimmy had collected everything we needed and was on his way down from Arlington to pick him up. He put their ETA at the cabin around noon. I ended the call and checked the time. 0900 hours. We needed to move.

Pop had two chainsaws in the basement next to a gallon container marked oil-gasoline mixture. I grabbed them, a couple pairs of gloves, and a quart of bar and chain oil. I put everything in the back of the jeep, then grabbed a hank of rope and a tow chain.

Nicole climbed into the passenger seat. "Where are we going?"

"Not far. Coop and Jimmy will never make it in if we don't clear the road."

I backed out of the driveway and drove up the road about three hundred feet before I had to stop.

I turned the engine off and looked at Nicole. "We're here."

"You've got to be kidding. How are we—"

"Same way you eat an elephant." I tossed a pair of gloves in her lap. "One bite at a time."

I grabbed the larger of the two saws from the back and set it on the three-foot diameter tree trunk that dissected the road. The little two-cycle engine sputtered on the first three pulls. Nicole watched me prime it again and pull three more times. This went on for two minutes that seemed like twenty. If I didn't get the damn thing started soon, we wouldn't make it.

I unscrewed the gas cap, turned the saw upside down, and shook out all the fuel. I refilled the tank and tried again. This time it coughed. I resisted the urge to throw it down and grab the other saw. I held it against the tree with my foot and gave it a Chuck Norris pull. The tired little engine roared to life. I revved it a few times before I touched the spinning chain to bark.

As I neared the bottom of the trunk five minutes later, I called Nicole over and instructed her to turn the truck around and attach the chain to the trailer hitch. I'd cut the trunk closer to one side of the road, hoping to pull the larger piece around—like opening a door—and drive the Jeep through.

As I watched the Jeep strain and the tires slip, I realized that I'd underestimated the weight of the wood. Five minutes later, I'd finished another cut. Nicole turned the Jeep around and pushed the smaller piece out of the way with the front bumper.

I climbed in and we drove another five hundred feet before we had to stop. This trunk was smaller, maybe eighteen inches across. I secured the chain, sliced through it quickly, and Nicole pulled it out of the way. I felt a little better about our chances.

We moved seventeen trees and made it to the main road by 1130. I needed a shower and a nap. We drove back to the cabin and cleaned up just before Coop and Jimmy pulled in.

Coop jumped from the truck before it stopped.

"I've been trying to call for the last hour. Where the hell have you been?"

"What's the matter?"

"We've got a problem."

CHAPTER 45

I held up my hands as he approached. "Relax, Coop. Whatever it is, we'll fix it." I'm not sure who I tried to convince, him or me.

"Bobby's in the hospital." He folded his arms across his chest. "How you gonna fix that?"

I took a deep breath, hoping Coop would do the same. "What happened?"

"They found him outside the campus pub, unconscious. Someone beat the crap out of him."

"Is he gonna be all right?"

"Yeah. He's got a couple broken ribs, and I guess he looks like hell, but he's gonna be okay."

"And you think Josh did this?"

"Don't you?"

Unfortunately, I did. More collateral damage. My hands tightened into fists. "This is because of me—Bobby, Amanda, Nicole's house. I'm gonna have to put a stop to this once and for all."

Coop squeezed the back of his neck, no doubt worried about his family.

"We have to assume that Josh knows Bobby won't be here tomorrow," I said.

"You think he'll still come?"

"I'm the one he wants. I just used Bobby to sweeten the pot."

"And now he's in the hospital."

"I'm aware, Coop. Don't rub it in."

"Sorry. I didn't mean it like that."

I turned and walked toward the door. "C'mon. We've got work to do."

Nicole had been listening from the deck. She chewed her bottom lip as she held the door.

I stared out the window at the lake while Jimmy unpacked his equipment. "The way I see it," I said, thinking out loud, "our biggest challenge now is that we lost our advantage. Josh had a reason to be here at a certain time. For all we know, he could be on his way over here right now."

"Shit." Coop joined me at the window. "That would suck. Bill's not here with the wire… and his Hulk-like, Ranger self."

His words hung in the air for a moment.

"I think I speak for everyone in the room," he continued, "when I say I don't want to get shot."

"Coop. I won't let Josh shoot you. You have my word."

Jimmy placed a tiny, motion-activated camera on the fireplace mantle that would provide video coverage for the door and most of the room. He attached a microphone to a lamp shade in a more central location. Both devices transmitted wirelessly to a recorder hidden in my old bookcase in Pop's bedroom.

"That should do it for inside," Jimmy said.

"Inside? There's more?"

He grinned. "I brought a motion detector that I can install on the deck. It'll chime whenever anyone gets within twenty feet of the front door. I thought it might help."

"Absolutely. Let's do it."

Jimmy installed and tested the device. The handheld receiver gave a squeal as he approached the deck. He turned it down enough so an intruder wouldn't be able to hear it from outside. He suggested I keep it by my bed at night.

Jimmy closed his case. I put my arms around my two amigos and walked them to the door.

"When this is over, you're all invited out to the ranch for a barbecue."

As soon as I said it, I remembered Nicole was still in the room. I turned to her, and our eyes met. "Uh... you—"

"It's okay, Dillon. I don't think your friend Jenny Lee would approve, anyway."

Our eyes lingered for a moment, and I felt my chest tighten. I walked the boys to Jimmy's truck and stood on the passenger side. Coop climbed in and lowered the window.

"Be careful driving back," I said. "We had a helluva storm here last night."

"They cleared the road pretty quickly," Coop said. "There must have been twenty trees down between here and the main road."

"Seventeen." I smiled.

Coop scratched the side of his head as he stared.

"I need a big favor, Coop."

"This is gettin' to be a habit with you." He chuckled.

"I'm serious. Can you check in on Mama when you get back? Make sure she's okay and tell her I'll be home in a couple of days."

"Sure thing." More head scratching. "Why do I have the feeling there's more?"

"For this to work, I need to know when Josh is coming... way before he sets off the motion detector. I need to make sure Bill is here and set up, so he won't be able to keep an eye on Josh back in Bradley and let us know when he leaves. I'm sure he won't try anything at night. He doesn't know his way around."

Coop bent his arm and rested it on the door. "I got it. After I check on Mama, I'll find Josh and keep him under surveillance until dark, then pick him up again at first light."

"Thanks, man."

"I can't keep this up for long. Some of us have jobs."

"Roger that." I nodded. "He'll make his move tomorrow."

"I wish you didn't have to do this."

"Hopefully, your wife will still talk to me when it's done."

"Don't worry about Jo." He slapped my arm with the back of his hand. "You've got enough on your plate."

I leaned over and looked into the cab. "Thanks. You guys are the best."

I tapped the top of the truck a couple of times and Jimmy backed out of the driveway. I watched them drive away, thankful that I still had friends I could count on. We all had a lot riding on this, and I had no intention of letting any of them down.

Back inside, emotions were strained, and an awkward silence hung in the air.

I waited until it became uncomfortable. "I'm sorry."

"You're sorry? You have nothing to be sorry for. I had you a long time ago, and I let you go. No, I chased you away. I burned it all down, and I have no one to blame but myself."

For years, I'd thought the same thing. I guess Jenn taught me that we don't always know what we want, or even what's best for us. It's only when we let go of those old feelings that we make room for bigger and better things.

"Don't you think you're a little too hard on yourself?" I asked.

"There you go again. Why aren't you mad? Why don't you want to punch me in the face?"

"You think I should punish you, is that it?"

"Maybe." She pulled in a ragged breath and struggled to hold back tears. "Maybe then I'd know that I meant something to you."

"Don't you realize you meant everything to me? That's one reason I left."

Her eyes overflowed and tears rolled down both cheeks. She made no attempt to stop them.

Silence descended again, but not as awkwardly. All the malicious feelings I'd ever had toward her were buried in the past. I felt only a connection to an old friend. She'd been a painful, but important, part of my journey. Pain is our greatest teacher. Mama told me that.

"When you returned to Bradley," she said in a small voice, "I thought maybe we could rebuild something from the pile of ashes I'd left ten years ago."

"There will be bigger and better things for you to build. I'm sure of it."

"You'll always be the best man I've ever met."

"Are you sure you haven't been drinking?"

Her lips twitched in a weak smile. "No, but I could sure use one."

I pulled two beers from the fridge, handed her one, then sat next to her on the couch. She held her bottle up, and I tapped it with mine. No words were spoken. This time, the silence felt comfortable.

CHAPTER 46

Coop called two hours later with an update. Mama was fine, but she didn't like our plan. Said it was too risky. She threatened to drive down here with Pop's shotgun, so he took her with him. They'd followed Josh to the racetrack and kept an eye on his car in the parking lot. He said he'd call again when Josh was in for the night.

Bill arrived shortly after I'd hung up with Coop, all smiles and handshakes as he puffed on a big cigar. He said he hadn't been to the cabin in years, but he had no shortage of stories about the good old days with Pop and Mort.

He offered to spend the night when I told him about Bobby and how we'd had to change our plans. I thought it would be better if he stayed in nearby Whitney. I promised to call him as soon as I heard from Coop that Josh was on his way. In the meantime, he showed me how to attach the wire, and we tested the communications. He also gave me a tiny receiver for my ear so the comm could go both ways.

Nicole had made herself scarce after Bill arrived. When he left, she was quick to explain. "If he stayed, I'd have left."

"What are you talking about?"

"He gives me the creeps."

"Bill's full of himself, but he seems pretty harmless to me."

"Did you see the way he looked at me? I had to leave the room. I feel like I need a shower."

"I imagine a lot of men look at you that way." I smiled.

"He was... leering."

"Hopefully, this will all be over after tomorrow, and you'll never have to see him again. Until then, we need to focus."

"Promise me you'll kick his fat ass if he tries anything."

"If he ever touches you, I'll whip him like a redheaded stepchild."

Despite the tension, Nicole laughed.

The rest of the evening passed uneventfully. Coop called a little after nine to say that Josh had gone home, presumably for the night. I asked him to stay for a while to make sure Josh didn't leave. I needed to get a good night's sleep, which would be easier if I knew Josh was at home in Bradley.

If Josh was smart, he'd wait a few days. Turn up the pressure. He had the advantage. Uncertainty had already taken a toll here, and it would clearly grow as the days wore on.

I made a cup of tea, took a deep breath, and dialed Jenn's number. She sensed my apprehension immediately, and I second-guessed making the call, but I needed to hear her voice. I'd never been able to keep things from her, so before long, I explained the details of our plan.

Jenn offered to drive down that night, but I said no. I could use someone with her skills, but putting her in that position would be unforgivable. Besides, her presence here would create a vulnerability that Josh could exploit.

"Don't need another *distraction*, is that it?"

"That's not fair. I said I was sorry."

"I know." Her voice softened. "I'm scared, Dillon. I want you here with me, not doing battle with some crooked cop hundreds of miles away."

"This will all be over soon, and we'll be together. I promise."

"How am I supposed to sleep tonight?"

I wondered the same thing about myself as I took another sip of Leotie's tea.

"Call me in the morning?"

I hesitated. I wouldn't be able to make that call if Josh were here in the morning. I'm sure he wanted to finish this as quickly as I did.

"Dillon?"

"What?"

"Do you love me?"

"Like I've never loved anyone before."

"Good answer." She sighed. "I love you, too. Be safe."

Hanging up was harder than I thought it would be.

I hadn't heard from Coop again. I assumed no news was good news and went to bed.

Sleep did not come easy. When I was young, Christmas Eve had always been the most difficult night of the year to fall asleep. Christmas Day held the promise of presents under the tree. What did tomorrow hold? A face full of lead?

I shook my head to clear it. Negative thoughts were not something you wanted marching through your head on the eve of battle. I closed my eyes and saw Leotie's face through the smoke that rose from the bowl in her hand. She waved an eagle feather above the bowl, and I inhaled the sweet smell of burning sage.

I had an advantage over Josh. Besides the fact that he'd never been the sharpest tool in the shed, I was bigger, stronger, and a better shot. He had no training, and he was arrogant enough to come alone, so we'd have him outnumbered. We also had home field advantage. The more I thought about it, the more it sounded like a suicide mission for the poor bastard.

Still, I knew a hundred things could go wrong.

The perimeter alarm sounded, and I bolted upright in bed. I grabbed Pop's Glock 9mm from the nightstand and hurried downstairs. At the window, I moved the edge of the curtain two inches with the gun barrel and looked out onto an empty deck. Nothing in the driveway except the Jeep. I pushed the curtain back another inch and scanned my entire field of vision. I detected movement near the tree line.

I squinted for a better look and spotted a pair of green eyes glowing in the moonlight. They appeared to belong to a large animal—a coyote, or maybe even a wolf. Whatever it was, stared intently at the house like it knew what was about to happen. Like it knew *me*. There must have been a little cannabis in Leotie's tea because I felt a strange connection with this animal.

Movement behind me brought me back. I held the Glock out in front of me as I turned.

"Dillon?" Nicole whispered from the top of the stairs.

I lowered my gun and turned on the light. I surveyed the room from my vantage point at the front door, a picture of what Josh would see when he first entered the cabin. My eyes came to an abrupt halt at the fireplace. My stomach twisted. In the mirror above the mantle, I could see the entire room, including Nicole on the stairs.

Without a word, I walked to the fireplace and removed the mirror from the wall.

"What are you doing?"

"Redecorating." I scanned the room for any more strategic disadvantages, well aware that I wouldn't have known about the mirror problem if that wolf hadn't shown up at my door in the middle of the night.

"Why are you doing it now?"

"You wouldn't believe me if I told you." I looked up at her. "Go back to bed, Nicole."

CHAPTER 47

I received the call from Coop at 0830 the next morning. Josh had just turned south on 174, driving alone in a patrol car.

"Where's Mama?"

"Right here. She stayed with us last night."

"Thanks, Coop. I'll take it from here."

I called Bill and told him that Josh had just left Bradley—ETA: 0930. I glanced around the living room to make sure I hadn't missed anything.

Nicole watched from the bottom of the stairs as I attached the wire and buttoned my shirt. "What am I supposed to do?"

"Stay out of sight. You're strictly backup." I handed her the Glock and showed her how to release the safety. I tucked the heavier Beretta M9 in my belt behind my back. "He thinks you're dead."

"How will I know if you need help?"

"I want you to listen from the upstairs hall. If I say *I could really use a drink*, you come down the stairs halfway, holding the gun in front of you like this." I pulled the Beretta from my belt to demonstrate.

She followed my lead.

"Don't forget to remove the safety."

She lowered the gun. "Dillon, I don't think I could shoot Josh."

"You'd be surprised what you can do when your life is on the line."

"Josh wouldn't shoot me."

"Really? Then maybe he'll just blow the place up, and he won't need to shoot you."

She sat and placed the gun on the bottom step beside her.

"If this goes south," I said, "I'm going to need you." *Please don't let me down... again.*

Nicole nodded less than reassuringly.

I paced around the room, thinking about something I'd said to Nicole. Josh had already attempted to take us out once with a big bang. What if he tried it again? I didn't know what kind of arsenal he had at his disposal, but something like an RPG through the front window could end this dance before it even started.

I took a deep breath and remembered what Leotie had said about how Luke watched over me. I had a feeling that he'd had something to do with the mirror incident the night before.

At 0920, I inserted the earpiece for a comm check. "Bill? Are you there?"

Static crackled in my ear. "You're coming in loud and clear," Bill said. "I'm in position with an unobstructed view."

"Copy that."

Seven minutes later, Bill's voice filled my ear. "I've got a visual. Target is approaching on foot with his sidearm drawn. No other visible weapons."

The perimeter alarm sounded, and I took my position behind the door.

"He's on the deck."

"I'm ready."

The next five seconds felt like an eternity. I watched the knob turn and heard the click as the bolt cleared the strike plate. The door opened slowly into the room.

My mind slipped back to a little village north of Kandahar. I had waited alone by the door, the sole survivor of a bloodbath. *The intruder appeared to be alone. I glanced outside for the rest of his unit. There had been more—plenty more. They shot the building up good. Probably figured there were no survivors and sent someone in to make sure.*

He wore a strange uniform. He wasn't Taliban. Who was he? I had no time to think. He turned toward me. I kicked the pistol from his hand and tackled him. We hit the floor hard with me on top. He struggled, but I grabbed him by the neck with both hands and squeezed. I pinned his arms under my knees, then straightened up to get a better angle. I applied more pressure, and his eyes bulged in their sockets.

"Dillon. Stop!"

A woman's voice. Something wasn't right. I squeezed my eyes shut for a second. When I opened them again, Josh lay on the floor beneath me, my hands wrapped around his throat. I pulled my gun from my belt and pointed it at his head, then quickly gained my feet.

Josh pulled himself up to a sitting position and rubbed his neck. "Nicole?"

"Surprise," she said from somewhere behind me.

"I thought you were—"

I pulled him to his feet. "You thought wrong." I dragged him to the chair in the middle of the room and pushed him down on it.

He continued to stare at Nicole.

"Look at me," I shouted. "I want the truth about Amanda's death."

He turned. "How did you know about the suicide note?"

"I'll ask the questions."

I took a moment to clear my head. Another flashback. The first in over a month, and it had to happen today?

The sound of splintering wood broke the uneasy silence as the door swung open and crashed against the wall. Harley Wilkerson, dressed in street clothes and holding a shotgun, stepped inside.

CHAPTER 48

Harley leveled his weapon at Nicole. I turned and held the pistol in front of me with both hands. I glanced at Josh to make sure he wasn't stupid enough to make a move.

"You best set that piece down, boy," Harley said, "or I'll blow that pretty little head clean offa your girlfriend over there."

I glared over the top of the gun that I held pointed at his head, then relaxed my arms and slowly set the gun on the floor.

"Step back, war hero," he said with a sneer.

I moved closer to Nicole.

Harley turned the rifle on me, then looked at Josh. "Go on, boy. Pick up his gun." He snorted. "And you might as well get yours while you're at it."

Josh picked up the guns and pointed his in my direction.

"You'd think after almost thirty years, I'd have learned that you can't send a boy to do a man's job." Harley shook his head. "What were you waitin' for, boy?" He continued. "Your daddy to show up and hold your hand?"

"Shut up!" Josh turned the gun on Harley.

"What you gonna do? Shoot me? Hell, you couldn't shoot these two, an' they ain't even kin."

"I'm done listening to your bullshit."

This showdown had taken an unexpected turn, one that I might be able to use to my advantage.

"Well, look at this." Harley chuckled. "Little Joshie grew himself a pair. Does that mean you're a man now?"

Years of pain and frustration bubbled up in Josh's eyes as the two stood at gunpoint. If this is how Josh grew up, it might explain why he'd always been such an asshole.

Josh turned his gun back to us.

"Don't be such a pussy next time," Harley mumbled.

I watched Josh, waiting for him to snap and shut his old man up for good. No such luck.

"Now go over there and unbutton soldier boy's shirt."

Busted! I held up my hands as Josh approached. "I'll do it."

Relief washed over Josh's face.

He stepped inside the circle of death, but I couldn't risk taking him down with Harley's gun pointed at my head. "I don't usually do this kind of thing unless you've bought me dinner," I said as I unbuttoned my shirt. "But in this case, I'll make an exception."

Josh's eyes widened. "He's wearing a wire."

"No shit, Sherlock." Harley waved his gun at my head. "Check his ears."

Josh blinked in confusion, then turned to Harley.

"Go on, boy. What are ya waitin' for?"

Again, I held up my hands. I removed the device and handed it to Josh, who flashed a smug grin just before he ripped the wire from my chest.

"Now bring 'em both over here," Harley ordered.

Harley dropped my earpiece on the floor and crushed it with his heel, then instructed Josh to remove the battery from the transmitter he'd torn from my chest.

"Who's on the other end of this?"

Nicole pulled a small electronic device from her pocket and held it in the air.

"She was hiding upstairs when I got here," Josh offered.

"The dead woman comes back to life," Harley said with a smirk. "Too bad she won't be staying long."

Josh grabbed the device from her hand and inspected it. "Looks like a recording device, all right."

"You know what to do."

Josh threw a fastball at the fireplace, and the device shattered against the stone. He'd chosen football over baseball, but as I recall, it could have gone either way.

I guess Bill had told the truth when he said this wasn't his first rodeo. The device that Josh had just destroyed was a dummy. Perhaps our captors would speak a little more freely, if they thought their words would never leave the room.

"So, which one of you killed my brother?"

Harley chuckled. "You Bishops never were much for small talk."

"Like you said, we won't be staying long."

"I *had* to kill that boy," Harley said.

"What did he ever do to you?"

"You gotta understand, the only thing Josh's ever been good at was sports. He'd earned a football scholarship to LSU, and I sure as hell wasn't going to let another DWI charge derail those plans."

"Josh wasn't driving," Nicole said. "I was."

Harley's eyes grew wide, and he looked like he might topple over in a stiff breeze.

"You didn't know that, did you?" I considered rushing him before he recovered.

Harley set the shotgun down and pulled a pistol from his belt. He turned to Josh. "All these years you've been covering for this bitch?" His face reddened, and he raised his voice. "You stupid shit. This whole goddamn mess could have been avoided if you'd told me the truth. I wouldn't have given a rat's ass if your girlfriend went to jail. And you shouldn't have either."

I continued to push him and hoped that his contempt for Josh might somehow work in our favor. "You disposed of the body, destroyed the evidence."

"I wish it was that easy," Harley said, gaining his composure. "The little bastard wouldn't die. I had to put a bullet in him like I'm about to do with you."

I finally knew the truth, but it would be a hollow victory if Luke's killer walked out of here and I didn't.

"What about my daddy?"

"He's another one." Harley shook his head. "What is it with you Bishops?"

"So, you killed him, too?"

"Believe me, I thought about it." He pointed a finger in Nicole's direction. "But someone saved me the trouble."

"I didn't kill anybody," Nicole protested.

"Well, I didn't inject him with all that adrenaline a few minutes before he died."

"I gave him his regular morphine shot," she said through tears. "I filled the syringe myself."

"Appears that I'm not the only one who had something to lose if he—"

A gunshot echoed outside. Both Harley and Josh turned their heads toward the sound. I had to act fast. No time to consider what might have happened out there.

In the two seconds it would take for Harley to turn, level his gun at me, and squeeze off a round, I surprised Josh and grabbed his firearm. I wrenched his body between myself and Harley as we struggled.

The first bullet struck him in the back. Even with Josh in front of me, the impact felt like a punch. Josh let go of his gun just before the second bullet knocked us backward. On the way to the ground, I reached the gun around Josh and double-tapped Harley in the chest. Harley's third shot missed its mark as he dropped to the floor.

Nicole screamed. She knelt beside me as I rolled Josh onto the floor. "Are you okay?"

I stood. "A lot better than him."

Josh lay on his back, bleeding, but still alive.

CHAPTER 49

The motion detector startled me. I looked at Nicole and nodded. "Bill." Could have used him a couple of minutes sooner, but with our communications down, I'm sure he had reacted to the shots fired.

I lowered my gun when I saw Bill's face in the open doorway. I choked on my last words when he pulled Mama into the room, her eyes wide with fear.

"I ran into some friends outside," he said as he closed the door behind him with his foot.

"Mama? What are you doing here?"

"Cooper and I—"

"Coop's here?"

"I made him bring me." She cried. "I'm sorry, Dillon."

I shifted my gaze to Bill. "Where is he?"

"Takin' a dirt nap outside." Tiny muscles flexed and tightened around his stony eyes. "Unless the wolves have dragged him away by now."

Confusion clouded my thoughts. "Wolves?"

"One of 'em nearly attacked me on the way in."

I raised my weapon. "You're gonna pay for that, you—"

Bill wrapped a beefy arm around Mama's neck and pressed the end of his pistol against the side of her head. "Let's all just take it easy," he said in a calm voice. "I need you to put down your weapon."

Mama looked small and fragile against his king-size frame. Thinking that Bill cared for her may have turned out to be a fatal mistake. I knew now that greed was his only lover. Fear turned to terror in Mama's eyes as Bill tightened his grip around her neck.

"I said drop it, boy."

"Dillon," Nicole urged from behind me.

I held up both hands to indicate submission, then set the gun down on the floor.

"Kick it over there," he ordered with a sideways nod of his head.

Reluctantly, I complied.

"There. Now let's all take a breath." He lowered his gun and loosened his grip on Mama, allowing her to breathe a little easier.

I glanced at the two bodies on the floor, one dead, the other bleeding to death.

"You saw Harley, and you didn't say anything. You hoped he might save you the trouble, didn't you?"

"The thought had crossed my mind. I underestimated your resourcefulness. I won't make that mistake twice."

"So, it's been you all along?"

"I had nothing to do with your brother's death." He wagged his gun at Harley's body. "That was all him."

"And Pop?"

He shook his head. "Eli wouldn't listen to reason."

"I know about the clause in your contract."

"He was a stubborn old drunk."

"You found oil under that land."

"You're damn right I did. I spent a small fortune doing it, and I wasn't about to let some crack whore waltz in here and steal half my fortune."

I glanced at Mama, and my heart broke for her. I wanted to shove Bill's gun down his throat and make him take it all back. "So you killed him."

"I had to. Eli was dying, but not fast enough."

"I thought you had feelings for Mama."

"That's one thing I never lied about."

"You lied about everything else."

"When Harley framed your mama for Eli's murder, who got her out of it?" Bill's voice rose. "And who bailed her son out of jail so she could sleep at night? Huh?"

I stared into his arrogant eyes. "You're sick."

"This isn't all my fault." He motioned to Josh on the floor. "Lover boy over there screwed the pooch when he destroyed the suicide note I left with your friend Amanda. I reckoned he didn't care for the way you were sniffin' around his girl."

"I'm not his girl."

Bill glanced at Nicole, then back at me, and the flicker of a smile crossed his face. "When your prints turned up all over her stuff, Josh saw an opportunity to get you out of the way. The dumbass didn't realize that the note would have let everyone off the hook, including himself."

"Maybe now the truth will come out."

"Too bad y'all won't live long enough to tell anyone," Bill said with a sneer.

"So that's your plan?" I glanced at the bodies on the floor. "Kill everybody involved?"

"Truth belongs to the victor." He shifted his weight, and Mama gasped for air as her feet left the ground. "I see what you're doin' here, but the wire's been destroyed. Nobody's listening."

"You don't have to kill us," Nicole pleaded. "We won't tell anyone."

He looked at Nicole with an evil grin. "Be a shame to kill such a pretty little thing... without havin' a little fun first."

"You pig," Mama said, struggling against his grip. He pulled her closer, then turned his attention back to Nicole.

"After I kill your boyfriend and his mama, we're gonna have the place to ourselves. Hell, if you play nice, I may even let you live till mornin'."

"Dillon, please..." Nicole whispered from behind me. The terror in her voice sent a chill down my spine.

Bill's eyes drifted for a second. I'd waited for a distraction, an opportunity. Had I just missed it? I took a step toward him.

"Any closer and you're gonna be an orphan." He pressed the gun harder against Mama's head. She winced in pain.

I froze. A heartbeat echoed in my ears. Was it mine or Mama's? I stared at his finger on the trigger, every little twitch magnified by a growing feeling of helplessness.

A frontal attack was too risky. My only chance was to attack his flank. I saw my gun on the floor, but it was too far away for me to grab before he got two, maybe three, shots off. I didn't like the odds. Harley's pistol was closer, but it appeared to be wedged under his lifeless hand. I could dive and roll, hoping Bill's first shot missed its mark, but if I had any trouble freeing Harley's gun, I'd be a dead man. I'd be a dead man for sure if I didn't try.

Bill was experienced and undoubtedly trained in threat assessment. If I made a move, I'd immediately become his highest priority target. Mama became secondary. But in order to have a fighting chance, I needed him to take his eye off me for just a second. I sent Mama a look that said I needed her assistance. Her eyes conveyed a silent confirmation.

Seconds later, Mama went limp. Bill turned as her slumping body pulled on his arm. I dove toward Harley.

The room exploded with gunfire. I felt the wake of the first bullet. It splintered the wood floor a fraction of an inch behind my head. Harley's body had been farther away than I'd estimated. I rolled again, waiting for the second shot.

Time didn't stop altogether, but each second became a minute. Another shot rang out from a distance. Glass shattered behind me. I slammed into Harley in mid-roll and pried the gun from his dead fingers. *Why hadn't Bill taken another shot?*

My head came around just in time to see a red circle in the middle of Bill's forehead. His eyes grew wide for a second before his body dropped to the floor like a bag of hammers. Mama screamed as she went down with him. I scrambled across the floor toward them.

I stood, kicked the gun from his hand, and pulled her to her feet.

"What happened?" she asked in a shaky voice.

I turned toward the broken window, then back to Bill. "I'm not sure."

A pool of blood widened around Bill's head, and I glanced at the broken window. *Coop?*

Mama's legs gave out, and I grabbed her arms with both hands.

"Mama? Did you actually see Coop get shot?"

She nodded as tears fell.

I glanced at Bill. He died too quickly. I wanted him to suffer more. A lot more.

The cabin door opened. I looked up and confusion set in again.

Jenny Lee stepped into the room with Pop's Mossberg slung across her shoulder. Tears rolled down her cheeks.

"If y'all are trying to ditch me, Dillon Bishop," she said in a shaky voice, "you're going to have to try a little harder."

I blew out my breath and emotion nearly overwhelmed me. "If I was trying to ditch you..." My throat tightened. "We wouldn't be having this conversation."

She turned her head toward Bill's body. I went to her and gently turned it away until her eyes met mine.

"You saved my life. All our lives."

Her bottom lip quivered. She held my gaze for a moment before burying her head in my chest. I stared through the open doorway. A pair of green eyes watched from the tree line.

I felt Mama's arms close around Jenn and me. Before I said anything, Jenn motioned for Nicole to join us. Jenn smiled and shrugged as she looked up at me. Another tear rolled down her cheek.

A voice from the open doorway interrupted our group hug.

"Hey!" Coop held out his arms. "What about me?"

Mama yelled, "Cooper!"

I blew out a breath and shook my head. "I don't understand. Mama saw Bill shoot you."

"Like I told you, Bish, you need to watch more TV." He grinned as he pulled the neck of his t-shirt down to expose a bullet embedded just above his heart in a Kevlar vest.

"Where did you get—"

"I found two police cars parked up the road a bit." He shrugged. "Who leaves their doors unlocked anymore?"

Despite my shock, or maybe because of it, I laughed.

Coop scanned the room. "Jeezus, Bish, what the hell happened in here?"

"I think Josh might still be alive."

"And you want to save him?"

"Shut up and give me a hand."

Coop shook his head. "I didn't think I'd ever say this, Bish, but you're a better man than me."

"By the way," Coop continued as he followed me, "you promised me you wouldn't let me get shot."

"I said I wouldn't let *Josh* shoot you."

CHAPTER 50

Josh lay in a hospital bed, probably wishing he'd left the cabin in a body bag like Harley and Bill. After his recovery, he'd face conspiracy charges for Luke's murder, as well as attempted murder charges for blowing up Nicole's house.

Mort stopped by to deliver the news that all charges against me had been dropped. There would be no trial. The recording devices I'd planted at the cabin provided enough evidence to convince the District Attorney of my innocence. No charges were filed against Jenny Lee, either. They deemed her actions justifiable. She vowed to whisk me away from Texas before I got us into any more trouble, but I convinced her to stay another week so I could tie up a few loose ends.

We tied up the biggest loose end on Saturday in a dusty field outside Alvarado, Texas. The crowd that gathered for Luke's memorial service brought a tear to my eye. I removed Luke's star from my pocket and pinned it on my chest. Lawman Luke would always be my hero. When he was seven years old, he'd proudly worn this star and talked about cleaning up the county. The world had become a better place for his being here.

We stood around a large rock in the southwest corner of Pop's property—the only rock outcrop visible on this dusty prairie, and the only rock in Texas that held a bronze plaque that read: *Luke Bishop 1994-2009, Little Brother, Big Heart.*

After Luke's service, a few friends and family stayed to watch me scatter Pop's ashes around the rock. Ironically, the land he thought would save him had ultimately contributed to his demise.

I watched a pair of hawks circle effortlessly overhead. Mama's words, *Spirit never dies,* echoed in my mind. With Mama and Jenn at my side and my eyes looking up to the heavens, I tipped my hat to my old family and put my arms around my new one. At that bittersweet moment, Bradley, Texas, let go of its hold on my heart.

Jenn received a call the following day as the three of us sat and talked freely in our recently sanitized, bug-free living room. We'd just convinced Mama to come live with us in Colorado. Jenn stood and walked outside with her phone. I looked at Mama and shrugged, resisting the urge to eavesdrop by the door.

Upon returning, Jenn announced that she needed to leave for Colorado that afternoon. Mama and I would follow after we'd packed her things and settled the rest of her affairs.

"Is something wrong?"

"No," she said matter-of-factly. "It's nothing."

"It has to be something. You don't just take off early and leave us behind for nothing."

"Leave you behind?" She put her hands on her hips. "Does that mean you're not coming?"

Her question put me on the defensive. "Clever girl," I said, looking at her through squinted eyes. "I see what you're doing. That's not what I meant. This isn't about me."

Jenn stood directly in front of me. "Dillon Bishop, do you trust me?"

"With my life."

"Good answer." She stood on her toes and kissed my cheek. Her hand brushed the back of my neck, and I went into a full-body shudder.

I glanced at Mama as Jenn turned to leave. She raised her eyebrows as if to say, *What are you waiting for?*

"I'll help you pack," I said and followed Jenn down the hall and into her room.

"Another good answer." A mischievous smile played on her lips. "Clever boy." She closed the door behind me.

A half-hour later, we stood by the front door. I dropped Jenn's overnight bag on the floor and leaned in for another kiss. Mama cleared her throat from the kitchen doorway.

"You two must be hungry after all that *packing*." She glanced at the small bag at Jenn's feet, unable to conceal a knowing smile. "I made us lunch."

I tried one more time to change Jenn's mind about leaving so soon, but she politely resisted my efforts. She wouldn't say why she had to leave, just that important business had come up unexpectedly. I assured her that Mama and I would be on her doorstep within a week.

We stood outside an hour later and said our goodbyes. Mama insisted on a group hug right there on the front porch. I think she enjoyed having a family again. I know I did.

Mama and I arrived at Mort's office early Monday morning to discuss the transfer of Pop's land to Bishop Oil, the newly formed partnership between Bonnie Bishop and her son, Dillon. The first order of business would be to retain Mort as legal counsel. The second would be to transfer the house in Bradley and the cabin on Lake Whitney to Bishop Oil for immediate liquidation.

Finally, we extended an offer to Coop to act as trustee and part-time operations manager. With boots on the ground in Bradley, Mama and I could manage the business remotely from Colorado. Mort promised to have all the necessary papers drawn up for our signatures by Friday.

We drove down to the cabin one last time to retrieve a few personal items. The professional cleaners we'd hired had completed their work, but the disturbing memories remained. We moved quickly and left in a hurry, eager to put the events of that night behind us for good.

The house proved somewhat easier to deal with, but it held some bad memories of its own. By Friday afternoon, the place was empty and everything we kept sat under a big, blue tarp in the back of Pop's truck. We each said our own silent goodbyes before we left for Mort's office.

The mood was somber as we sat across from Mort. He slid one paper after another across the small conference table for our signatures. When we finished, he looked from Mama to me, then back to Mama.

"I'm going to miss you both. Are you sure you have to leave?"

Mama looked down at her hands. "We can't stay here."

Mort's eyes pleaded with her, and I knew why she had looked away. "It's not such a terrible place to live." He leaned forward and attempted to make eye contact with Mama. "And with a new Police Chief, we can all breathe a little easier."

"It's time to move on," I said.

With all the necessary papers signed, we headed for Coop's. Jolene had invited us for a goodbye dinner, Texas-style. We also took her up on her offer to put us up for our last night in town.

After a kickass dinner—did I mention Coop had his own smoker?—we talked over drinks on their patio. Fireflies glowed all around us as dusk turned to dark. Our conversation slowed, and our hearts became heavy. I vowed not to stay away so long this time and reminded Coop that his family was welcome at the ranch anytime. Jenn had assured me she had plenty of room.

I found myself alone with Jolene after Mama had gone to bed and Coop had disappeared into the house.

"Did you say goodbye to Nicole?"

I shook my head.

"Why don't you stop by the hospital tomorrow morning around 9:30?" She smiled. "I'll make sure she takes her break in the park."

"I wouldn't know what to say."

She stood, bent down, and kissed my cheek. She whispered in my ear. "You'll think of something."

I finished my beer alone in the glow of the citronella candles. Coop approached as I stood and collected the empty bottles.

"Leaving me again, I see."

I shrugged. "It'll be different this time."

"You mean I'll get to say goodbye, or I'll see you again sometime this decade?"

"Yeah, that was kind of shitty, wasn't it?"

"I've got something for you," he said and reached into his pocket.

I set the empties on the table.

He placed a small piece of lead in my hand. "I want you to have this."

I examined the flattened bullet. "Coop…"

"If you ever get to wonderin' who your real friends are, remember the one who took a bullet for you."

I smiled. "I guess you win."

"Win what?"

"The most Nicole ever did for me was—"

"Whoa!" Coop held up his hands to stop me. "Too much information."

"Seriously, Coop, you've always been my best friend. That's not going to change."

He raised an eyebrow above a crooked smile. "What about Jenny Lee?"

I grinned. "I reckon she's gonna give you a run for your money."

Coop surprised me when he pulled me in for a hug. Not one of those shake-your-hand-and-pat-your-back, man hugs. This one was the real McCoy.

We pulled into the hospital parking lot at 0930 on Saturday. I told Mama that I would only be a few minutes and left her in the truck. Jolene smiled from the nurse's station when she saw me and pointed to the back door. I found Nicole at one of the picnic tables in the park.

"Why are you here?" she asked.

"I came to say goodbye."

Nicole hung her head for a moment, then raised her eyes just enough to meet my gaze. "I still have that rain check."

I smiled. "Hang on to it. It's good for more than one lifetime."

A faint, fleeting smile crossed her face.

"Our hearts have history," I whispered. "I don't want to change that. But this future belongs to Jenn."

She stood. "Will you at least kiss me goodbye?"

I leaned in to kiss her cheek, but she turned her head and our lips met. She held on tight. I pulled back gently. Her eyes searched mine for something that wasn't there.

"I'm sorry, Dillon. I've made a lot of mistakes and I hurt you. If I could do it all over again..." Her voice cracked. "I would do it differently."

I nodded. "I know you would."

She rested her head on my chest. We stood in silence for a moment before I took a half-step back. Nicole looked up at me with those eyes.

I brushed the hair back that had fallen across her face. "I need to go."

She remained silent until I reached the hospital door. "Dillon?"

I turned.

She forced a smile. "If you're ever back in Bradley..."

"I'll be sure to look you up." After a deep breath, I tipped my hat. "Bye, Nicole."

I opened the door and resisted the urge to take one last look. I smiled and touched the brim of my hat as I passed Jolene on the way to the parking lot.

CHAPTER 51

I slid the seat back and settled in for the long ride. I stole a glance from time to time in the mirror and calculated the growing distance between myself and Bradley, Texas. With a sense of optimism, I realized that, for the first time in my life, I found myself more intent on running toward something good than away from something bad.

We stopped for dinner at a roadside diner in New Mexico, and made Trinidad, Colorado, by 2030. Mama told me she wouldn't mind if I told time like regular folks. We found a Days Inn and called it a night around 9:30.

Shortly after sunrise the next morning, we set out on the final leg of our journey. The next three hours took us through some of the most beautiful country I'd ever seen. Majestic, snow-capped mountains reached for the sky all around us. Clearly, we weren't in Texas anymore.

We skirted the city of Colorado Springs to the west. The landscape turned to rolling hills, where horses grazed behind miles of white fence. The snow-covered summit of Pikes Peak stood majestically in the distance.

The rolling hills soon gave way to steeper grades and twisty mountain roads. A sign for the Red Valley Ranch marked our destination, and I turned down a long drive. We passed several barns and smaller outbuildings before I spotted Jenn on the wraparound porch of a large, two-story wooden homestead.

She strolled out to the truck to greet us, and we followed her through the wood panel front door into a great room that could have come out of a Country Living magazine. A large, stone fireplace, like the one at the cabin, took up most of one wall. Heavy rustic furniture filled the room under three fans that hung from a twelve-foot vaulted ceiling. Four large windows with arched transoms allowed a picturesque view of the countryside and made nature an integral part of the room's decor.

"There's someone I'd like y'all to meet," Jenn said before she disappeared into an adjoining room. I caught Mama's stare, and I shrugged.

Jenn returned two minutes later with a young boy. They held hands as she led him into the room. I scratched my head, confused by his dark skin and jet-black hair. Clearly, he wasn't a blood relative.

They stopped directly in front of us and smiled. "His name is Rafi Alexander Ahmadi." Jenn smiled as she ran a hand through his thick, black hair. "Alex is going to stay with us for a while."

I offered my hand to the boy. He stared at it but didn't move. I looked at Jenn.

"GI Joe," the boy said.

My head snapped in his direction. "What did you say?"

He pointed at the tattoo on my still-outstretched arm. "GI Joe."

His English was better, but his voice was the same one that had haunted my dreams for the past three years. The terror that I'd once seen in his eyes had dissolved into something more tranquil, but a measure of uncertainty remained in his expression.

I squatted down to his eye level. "We've met before, haven't we?"

He nodded.

I glanced at Jenn, her eyes wide, and her knees about to buckle. Mama, the only soul with whom I'd confided about *the boy,* sat on the edge of the sofa.

I looked at Alex. "You want to tell her?"

He explained in a concise manner how his home had been attacked and his parents killed. He feared for his own life when the American soldiers arrived, but the soldier he called GI Joe picked him up and carried him back to his vehicle. That soldier saved his life when a bomb exploded a few minutes later. They wouldn't let him ride in the ambulance with GI Joe, so Captain Driscoll escorted him to the base and put him on a plane to Germany.

I held out my hand. "It's great to see you again, Alex. You can call me by my real name. Dillon."

He shook my hand with a great deal of enthusiasm. When he finished, he threw his arms around my neck and nearly knocked me over backwards.

I looked up at Jenn with Alex still hanging around my neck. I raised my hands and mouthed, "How?"

Jenn smiled, apparently pleased with our little reception. "Let's have something to drink on the patio, and I'll tell y'all the story."

A well-tanned, thirty-something male walked in from outside. Jenn introduced her cousin Seth, and invited him to join us.

"Can I get you a beer, Dillon?" Seth asked.

"You sure can. Thank you."

"Great. Two beers coming up."

"Make that three," Jenn said.

"Four," Mama added.

"How about you?" Jenn asked Alex.

He shook his head. "No beer for me, thank you."

We all laughed.

"I meant, what would you like to drink?"

"Oh." Alex thought for a moment. "A Pepsi-Cola, please."

We all took a seat at a table under a large umbrella at the back of the house. Jenn launched into the story of how a boy named Alex Ahmadi came to be sitting among us in Redfield, Colorado, USA.

In 2010, Jenn's transfer from combat duty landed her at the US Army base in Wiesbaden, Germany. Shortly before her discharge in 2012, an Afghan refugee—a seven-year-old boy named Alex—arrived at the base on his way to foster care in the States. Due to an administrative snafu, he spent three months at the base under the supervision of Jenn's friend, Sarah Porter. Jenn spent a good deal of time with the two and felt a sense of loss when Alex was shipped stateside.

Jenn returned home to Dallas a month later, wondering where Alex had landed. Unable to forget his frightened little face, she contacted Sarah, who put her in touch with a friend at the agency in Washington that had placed him. Sarah's friend, Kate, couldn't release any information beyond the fact that Alex had been placed in a foster home. She apologized and took Jenn's number in case his situation changed.

After Jenn moved to Colorado, Kate called to let her know that, through no fault of his own, Alex went back into the system to live in a group home in Virginia. Ten-year-old American children were hard enough to place, so when someone showed interest in an Afghan boy, special arrangements could be made. After a surprise home assessment visit by the adoption agency last Monday—the reason Jenn left Bradley in such a hurry—a one-month trial had been approved.

"I wanted to tell you, Dillon," Jenn said, "but I didn't know for sure until yesterday." She placed her hand in mine and looked into my eyes. "Are you okay with all this?"

"Uh... yeah, sure."

"You don't sound very convincing."

"It's so... unexpected." I glanced at Alex, then lowered my voice. "I think I just need some time to get used to the idea."

Jenn stood. "C'mon, Bonnie. I'll show you the guest house. I'm so happy you're here."

"Honey, you can call me Mama."

"I will... Mama." Jenn led her down a flagstone walk with Alex in tow.

Seth waited until they were out of earshot. "Don't get too comfortable here."

"Excuse me?"

"You and your Mama should go back where you came from. We don't need you 'round here."

"That's up to Jenn and me. You don't get a say."

"It's rough country up here. I wouldn't want to see anybody get hurt."

It sounded to me like that's exactly what he wanted to see. "Are you threatening us?"

Jen returned and asked about Mama's bags.

After a lengthy glare in Seth's direction, I excused myself and grabbed Mama's things from the truck.

Back inside the main house, I dropped my duffel bag by the door.

Jenn looked at the bag, then back at me. "I thought you were movin' in, not just stayin' overnight."

I brought plenty of baggage, just not the kind you can see. "There are a few more things in the truck. I'll get 'em in the morning."

She locked her arms around my neck and washed away some of the tension caused by my conversation with Seth. I decided not to mention it just yet.

I glanced around the room. "This is a real nice place you got here, Jenn. I could get used to this."

"That's the plan." She gave me a quick kiss before her eyes widened. "Want to take a ride?"

"What about the boy?"

"You mean *Alex*?"

"Yeah, sorry about that. It's just so—"

"Seth will keep an eye on him."

I wondered if that was such a good idea. "So, where are you taking me? I'm not sure I can handle another surprise."

"It's a special place."

We climbed into her Ford Bronco and drove to the edge of her property. She turned onto a dirt road that wound its way up into the hills between stands of aspen and blue spruce. I hadn't yet acclimated myself to the thinner air at this altitude. My breath quickened, and I felt lightheaded.

She pulled over next to three rocks that looked like giant teeth that had grown out of the ground. She hopped out of the jeep. "C'mon."

"Where are we going?"

"We're almost there."

I followed her down a dirt trail that disappeared between two of the teeth.

"Close your eyes," she said as we neared a clearing in the pines. She took my hand and led me the rest of the way.

"Can I open them now?" I asked when we stopped.

She placed her hands on my shoulders and turned me about 45 degrees to the right. "Open."

We stood at the edge of a cliff, high above a narrow river that snaked its way between jagged red rock and rolling, evergreen-studded hills. Majestic snow-capped mountains guarded the land below on two sides, creating a breathtaking vista.

Jenn pointed to the top of the highest mountain. "That's Pikes Peak."

I had no words. I probably couldn't have spoken them if I did. I'd been here before... but I hadn't. I turned around to see if perhaps a young Leotie watched us from behind.

"I've seen this place before," I whispered. "In a dream."

"You're kidding."

"I remember every detail." I put my arm around her shoulder as we watched an eagle soar high above us. "The only thing missing was you."

I told Jenn about Leotie and the dream. Clouds rolled in while we talked, and raindrops fell. A clap of thunder warned us to take cover. We made no attempt to leave.

The rain came down harder, and I felt an irresistible urge to dance.

***

A Note from the Author

Thank you for investing your valuable time in reading my novel. I hope you enjoyed the story. Please take a moment to visit **www.davidhomick.com** for more information about me and my books and to sign up for my mailing list using the link at the bottom of the home page. You can write to me through the site if you're so inclined. I'd love to hear from you.

Word of mouth is the most powerful promotion any book can receive. If you enjoyed this book, please tell your friends. A shout-out on your favorite social media sites would be cool, too.

I want you, the reader, to know that your review is very important to me and to others that may be considering buying this book. Please leave an honest review on Amazon. It doesn't have to be long, just a sentence or two, unless you're so inclined. Your comments are greatly appreciated.

Thank you, and I wish you all the best.

What's next for Dillon and Jenn?

Separating truth from lies continues to be a messy—and dangerous—business.

Dillon Bishop thinks he's leaving trouble behind when he moves from Texas to live on the Colorado horse ranch that girlfriend Jenny Lee inherited from her Uncle Roy. But it doesn't take long for him to realize that trouble has a way of finding him wherever he goes.

When Buck, the ranch foreman, suggests that Roy was murdered, Dillon writes it off as the ramblings of a crusty old cowboy who likes his liquor a little too much. But Buck's not alone in his opinions, and Dillon pokes a sleeping bear when his accusations put him at odds with the local sheriff.

When Jenn is arrested for Roy's murder, Dillon must find the real killer as dangerous lines are drawn within the community. Dillon is once again forced to do battle with corrupt law enforcement, as well as the large marijuana farm that wants Jenn's land, and others closer to home whose motives are thrown into doubt.

Truth is in short supply in this little Colorado town, and Dillon finds himself drawn into another conspiracy that could cost him everything.

Rain Dance (Rain Mystery Trilogy Book 2)
is available at Amazon.com

Other Books by David Homick

From Time to Time

They say the past is the past. An MIT grad student with a time machine is out to prove otherwise. Having lost the love of his life in a tragic car accident the year before, he is determined to jump back in time to rewrite history. But a new love interest has a secret that can stop him dead in his tracks.

When Zac Taylor loses his fiancé in an auto accident, his promising academic career crashes and burns with her. After a year of self-imposed exile and an unsuccessful suicide attempt, he returns to MIT, where his advisor persuades him to complete his dissertation in quantum physics.

Rachel Lockhart moves to Cambridge looking for information and lands a job as Zac's research assistant. Zac doesn't want an assistant, especially one who reminds him of his dead fiancé. Despite his reluctance and her ulterior motive, they grow close.

Zac's experiments produce an unexpected result—time travel. When his time machine is stolen, he must retrieve it and outrun everyone on his mission to save the love of his life.

Broken Angels

A missing father, a long-lost love, and a precocious little girl force a jaded young man to face his demons, but his salvation has an expiration date.

Abandoned by his father as a child, Jack DiLuca cannot see that his self-destructive behavior and one-night stands are preventing him from finding the love and the life that he desires. Driven by recurring dreams about his father, he walks away from his first meaningful relationship to settle the score with the man who destroyed his life.

When Jack finds his father in Philadelphia, he discovers that everything is not as it appears. He gets more than he bargained for as family secrets are revealed, and he learns that even he is not who he thought he was.

A chance meeting with Maggie, an old high school flame, rekindles his desire, but she resists his attempts to get too close. After building a bond with her ten-year-old daughter, Jack longs to be part of a family. But when tragedy strikes, he discovers that Maggie hides a secret that threatens to destroy everything.

Reason to Live

He's on a mission to win back the heart of the only woman he's ever loved, but there's a problem. He's stuck in the body of a man she's never met.

Richard Dunham awakes in a hospital with no memory of the accident that allegedly killed him. He thinks he knows his name, but the hospital staff disagrees. Confusion turns to terror when he looks in the mirror and a stranger looks back.

When a mysterious old man shows up at his bedside with tall tales of a life—and death—for which he has no recall, Richard realizes that he's not in Kansas anymore. He has no point of reference, no memories of his own, no idea of the kind of man he'd been. When a series of flashbacks begin to paint a picture of his past life, Richard doesn't like what he sees.

Richard, now Michael Riordan, must navigate his way through an unfamiliar landscape as he embarks on an unexpected life-or-death mission. When the obstacles in his path appear insurmountable, Richard must make a choice. Will he let his past determine his future, or will he discover that it's never too late to be what he might have been?

Disclaimer: Reason to Live is a re-write of my first novel, A Lifetime Last Night, that more closely follows the screenplay adaptation. While the story is told differently, many of the characters and the premise are the same.

Made in the USA
Middletown, DE
27 October 2022

13576991R00191